A NOVEL OF THE KRAKEN MC

CUTTER'S HOPE

The Virtues BOOK I

AJ Downey

Second Circle Press

Published 2015 by Second Circle Press
Book design by Lia Rees at Free Your Words
(www.freeyourwords.com)
Cover art and Virtues logo by Cover Your Dreams
(www.coveryourdreams.net)

Text copyright © 2015 AJ Downey

This is a work of fiction. Names, characters, businesses, places, events and incidents are either the products of the author's imagination or used in a fictitious manner. Any resemblance to actual persons, living or dead, or actual events is purely coincidental.

All Rights Reserved

ISBN: 978-1519689818

Author's Note

The events of this trilogy take place *after* the events of Damaged & Dangerous, The Sacred Hearts MC Book VI. If you have not read the SHMC series, references and events that are talked about in this book may not make sense to you. I highly suggest reading the SHMC series first. Shattered & Scarred is the first book.

Dedication

To the first responders. No one knows what you go through... I include Dispatch, Police, Fire, Medical, and Military in there. If I've missed anyone or any particular branch of the first responder tree I apologize. Just the same, you save people and that takes a real toll, especially knowing how badly people can treat one another.

The Virtues Books in Order

1. *Cutter's Hope*

2. Marlin's Faith

3. Charity for Nothing

Special Thanks

A special thank you to 'Sweatpants and Coffee' a special blog that's not only informative but full of some great laughs. Also to Shandle Blaha for keeping me above board. Much love <3

Contents

Prologue	*1*
Chapter 1	*3*
Chapter 2	*9*
Chapter 3	*15*
Chapter 4	*19*
Chapter 5	*25*
Chapter 6	*37*
Chapter 7	*40*
Chapter 8	*50*
Chapter 9	*55*
Chapter 10	*63*
Chapter 11	*70*
Chapter 12	*76*
Chapter 13	*86*
Chapter 14	*94*
Chapter 15	*100*
Chapter 16	*106*
Chapter 17	*111*
Chapter 18	*118*
Chapter 19	*124*
Chapter 20	*130*
Chapter 21	*143*

Chapter 22	*151*
Chapter 23	*157*
Chapter 24	*165*
Chapter 25	*170*
Chapter 26	*178*
Chapter 27	*181*
Chapter 28	*186*
Chapter 29	*193*
Chapter 30	*202*
Chapter 31	*204*
Chapter 32	*212*
Chapter 33	*213*
Chapter 34	*221*
Chapter 35	*225*
Chapter 36	*233*
Chapter 37	*237*
Chapter 38	*244*
Chapter 39	*250*
Chapter 40	*253*
Epilogue	*259*
Marlin's Faith: Cover	
About the Author	

PROLOGUE
Faith

You never imagine it would happen to you, but it happened to me. I was sold, that's right, *sold* like a prime piece of meat at a butcher's counter, which is what I felt like at the moment. Like so much tenderized raw meat.

The drugs were wearing off and it had devolved into this... hoping that my captors would bring around the next dose of whatever they injected me with. Praying for the sweet bite of the needle and wishing for the oblivion and euphoric haze. Whatever they kept me on would give me at least a mockery of peace as it rushed through my system, through my blood. I needed it. I craved it. It was the only thing I had to look forward to nowadays.

I didn't need the drugs to keep me docile anymore. I figured out quickly that fighting them was no use, it only made them hurt me more.

I drew my knees up to my chest, listening to the steel chain padlocked around my ankle scrape across the cement floor of the storage locker. This is where I called home while they weren't using me. It wasn't much. A vinyl covered mattress on the floor. A bucket in the corner. A dim lightbulb hanging from the middle of the ceiling.

Fuck that fucking cunt Tonya.

I never should have gone. Never should have trusted her or let her talk me into coming here. It was supposed to be just me and her, a girls' weekend in the Big Easy. I never should have tried to save money by living off campus, never should have answered her ad for a roommate. I never, I never, I never... but I had, and she'd sold me.

Sold me and I didn't even know for how much... not that it

made a difference. Now my only hope *was* Hope.

I had to have *faith*.

Faith.

Hope, Faith, and Charity…

God, would I ever see Charity again? Would Hope find me?

The lock on the outside of my storage locker rattled and I sat up, smoothing my hair behind my ears as the door opened. The light from the corridor cast him in shadow but he was only here for one thing… they all were. He stepped into the unit and shut the door behind him and I found myself bitterly wishing he was what I called a one hit wonder; as in he stuck it in, a stroke or two, and he'd come so I didn't have to deal with him being on top of me for very long.

This is what my life had devolved into and I honestly didn't know how long I'd been here… or how long I would stay.

CHAPTER 1
Hope

I stopped in front of the bar and double checked my notes on my phone. This was the place. For *sure*, this was the place. The Plank. The sign was just as the name implied, a plank of wood nailed above the doors, the name burned into the surface in big block letters, but below that in a flowing gilded script the words *'It's beachy, it's manly, it's made of hard wood'* were inscribed which made me choke on a laugh. That part hadn't been in my notes, just 'The Plank' and the street address. I put my phone into my concealed carry purse, not that I really needed a gun. I was almost more lethal without one.

I quickly assessed the bikers standing around the line of motorcycles that were backed in at an angle to the curb. All of them were so much shiny chrome and black leather, the brightly painted gas tanks sparkling under the punishing Florida sun. I was a California girl, so I was used to sun and even heat, but the humidity here? Only one word for it: gross.

I continued up the sidewalk; back straight, lightweight summer halter dress ending mid-thigh, swishing against my legs. I knew I looked good to these guys. I didn't need the lascivious grins to tell me that. I was a tall girl with a lot of toned leg and tanned a deep bronze. My hair, I kept tightly braided with a flirty length of side swept bangs. My make up? I kept it natural, but every bit of it I used to full advantage to accentuate my wide brown eyes. I looked like a pretty doll. You'd never guess I was a defense contractor by trade and that I went from city to city assessing police forces and their hand to hand combat skills.

That was me. I went in, assessed the personnel on the force with a series of tests then created a training regime to fill in all the gaps. My specialty? Non-lethal tactics designed to disarm an armed assailant. I was damned good at my job and had a hell of a resume to back it up. A decorated Army Veteran with an exceptional record and a specialty in Krav Maga. With the recent race relation media explosions over cops versus citizen scenarios playing out over the nightly news, yeah, business was booming.

So why was a girl like me about to step into the den of a motorcycle gang notorious for their illegal dealings up and down Florida's coast? One word: family. My sister to be exact. She'd gone missing almost two years ago on a vacation to New Orleans with her roommate. The roommate hadn't exactly stuck around after my sister had disappeared either. Hopping from one place to the next. Her last known whereabouts had been with a motorcycle gang from up north of here, The Suicide Kings. The Private Investigator I'd hired had finally come across some information that Little Miss Tonya had last been seen with these guys, headed to Florida.

Armed with an almost three year old mugshot of the girl from when she'd been busted shoplifting, I was here to try my luck with these Neanderthals. The door to the bar was open. No air conditioning... *Great.* I stepped into the dark of The Plank and lifted my sunglasses off from over my eyes and perched them on my head. Several guys in denim and leather turned from the bar and eyed me. I gave them a flat look back.

"Man in charge?" I asked raising my eyebrows. One of them, a young man behind the bar polishing the top with a rag jerked his head toward an alcove at the back. I stepped in that direction but was immediately blocked by a wall of muscle going soft around the middle. I sized up weak points on the man who looked to be in his fifties before I could blink. I held my ground and shifted my weight onto my back foot.

"Who might you be?" he asked and I half expected him to add 'little lady' to the end of his sentence.

"You're not the man in charge," I said slowly, with my most disarming smile.

"Why do you say that?"

"Because the man in charge doesn't hold court out front. He keeps his business private and in the back."

The man who was taller than me crossed his arms over his chest and smirked down at me. I glanced at the name tag on the front of his vest, it read 'Tiny' and under that 'Sgt. at Arms'. I gave him another once over. Again, he was muscular, but it was starting to go soft with age. He held himself tall, but it was a posture filled with arrogance, not with any kind of military precision. His graying hair was held back by a wide swath of orange bandana across his forehead. His hair was shoulder length and, curled above his shoulders which were broad and tinged red by too much time spent in the sun. His light blue eyes were sparkling with smug humor and he almost reeked of bully, but bullies had never bothered me. His gaze skated over my tits, or really what passed for them. I was almost as flat as a teenage boy but I couldn't be too sorry about it. It was hard to hold onto feminine curves when you were all lean muscle, and I would take *that* over boobs any day of the week.

I felt a trickle of sweat slide down my spine as we stood there, neither one of us budging, both of us just coolly assessing the other. Finally with a chuckle the man stepped aside. Yep, that was me, all harmless and girly, no threat here, *now get the fuck out of my way*.

I smiled sweetly and silently stepped past him. I could feel him check out my ass as I went by and I fought not to roll my eyes and do something unladylike, like kick him in the balls. There were way more of them than there were of me, and while I was pretty sure I could handle most of them, some of them might give me a run for my money…

Like the man in charge, the cocky son of a bitch.

He lounged in an electric chair, either a replica, or a real relic from some mothballed penitentiary, I couldn't tell… I didn't really care either. The man on the 'throne' which sat on a slightly raised dais screamed *'danger'* in every sense of the word. He worked out, clearly, but it was more than just chiseled abs and corded arms. It was the way he held himself. He appeared nonchalant, leaning to one side, leg hitched up over one arm of the chair. He wore a pair of frayed cargo shorts and no shirt, just one of the leather vests that seemed to be the uniform code around here.

"You Anders – "

He held up his hand abruptly and my voice stilled in my throat. I swept him one more time. Tattooed, sure, but one of them was damn sure a war memorial. A tattered American flag decorating the swell of one shoulder. He was more attractive than not and he knew it which should have been a total turn off, but hey, it'd been a while, okay?

"We don't use last names around here, Sweetheart. Truth be told, we don't use first ones either."

"What do you want to be called then, Sunshine?" I asked warily.

"I'm Cutter."

I snorted, "Right."

"What's a pretty *Civilian* girl like you doing in a place like this?" he asked and he was smiling but it didn't quite reach his eyes. I took my eyes off him and opened my purse, a flicker of movement brought my attention up and I stilled. He'd sat up abruptly and I looked him over warily. His hair was a little longer than mine and curled in a loose horsetail over his shoulder. He had a neat, trim beard that was graying at the corners which matched the gray at his temples. He didn't look that old, late thirties, early forties maybe? He moved quickly though. Quick and quiet.

"Problem?" I asked sweetly. Couldn't resist yanking his chain juuuuust a little.

"We aren't a big fan of sudden movements around here."

I raised an eyebrow and withdrew the mugshot from my purse holding it out in front of me. "Seen her?" I asked. He stared at me and didn't even bother to look at the picture, his eyes were a warm brown with those golden undertones. Not like mine which sparkled with hardness, a cold deep brown, almost black. Like obsidian or coal.

"Nope," he said and still hadn't bothered to look. His face was impassive. *Too impassive.* He was trying not to show a tell and his obvious trying was a tell in and of itself.

"Would you mind bothering to look?" I asked just to force the issue, see if he would give anything away.

"I'm looking at all I want to see," he said, lips spreading into a slow and lazy grin, his eyes riveted to my face. It was already a million degrees in here but the look he was giving me turned the thermostat up even higher.

"I really need to find her."

"I really need to get to know you. Girl like you doesn't come around these parts every day."

"Not happening," I said.

"Then I can't help you."

"No, you're saying you won't help me."

"Call it what you like," he smiled, teeth even and straight.

"Will you please just look at the picture? I really need to find her."

I don't know if some pleading had crept into my tone or if it was the enticing or insistent little shake I gave to the photograph but his eyes finally slid from my face to the picture in my hand. I'd never had a look do me like that. Where his eyes slid along my skin, I don't know, it felt like a very real thing with weight and substance to it. Like a very physical caress had just gone across me. I suppressed a shudder.

His eyes alighted on the photograph and his entire expression went dark, like someone had flipped a light switch and just nobody was home anymore. Ooooooh yeah. Cutter was a very dangerous man. A very dangerous man indeed.

"Nope. Never seen her," he lied right to my face. I felt my lips curl into a nasty little smile full of derision.

"Okay. Fair enough. I'll be in town for a few days asking around about her… if anything, you know, comes to you, I'm staying at the Nautilus Beach Front B&B."

"You can ask around all you want, Sweetheart, ain't no one stopping you," he smiled, the charm back on, "Now you telling me where you're staying, is that an invitation?" he asked and bounced his eyebrows.

"Not interested in anyone that doesn't know anything about *her*," I said giving the picture a little flick making it snap. I stepped back, not taking my eyes off of Cutter whose vest proclaimed him the king of this twisted little bar room kingdom by the sea.

"Maybe I'll come see you anyways," he said with a wink, "What's your name?"

"Wasn't an invitation," I stated dryly, "and I thought you didn't do first and last names." I was almost to the alcove.

"This is my town, Baby. I don't need no invite, and we don't do given names, but Civilians like you? Well, you usually only got one name and that's your given one, so what's yours?" he winked at me and I gave him a nasty little smile.

"Hope, my name is Hope," I told him, before turning and striding back out into the sun, flipping my glasses down off my head and over my eyes. I wanted to be a bitch and not give in to him with my name, but I'd already said where I was staying and he might tell me what I wanted to know with some persuasion.

Not *that* kind.

When it came to a fight, I wasn't sure who would win in a match up, me or him. I didn't think it prudent to find out, either. I wasn't there yet, but I was getting close to being just about desperate enough to get another kind of physical, if it would get me a better lead. *Okay*, who was I *kidding*? Cutter was just plain my kind of hot. I loved a guy with a certain amount of perceived arrogance. I say perceived because I was betting that Cutter came by his arrogance honestly. Meaning he had the testicular fortitude to back his mouth up. It isn't technically arrogance if you're that good. Maybe confidence was the word I was looking for.

I sighed and derailed my runaway train of thought that my hormones had put on full throttle. The trouble wasn't so much what he'd said, but rather what he hadn't. I'd seen the spark and flare of recognition in his eyes. If I'd learned one thing for sure out of this exchange? Anders Martin AKA Cutter knew the girl in the picture, or at the very least, something about her and I wasn't leaving Ft. Royal until I knew what it was. Even if I had to use my powers for evil to get to the greater good. All joking aside, I *was* the kind of desperate at this point that wasn't opposed to anything as long as it got me results.

I walked up the street, away from The Plank at a steady clip and contemplated my next move.

CHAPTER 2
Cutter

"Atlas!" I shouted a few minutes after Hope sashayed that sweet, perfectly toned, ass out of my bar. My club's secretary jogged into the room a half second later.

"Yeah Captain?" he asked.

"Find out everything you can about that girl that was just in here. Said her name was Hope and she's stayin' down at the Nautilus," I said to him but my eyes were fixed on where she'd been.

She was a girl on *fire*, and I damn sure wanted to know what *she* wanted with the girl from the picture. I'd recognized her alright. Wasn't no way I was going to tell that cool drink of water though, not with how that run went straight to hell in so many ways.

"Aye, aye, Captain."

"Send Tiny back here," I told him when he turned to tend to the task I'd set him. Atlas gave me a half assed grin and an even sloppier salute. He could tell when I was in a mood and this particular shit show put my mood square in the middle of the black. Tiny didn't exactly have any fans around these parts and I think the club knew I was reaching the end of the line when it came to my patience with our SAA.

Tiny came in and said, "Wanted to see me Cutter?"

No fucking respect, this one.

"Sit down," I told him, tone cold. He scowled but complied.

"What's up?" he asked, crossing his arms over his barrel chest.

"What did I tell you when you came to me about that girl from The Sacred Hearts' Lake Run, and you told me what you'd done?" I demanded. He scowled.

"Why the hell you bring that up now, Man? That shit's over and done. It's been in our rearview over a year now."

"Answer the fucking question, Tiny," I grated.

"You said if anyone came looking my ass was on the line and you'd put it to a vote."

"Put what to a vote?" I demanded. I wanted to fucking make sure we were crystal goddamned clear this time. No mistakes. No fucking up. No Tiny going on his own fucking program.

"My standing as SAA and within the club, period. What the fuck, Man?"

"That's fucking right, and guess fucking what?" I pointed in the direction of the open bar room door and dropped both feet to the floor, the flip flops slapping loud against the concrete. "Someone, and by the set of her I'd say some sort of LEO, just came looking!"

"Oh Jesus Christ, Man! It's been over a year, even if she was a fucking cop she ain't got shit," he tried to blow it off and I turned my pointing finger to a fist and brought it crashing down on the arm of my chair.

"You don't get to decide that! Now I kept you on as a favor to Mac but this ain't his club anymore. It's *mine* and you have proven, time and fucking time again that you ain't interested in falling in line and now you've put all of us, every single fucking one of us, in the goddamned hot seat! I told you, *consequences*, Man." I crossed my arms while Tiny looked at me poleaxed.

"It ain't nothing to make this bitch disappear too…"

"Have you learned *nothing*?" I bellowed, "This isn't some girl with no family! No, you sit your ass right there." I pulled my phone out of my cut and dialed Marlin, my VP. He answered on the third ring.

"Yo."

"Marlin, Cutter, we have ourselves a situation. Get your ass and the rest of the council in here pronto."

"Can you give me a heads up, Man? How bad is it?"

"No; talk when you all get here." I hung up. The entire dialogue my eyes were locked with Tiny's watery blue ones and he looked positively mutinous. He was standing alone on the sentiment. Dumb fucking cunt.

"You're really blowing this shit out of proportion, Cut."

"We'll see what your brothers have to say about that."

Stalemate. Tiny and I sat in an angry uncomfortable silence while we waited for the rest of the boys to arrive. Atlas, who was at the bar on his cell making calls, leaned back and gave me a chin lift, indicating Marlin had called him and he would be in with the rest when they came. Nothing showed first, then Marlin. Pyro took the longest but I knew what he was doing. He was out on a salvage tow, bringing a boat back into the harbor. There was no cutting corners in our line of work.

By the time my best friend rolled in, the boys had moved enough bar tables into the room down in front of my chair so that we had a meeting table. Without a word, Pyro closed up the big wooden doors leading back here. We were effectively plunged into silence. I slid the gavel out of its pocket where it hid behind the back of my chair and cracked it sharply on the arm.

"To order," I called.

"What do you have, Brother?" Marlin asked me calmly. He was a good man, not my best friend, not my worst, but one of the most dependable dudes I had ever met. His eyes were a deep blue, the color of the fish, but that isn't how he got his name. He got his name for pulling in one of the biggest motherfucking Marlin's in state history. He was a sport fisherman by trade and ran a deep sea fishing outfit out of a slip a few down from my maritime salvage vessel.

"The Sacred Hearts Lake Run. The first one, I agreed to return one of The Suicide King's girls to Tallahassee." I watched frowns crush the expressions of my brothers around the table.

It was a big fucking tragedy what'd happened to that girl, and it was all my fucking fault. I'd put the matter into Tiny's hands, him and a prospect's. Told Tiny to 'take care of her.' I should have chosen my fucking words more carefully. When we went to head out the day after seeing The Sacred Hearts off, she'd gone missing. Tiny had choked the life out of that girl, scattered her parts all the way down the fucking highway to hell and gone… on my order.

"Why we revisiting this now?" Pyro asked, grim.

"I told you what would happen if anybody came looking and now someone has – "

Tiny interrupted me, "Aw come off it, Cutter!" Marlin stood up, Pyro right on his heels.

"That's your President, Dude. Show some fucking respect," Atlas grated.

Pyro and Marlin sank into their seats and I could read it on all of their faces. They were all sick and tired of Tiny's fuck ups and he'd run clean out of good will with every last one of them.

"Who was she?" I asked Atlas.

"Not sure yet," he said honestly, "I've got calls out to every contact I've got. It'd be easier if I had a last name but that'll come in time. Whole town is lookin' out now. Won't be long." His phone vibrated across the table.

"Speak of the devil." He scrolled down the screen and nodded, "Andrews, Hope Elizabeth Andrews." He gave a low whistle like he was impressed.

"What is it?" Nothing asked.

"She's a fucking badass, but she's not exactly a cop. She works for 'em though. Ex-military," he glanced in my direction, "Army," he clarified for my benefit, "Tested high with an aptitude for teaching so they made her into an instructor. A good one."

"Relation to the girl?" Pyro asked for me.

"Nothing yet."

"How the fuck did you get all that so quick?" Pyro asked with a frown.

"Linked In. Her whole work history is up," he turned his phone and sure as shit, there was Hope, hair pulled up into a severe bun, face flawless and her dark brown eyes sparking into the camera. She looked every inch the professional badass. Mercenary style. Interesting.

"Names are powerful things, fellas. First and last and you can find just about anything on someone." Atlas tucked his phone away.

"We need to vote this, I can't have a Sergeant at Arms bringing down this kind of heat with piss poor fucking decisions. Going off halfcocked on his own fucking program all the time."

"Now that's bullshit! *You gave me the order…*"

"I say strip him." Nothing said and stared coldly at Tiny, effectively silencing him.

"Of his rank or his whole goddamn patch?" Marlin asked disgustedly.

"Rank for now, probation for the patch," Nothing clarified.

"I second," Pyro said while Tiny sat there gaping like a landed fish.

"In favor of stripping rank say 'yay'," I said and immediately followed it up with, "Yay."

"Yay." Atlas.

"Don't fucking look at me, I suggested it!" Nothing said flatly and I gave him *the look*. He looked sheepish for half a second and entered his proper vote for the record, "Yay."

"Yay." Pyro

"Nay." Tiny spit on the floor.

"Shut the fuck up! You don't get a vote when you're the one getting' voted on. Yay," Marlin finished. I picked up the gavel and clapped it against the arm of my chair.

"So entered, so ordered."

Tiny made to stand up but Marlin and Nothing were already there, pressing him down into his seat. I got up and snapped open the Panak switchblade Reaver had gifted me upon leaving with his woman, six months or so back. Tiny made a noise of protest and jerked against the hold of the men to either side of him.

"I'd hold still, wouldn't hurt my feelings none if he cut you on accident," Pyro's smile was decidedly unfriendly. I went in and slashed the SAA flash off his cut and straightened. Tiny was glaring daggers at me but he kept his fucking mouth shut. Marlin and Nothing let him go and he jerked his cut straight on his body over his black tank.

"I could have done it," he said gruffly.

"You ain't exactly been on the level with us lately brother," Atlas said and he sounded sorry. None of us enjoyed this but we enjoyed dealing with cleaning up after Tiny even less. I knew the minute he'd told me he'd killed that girl that some serious bad juju would come our way. Now the storm was just on the horizon and maybe coming in fast, hard to tell.

"Just be grateful you're still even here, Man." Marlin shook his head and jerked his chin towards the door. Tiny scowled and went out to the bar, took two shots in rapid succession and went out. A second later his bike fired up and he peeled out. Fuck man. We all traded a look.

"Radar?" we all said in unison then broke into grins. Tiny was seriously the only fucking dude in this club not on the same page with the rest.

"Yeah, call him," Marlin said. We brought Radar in. The rest of the club's patched members were contacted, brought in, the vote cast and not surprisingly unanimously so. I bailed earlier than I intended and rode out along the strip. I'd be lying if I said I wasn't looking for that set of long, tanned legs out from under that short, white, fluttery skirt she'd been wearing. I was pretty sure I would see her again… The town just wasn't that big and she'd gotten my attention for sure. Hope Elizabeth Andrews didn't know it, but she was under my mark now. It'd be interesting to see where this was going to go. I just hoped for her sake and my club's that it didn't go anywhere tragic.

CHAPTER 3
Hope

I took my coffee off the marble countertop from the smiling barista and thanked her. I sipped the frosty confection and turned to head back out into the overcast, Ft. Royal afternoon, and stopped cold. Cutter, president of The Kraken motorcycle gang, was just outside the door to the place, shoulder leaned nonchalantly on the building's overhang support pillar. He was the picture of smug carelessness, arms crossed over his cut, but narrow chest, clad only in his leather motorcycle vest. A pair of ratty cargo shorts hanging low on his hips. His well-defined hip flexors carved that delicious damn 'V' inviting my gaze lower and I wasn't ashamed to take the invitation. Never have been, and never would be.

I caught his smug smile turning into a full on grin as I swept my gaze lower, pausing just enough where it counted even though there wasn't terribly much to look at, the shorts just loose enough to leave you wondering. He had one foot crossed in front of the other, the toes perched against the cracked sidewalk, while the leg behind it remained flat to the ground. He was balanced well. Weight evenly distributed, and in total control of himself. I guess he hadn't let his training lapse either.

"You following me?" I asked, arching one brow. His full lips crushed down in an attempt to look sincere as he suppressed his smile, and shook his head but his warm brown eyes sparkled with mirth.

"Nope, just coming in to get a cup of coffee. Small town, best place for it."

As if on cue the barista at the register called out, "Usual, Cutter?"

"That would be fantastic, Lily," he called past me.

I slipped out the door and onto the corner and waited for traffic to clear before I crossed.

"So? You find what you're looking for yet?" he called nonchalantly, when there was nothing nonchalant about it, I looked back over my shoulder at him where he looked back over his at me. Our gazes locked and sparks flew.

"How do you know her?" I asked, point blank.

"I told you, I didn't." His eyes shut down, became calculating and I felt mine narrow.

"Oh, come on, Lieutenant. You can't bullshit a bullshitter," I raised my eyebrows and took a sip of my drink, holding the straw to my lips, and even though I didn't show it, I let myself have a self-satisfied smile on the inside when his eyes fixed on the straw where I pressed it into my bottom lip. He smiled and it wasn't warm nor cold, it spoke of a total lack of surprise on his part.

"You've done your homework," he said quietly and the mock friendliness of a moment before crystallized and snapped into something much more real. We weren't playing anymore. Good. Faith wasn't a game to me, she was my sister and I needed to know what happened. Dead or alive, I had to find her.

"No doubt you've done yours too," I said.

"No doubt about that, Sweetheart," he winked at me and there was a lull in the conversation.

"How do you know her?"

"Why are you looking for her?"

"I asked first."

"Uh huh," he dropped his arms and buried his hands in his pockets, his shoulders hitching once in that thoughtful sort of physical expression people so often do but are completely unaware of. He chewed the inside of his cheek and stared off into space for a few heartbeats before shuffling into the coffee place. He picked up his drink off the counter and shuffled right on back out. It did not go unnoticed by me that he didn't pay and the girls behind the counter paid it no mind.

I wasn't really surprised, I'd been around law enforcement enough to know how this worked. Small town like this? The MC probably had more clout than the local P.D. I decided to test the theory some as Cutter drew up even with me after retrieving his drink.

"Let me guess, they pay you protection money or you have some other kind of racket going on with them?" I asked. Cutter grinned and goddamn it was disarming. I'm pretty sure if I'd been wearing any, my panties would have gone up in flames.

"Ha! What kind of thing you think we got going around here? Never mind, don't answer that," he stepped off the curb with me as I made my way up the street, the skirt of my summer dress swishing with each step. Okay, fine, *maybe* I put just enough swing into my hips to make it sway. It had the desired effect though. I stopped on the opposite side of the street and turned to look at him and most definitely caught him checking me out.

"What *do* you have going on around here?" I asked, since he opened the door, I would walk right through, thank you very much.

"You show me yours I'll show you mine, Sweetheart," his voice dipped low, for my ears alone and it was one hell of a sexy sound. He compounded the sexy by stepping just inside my personal space, I looked up defiant and he looked down the few scant inches separating us. His eyes flicked from my eyes to my lips and I *almost* wanted him to go there. God *damn* this guy was sex on a stick and it had really been too fucking long.

Hardcore attraction aside, I was always one to push my limits and to take things up a notch when challenged. I stepped just that liiiiiiittle bit closer and tipped my head back *just so*, so that our lips *almost, almost,* touched. I curled the edges of *my* lips into a heated, nasty little smile, and said, "I don't give it up on the first date."

I meant it to be a joke, a smart assed little remark because let's face it, dry sarcastic humor and smartassery has always been my thing, but Cutter… fuck if he didn't give me as good as he got.

The bastard smiled as if he'd won a fucking prize or something and touched the tip of his nose to the tip of mine rubbing out an adorable little Eskimo kiss. With a wink he said, "Fair enough, Sweetheart. What're we doing?"

My brain went out to lunch without me for a second while the tip of my nose tingled from the contact, his warm, solid, energy pouring over me in a rush at our proximity, right along with the masculine scent of whatever cologne he wore. I blinked. Fuck, he got me... I wasn't one to go back on anything I'd said when confronted with it, even if I had said it in jest. Backpedaling hadn't, and would never be, my thing and now as a result I was at a disadvantage. I had somehow just put myself on a date with the president of a known illegal enterprise. This was *not* going to look stellar as a footnote on my resume but... *Faith.*

Fine, okay, I could let him have this if it got me closer to him opening up about what he knew about the bitch who was last seen with my sister. I took a half step back out of his personal space and his smile widened.

"Your town, why don't you tell me? What're we doing?" I conceded defeat for this round and kicked the shit out of myself mentally. He held out his elbow all gentlemanly like and I scoffed but looped my arm through it.

"How about a nice walk on the beach? Get to know each other some?" I looked out towards the water. I'd just run my ass off on the beach this morning, but sure. Sounded like a plan.

"Alright," I assented and we set off at a leisurely pace in that direction sipping on our frothy blended coffees as they melted in their ecofriendly plastic cups.

CHAPTER 4
Cutter

Oh boy, she was a hard ass, and did I ever love a chase! I held out my arm and she hesitated, she was even prettier up close under the cloudy skies, which were still a hell of a lot brighter than the dim interior of The Plank. She finally looped her left arm through my right and I led us at a leisurely stroll across the street and towards the water. I have to admit that I lost myself a bit in her damn good looks and my mouth got away from me.

"So what brings you to our fair town of Ft. Royal?" I asked. She dug into her purse and shoved the picture of the girl from the Sacred Hearts' Lake Run at me again.

"This girl, you seen her?" she looked at me pointedly and it wasn't friendly.

"Nope, I already answered that." I smiled grandly and she shoved the picture back in her purse, switching her drink back to her right hand and taking a sip.

"Well I already answered yours," she said tartly. The sass on this woman was out of this world, but I could tell, she would skate the line if not skate right over it into disrespect, which could either be problematic, or could lead to some really fun times.

"So tell me something I don't know, Sweetheart," I kept my smile on my face even though I let my tone carry some bite. She looked up at me and her dark eyes flashed emotion like lightning over the water, though what emotion specifically? I couldn't tell you. She was quick to get her shit under control. I liked that. Solid. Different, and not entirely unrefreshing. I felt a little guilty for that last thought, a pair of pained green eyes flashing out from my memory, but I quickly buried it. I wanted to know more about the enchanting creature in front of me. I already knew all there was about a woman I loved but could never have.

"I don't know what you already know, so how about you ask a question and I'll answer it." Hope's voice rattled me loose from my pattern of thought and I smiled and nodded.

"Alright, where you from then?" I asked.

She snorted, "I thought you did your homework."

"I did, but it seemed like a safe enough place to start," I shrugged, "Don't like that one? Okay, alright, let's see… where to begin?"

"California. I was raised in California." I could *hear* the eye roll in her voice and I grinned.

"West coast girl, nice. Your turn."

"Oh, I get a turn? Goodie!"

"Yeah and that was it, next question," she scoffed and gave me a little playful shove. I laughed.

"What branch of the military were you in?" she asked.

"Not your turn, Sweetheart… but, I'll answer you anyways. I'm one of Uncle Sam's misguided children." She nodded carefully, thoughtfully, and I could see the wheels turning.

"What about you?"

"Army, enlisted when I was eighteen, stayed in for 10 years," she shrugged a shoulder nonchalantly.

"See any action?"

"Some," and that was really all that needed to be said about that. I was the last person that wanted to relive any of that shit. We walked in silence for a few moments.

"Family?" she asked.

"Got a brother but I might as well be an only child for how much we talk. Parents live in Virginia."

"That where you're from?"

"I get two questions if I answer that?"

"That's one," she said and I laughed.

"Fair enough, Darlin', fair enough. What about you? Family?" she hesitated.

"Two younger sisters, mom died when I was eighteen, that's part of why I enlisted, I needed to support them. They stayed with our grandmother while I was in basic, but I had to feed and clothe two sisters that weren't even teenage girls yet and become sister-mom." Her posture was stiff, there was more there but now wasn't the time to press. I needed to find out what her agenda was when it came to my club before anything.

"Sorry to hear that, that's rough." She nodded and sipped her drink.

"Boyfriend?" I asked and she laughed.

"No. Girlfriend?"

"Nope."

I tried to steer us into safer conversational waters, "What do you like to do for fun?"

She was quiet for a long time, and I took the opportunity to study her, we were still a ways from the water but our steady pace would get us there. She closed her eyes and sighed out in obvious frustration.

"It's been a while since I've done anything fun, not sure I remember the meaning of the word," she confessed and it was probably the most honest thing she'd said to me since we'd met the day before. The thing that struck me was her confession seemed to carry with it the weight of the world. Her shoulders dropped, and her gaze became distant as she stared out over the water, pointedly not looking at me. I think she was regretting telling me.

"Well you're in a good place to fix that," I shared.

"Yeah, back at you. What do you do for fun?" she asked.

"You just going to keep asking me the questions I ask you? Or you going to come up with some of your own? Geeze – Hey!" she knocked her shoulder into mine and leaned into me and I let her put me off balance some. I hopped on one foot in the sand and laughed and we returned to walking along, only this time she had a smile on her face, a genuine one and it lit her up from the inside out. Turned her from a pretty girl to a fucking gorgeous one in the space of an eye blink. I think my heart tripped over itself in my chest and I felt my cock stir in my shorts. Damn.

"I get two more questions," she pointed out then with that smile that was a match for my most rakish said, "Answer me. I'd ask nicely and sound like less of a demanding bitch but I'm not falling for that and, well, I kind of am a demanding bitch so spill it."

I grinned, realizing I'd been quiet too long but it hadn't been in an attempt to fool her into asking me to answer, I'd just been stunned by that stellar smile of hers into total silence.

"I do a lot of things for fun; work, swim, surf, fish, and yes, fuck. That one has to be my favorite," she barked a laugh and it was a clear, musical sound. I liked that too. I couldn't tell with her deep tan but she may have even been blushing.

"Crossing..." she stopped, "Excuse me, crossed the line right into the sex questions I see. Okay, last time you got to fuck?" She wasn't pulling any punches and to be honest, the topic of conversation was right up my alley, not to mention it made me feel like a teenager again. Bonus points for anything that accomplished that.

"Few nights ago," I said honestly, "Some tourist I picked up at a bar. Wasn't anything special," I opened my mouth to ask her something and she stopped me.

"Ah! Ah! Ah! No way, I've still got one more question, Mister." I grinned and inclined my head. We were getting out closer to the water and the rhythmic crashing of the waves on the shore was both soothing and a nice dull roar. We had to raise our voices to be heard over the white noise of the surf but that didn't bother us any. I turned us gently to walk along the water back towards the marina where my boat was moored.

"Okay, Darlin'. Go ahead and ask," I urged.

"I'm thinking!" She looked like she was doing it pretty hard too, it also looked like she was enjoying our little get to know you game. I know I was.

"You a love 'em and leave 'em kind of guy, Cutter? A real heartbreaker?" she asked.

"Why, you interested in a good time?"

"Answer my question first and maybe I'll answer yours," she tilted her face in my direction, into the sun and shaded her eyes with her hand. She unhooked her arm from mine to do it and I have to say, I didn't much like that. She finished off her coffee drink and I sucked down the rest of mine, making her wait for it.

"No, I make sure the terms are set before anything happens," I said. "Never been a cheater and never found the girl of my dreams neither," which wasn't exactly a lie. Hayden was never mine to begin with. It was only my damn fool ass to blame for any heartache on my part where Li'l Bit was concerned. My fault and no one else's. I'd come to terms with that a while ago and she and Reave would never know just how deep those feelings ran, which was as it should be.

Hope's expression became somber, then calculating before finally becoming a mixture of regret and defeat in equal measure. She looked up at me, face hard as stone.

"Only thing I'm interested in is finding that girl," she stated flatly but it was too late. I'd seen the cracks in her armor. Tough as she was there was some vulnerability in there. Fuck that was hot.

"Well, you know, doesn't mean you can't have a little bit of fun while you're doing it, now does it?" I asked and put on my most charming smile. No dice. She was having none of it.

"That's exactly what that means. Good talk, Cutter. Small town and all, I'm sure I'll see you around." She spun as if to go and I caught her elbow, firmly but gently and she froze. I waited for her to swing on me. I knew she was trained and capable but she didn't so much as twitch a single muscle. Interesting. She was stiff, in a holding pattern of readiness, her body almost thrummed with barely contained violence and my respect and desire for her started a steady climb.

"Hey look, I'm just horsing around, I didn't mean to make light of whatever it is you've got going on. For real."

She looked like she was thinking that over hard, finally she shook her head, rounded her arm, and slipped out of my grasp with a classic evasion move. I let her do it and she turned, striding across the sugar fine sand, back towards town. I stood and watched her go, admittedly enjoying the view of that fine, toned ass of hers in its short skirt as she walked away from me. I waited to see if she would stop, or turn back, and just when I thought it was time to give it up, that there was really no interest there, she finally did it. She turned and looked back over her shoulder at me. I couldn't see her eyes for the distance but it was something.

Gave me hope that Hope and I would be seeing each other again. Truthfully, I already knew I would. It hadn't been hard to engineer my 'accidental' run in with her at Soul Fuel on the boulevard for this little chat. Lily had done what I asked and had texted me the second she'd seen her. The whole town knew I'd marked Hope Andrews. She shouldn't have any problems while she was here, at least not from the locals. She wouldn't be getting any cooperation from them either though. Not until I knew exactly what she was after. What she wanted with the Suicide King's girl from the lake.

I would definitely be seeing Hope again, all roads to the answers she sought ended with me. I just had to make sure whatever answers she got kept me, and my club, in the clear.

CHAPTER 5
Hope

I take it back. Cutter wasn't confident, he was an arrogant ass. Although truthfully, I think I was more butt hurt that I let myself be distracted, even for just a minute, by my hormones. Faith deserved better than that. Faith depended on me and I'd been letting her down for almost *two years*. My namesake was running out on me but I would be fucked if I would quit on Faithy before I knew for sure where she was or what'd happened to her.

I walked back to the Bed and Breakfast, fueled by my mounting anger, my fury at my helpless inability to find my sister. I changed into a set of workout clothes, wrapped my hands and went out the back of the B&B into the yard. First thing I'd done upon hitting this town was figure out what I could hit and not do any damage. There wasn't a gym around here to speak of, unless it was a heavy bag and a set of weights in some beach bum meat head's garage, so I settled for a heavy hand wrap and the use of one of the B&B's palm trees. This was only the second time I'd been out here... today.

I stretched, warmed up, and laid into the damn tree until my wraps were toast and I was pretty sure I was bruised *and* bleeding underneath. I didn't care. The pain helped me focus. I stood, chest heaving, body slicked with sweat and still didn't feel any real satisfaction. I wanted to cry, but crying was for pussies, and just because I had one, didn't mean I *was* one.

I stared out the back gate and over the white sand beach towards the clear turquoise water. I debated heartily for several moments between shower and swim. The sun was hanging low in the sky and the coffee on the beach had definitely worn off. I sighed and started to unwrap my hands. Food had to be next on the agenda. I needed to refuel. Once the wraps were off I flexed my hands. Two knuckles on my left hand were swelling and two on my right were indeed bleeding, the skin slightly split. No more punching things for a day or two. That was okay, I could still kick the shit out of the poor tree.

"You won this time sucka, but next time I'm taking you down," I muttered at it before trudging wearily back into the B&B, my wraps trailing forlornly from my leaden arms. I took the stairs two at a time to push myself, and once back in my room, treated myself to a hot shower. It was amazing how restorative they could be.

I spent a minute on my hair and makeup, blow drying the mass of chestnut waves kept it from getting frizzy on me and just a touch of product kept it looking sleek and shiny. I did my makeup, emphasizing my large brown eyes with bronze shadows. Some nude gloss on my lips and I felt put together, at least on the outside. I donned the same short dress I'd been in earlier but traded out the simple beachy flip flops I'd started the day in for some gladiator sandal heels. You know the kind, goldish metallic, the kind that wound up the leg. I liked them even if they were stereotypical white girl, trash-tastic. They were my favorite heels to wear if the shit got real. High enough to accentuate my legs, but low enough that I could still throw a perfect round house kick without fear of losing my balance in the slightest. I mean, why worry about function over form when you could have both with just a little extra effort?

I grabbed my purse, the weight of the gun inside kind of annoying, and slung the bag over my shoulder. Keys, phone, wallet, compact and lip gloss were all accounted for alongside the Ruger .38 revolver I was packing. It was a cute little gun, held five shots. I had some spare bullets tucked away but that was wishful thinking. If I were in a gunfight long enough to have a need to reload I was doing it wrong.

I left the Bed and Breakfast and started the walk back towards town. I'd ridden in on my 2013 Ducati Diavel. I loved her so much. She was a glossy black and leaned in the shade looking pretty badass, practically begging me to go for a ride. Wasn't happening though. Especially with the bikers in town. That would seriously lead me to having to whoop one of their asses. No one talked shit about my baby, but that pack of jokers, one of them would try it.

It was about a thirty minute walk from the Nautilus to the start of

The Boulevard, which is what the locals called the main drag through town. I thought a lot about Cutter on my way down the sidewalk. I was trying to pick a place to eat, which just about every place here was fish themed or devoted to fish. Not a bad thing, not at all, as a California girl, I grew up on the stuff but when every place had pretty much the same fare it made it hard to decide which one to go with.

I finally just picked one at random and went in. It was a little coastal themed bar and grill, and as soon as I went through the open air doorway, I wished I had picked any other restaurant but this one. Cutter was standing by the bar, beer in his hand talking to one of his motorcycle gang brethren or brothers or whatever the fuck they called each other.

"Whoa! Now who's following who, Sweetheart?" he called out with one of those pyroclastic, panty-vaporizing smiles. I still wasn't wearing any but it still had the desired effect. Damn it.

"Just looking for something to eat, I could find someplace else but, you know, fuck that," I said and slid up onto a vacant barstool next to him. He laughed.

"Sorry about earlier?" he asked.

Yes. I need you to tell me how you know Tonya, I need to know what you know...

"Nope." I said but I think my bravado failed me this time, Cutter's chocolate brown eyes softened, becoming liquid and deep. He kept his gaze fixed on mine, never backing down.

"Care to finish our date then?"

"No."

"Hey Pyro, shove off, Man. I'll see you around, I've got a date with the lady," Cutter said, his gaze still affixed to mine. I raised an eyebrow. Pushy bastard wasn't he?

"See you around Bro," Pyro clapped Cutter on the back of his leather vest, polished off his beer and slid the glass down the bar to the tender. I didn't see if the man serving caught it or not but there was no sound of breaking glass so he must have. Cutter slid up on the stool next to mine. Our eyes remained locked.

"I didn't mean to offend you out there," he said quietly.

"Noted."

"You don't give an inch do you, Sweetheart?" he asked, an easy smile gracing his mouth. Fuck I bet he tasted phenomenal. I scowled harder.

"Why won't you tell me?" I asked.

"Why won't *you* tell *me?*" he asked. We had this pretty bad track record of deadlocking, stalemating, whatever.

"I don't trust people with my personal business," I said. He tilted his head to the side considering.

"Personal huh?"

"Yep."

"Well it's pretty much the same for me, Baby. How do I know I can trust you?"

"Look, I don't care about whatever it is you do out here. I'm just looking for the girl."

"Why?"

Fuck, he was going to try and force this out of me and I wasn't about to go there. After the first few false leads when a reward had been offered, back in the beginning of this nightmare, I'd learned to keep my cards close to my vest. People, as it turned out, were inherently shitty, selfish, fucks who were only in it for themselves. More than once I had gone out on a wing and a prayer only to find that some dumb prick, or worse, some even dumber twat leading a meathead or two *around* by their pricks. They were all the same. All of them were confident they could get me somewhere neutral and roll me for the reward money I may or may not have been carrying. They didn't give two shits, they were preying on the hopes and prayers of someone just trying to find their lost sister. They'd all lost something too by the time I'd gotten done with them. Their freedom, or, in one or two cases an eye or a finger…

"Okay, let's make a deal," he said when I'd been silent and balefully staring at him for too long. I raised an eyebrow and I knew I didn't look impressed.

"I'll buy you dinner, we'll talk about the unimportant shit for a while, take a walk back with me to my boat, share a glass of wine and let's get to know each other some, eh?" he looked at me plaintively and I snorted.

"I said I don't give it up on the first date," I said dryly.

"Not looking for sex," he said softly. If he were, he'd be disappointed because I would probably… who the fuck was I kidding, if it weren't for Faith I would probably tap that ass and be slipping out of his bed pulling the walk of shame before the sun could even rise. I was about to smart off but there was something in the look he was giving me.

"Sure, yeah. Okay." I found myself saying. *Who the fuck was this guy that he could have such an effect on me after just a couple of meets?*

"Know what you like?"

"Haven't looked at the menu."

"Can you trust me enough to order for yah?" he asked with that disarming smile of his.

"I suppose."

He ordered for us from the bartender who nodded and said, "You got it, Cut."

"What'll you drink?" Cutter asked me.

"Water."

"You heard her, Man; water and I'll have another IPA." The bartender nodded, poured our drinks and wandered off to put our order in. "Where were we?"

"Lost track." I told him, certain he was referring to our earlier game of however many questions.

"Ladies first then."

I pondered him in the light from the sunset blaring in from the back windows. There was something different about him this time, like he'd committed to something. He had that soldier's resolve painted all over his face, in the set of his shoulders, which despite how he nonchalantly leaned against the bar, were stiff.

"Why Florida?" I asked.

"It was as far away and as filled with water as I could get from that crusted, dried, piece of shit country," he said and his expression grew steelier, not less. I nodded slowly. I didn't have much love for

Iraq or Afghanistan either, *especially* as a woman.

"What about you? Where do you call home?" he asked.

"Nowhere, I have some shit in storage, but that isn't 'home'," I answered.

"Why, you runnin'?" he asked. I gave him a smile.

"Not running."

"Not runnin'?" Now it really seemed as if I had piqued his curiosity but plates were set in front of us and music started up and started up loud. I quirked an eyebrow at him and took a bite of my pasta which was creamy and delicious and loaded with all manner of seafood.

We ate in silence, or at least we didn't talk. There was no point in shouting over the music pounding through the bar. It was a Friday or Saturday night by the looks of it, and the party started here as soon as the sun went down. We finished our food and Cutter threw down some rumpled bills on the bar. The 'tender whisked them away, nodded, and Cutter slipped off his stool. I followed suit and like earlier he held out his arm, the perfect gentleman.

I slipped my arm through his and he led me out front, out of the blaring noise and onto a lightly breezed sidewalk. He turned left, away from my B&B and towards the marina. We walked in silence for a time.

"Believe it's your turn to ask," he said after the bass thump from the bar was a distant pulsing beat behind us, echoing in time with my slightly elevated pulse.

"Why'd you start your gang?" I asked. Cutter choked on a laugh and patted my hand where it rested in the crook of his arm, then left his hand covering my own. His fingers were warm, calloused and rough against my skin, but I didn't mind. I liked a man who worked for a living and the texture of Cutter's hands had a lot to say about that.

"The Kraken MC isn't a gang, Sweetheart. It's a club. A motorcycle club, or MC for short," he explained. My face felt hot and I had to bite my lips together to stop myself from apologizing. He'd sounded genuinely offended for a second there. Cutter chuckled.

"Apology accepted," he said simply and I felt my face crush down into a frown. I did not like how he'd seemingly just plucked that from my mind.

"Anyways, I didn't start it. I just took over. Original guy who started it was a dude named Mac. Ran it completely different, when he died of cancer, I sort of stepped up."

"Sorry, that sucks he died."

"Naw, Mac was a bastard if there ever was one. This club was an anemic, half-assed version of what a club should be when I took over. Took me a couple of years but I got everyone on board with my way of thinking. It's pretty much the brotherhood it was always meant to be now."

"I'm not gonna lie, I have no idea how it all works," I told him and he nodded.

"I suppose I could tell you a few things," he said and we turned into the marina's parking lot. He paused, steps faltering.

"The thing about MC's that you have to understand, is that one, we don't play by civilian rules. We make our own rules – form a bond with our brothers more profound than blood. It goes beyond honor and loyalty. I'd do anything for my brothers and they'd do anything for me. It's the way it works." He started us walking again and we passed the harbormaster's office.

"A lot like the bond you share with your unit," I said nodding.

"Stronger than even that, Sweetheart. I may be willing to die for the next man in my unit, but I'm willing to do a lot worse for one of my brothers. You get me?" he asked. He took me down one of the docks and he stopped short in front of one of the sailboats.

"I don't think I understand that one, I mean what could be worse than dying for the next man?" I searched his face which shut down some as he searched mine. The clouds of whatever he was thinking obscured his true intentions before he flashed that blinding panty melting smile of his. I knew that was all I was going to get for now, still, some insight was better than no insight at all and he'd certainly given me food for thought.

"Here we are, home sweet home," he said with a grand gesture at what must have been his boat. No idea if it was his home too. I let him help me up even though I didn't need it. It was kind of nice that he was a gentleman, not only given that he was a biker, but more because you just didn't find many these days. Granted, I was a tough chick and as women's lib and progressive as they came, but there was something... charming about being treated like a lady by a man who I was almost certain knew what I was capable of. Most guys did it out of habit, or to be condescending, but for Cutter, well, it felt like a natural extension of who he was and I liked that. I liked that probably way too much.

There were a couple of canvas chairs, a rich wood to match the decking of the sailboat. The backs and seats to the chairs were sun bleached like I would imagine the sails to be, though with the sails in their downed state, there was no really telling. A small table sat between the two chairs by the white painted chain railing and the set up looked both intimate and homey.

"Have a seat, Sweetheart. You like red or white?" he asked.

I took a seat and placed my white, rhinestone studded purse by my feet, careful not to make it clunk and give away the presence of the concealed handgun inside.

"White, please?"

"Girl after my own heart, back in a sec."

Cutter disappeared down below deck and I closed my eyes. It was still warm out here, a slight breeze coming in off the water. I listened to it lap against the hull of the boat, the distant thrum and bump of bar music from the Boulevard and the metallic clinging sound and rustle and snap of the flags in the breeze was a soothing thing that I could probably get used to if I ever got to settle down.

I had to hand it to Cutter, this wasn't a bad way to live. Peaceful in fact. I opened my eyes when I heard his tread on the deck, appreciative that he wasn't trying to be quiet or sneak up on me. He set two wine glasses on the small table and poured a generous amount in each, setting the bottle between them. He sat in the deck chair opposite mine and handed me a glass, picking up his own. He clicked his against mine and we sipped the cool, sweet wine.

"What are we toasting to?" I asked after savoring the selection.

"New beginnings," he suggested with a wink.

"How do you mean?"

He let out a gusty sigh of satisfaction after taking another sip of his wine and set the glass on the little table. He leaned forward in his seat, forearms on his knees and looked at me hard.

"You always gotta be so suspicious?" he asked.

"You always have to avoid the question?" I countered. He chuckled darkly and reached down, gently cupping the heel of one of my feet with his hand. He gave the barest of tugs and I thought about it for a second and relented. More to prove the point that I did know how to trust… well okay, more that I still had one leg and two arms to beat his ass with if he decided to do something I didn't like. He placed the heel of my foot on top of his thigh and picked at the laces holding my gladiator heels on.

I watched him fascinated as he took off my shoe but fascination quickly turned to contentment when he pressed his thumb into the arch of my foot, his warm, rough fingers wrapping around the instep. He nodded carefully at my reaction and caught my eyes with his. We stared at one another across a chasm of silence for several heartbeats, each looking the other over, wordlessly sousing each other out.

"You need to relax, Sweetheart," his voice was low and soothing and sent a little thrill of desire down my spine. I shivered and his smile grew into a shit eating grin. I raised my eyebrows and wordlessly took another sip of my wine. It was sweet and crisp and really damned good. Cutter had taste. I looked at the bottle, some kind of Riesling.

"Good stuff," I complimented.

"Thanks," he kneaded my foot just a little more insistently and I couldn't help it, my eyes slipped shut and a tiny sigh of contentment escaped me. I didn't leave my eyes closed for long. Cutter was hot, he had the bad boy thing down perfect and I enjoyed looking. Not like he minded it. I watched as he took another mouthful of wine, savoring it before he swallowed.

"Gimme the other one, Baby."

I scoffed a laugh, "I'm not your Baby," but I did what he asked and gave him the other foot. The deck was smooth beneath my polished toes. He gave the other foot the same careful consideration and I had to admit, sitting here like this, with him, was nice. We'd stopped speaking and it was odd, we didn't have to. The silence was a comfortable one of two grown ass adults taking a chill at the end of a long day. For a minute it was easy to pretend that we weren't at odds. That he wasn't hiding something from me and I wasn't hiding anything from him.

"You know, I thought you were a looker before but when you're relaxed and not scowling all the time, you're a real knock out," he took a drink and winked at me over his glass. I raised an eyebrow, amused and gave him the finger. He laughed.

We sat in companionable silence for a long time. When Cutter had finished kneading that foot he brought the other up so both of them rested on his knee and we just relaxed under the star spangled sky of the warm Florida night, sipping our wine and just being comfortable. God it would be nice if I could get more of this in my life.

Too soon I finished the last sip of my wine and sighed out, setting the glass on the little table. Cutter lifted the bottle and gave me a considering look.

"No thanks," I murmured and gathered my purse. He wasn't going to tell me anything else and as much as my pussy, and inner wanton sex goddess disagreed with me on this, I wasn't going to fuck him, so I needed to head back to my room and get some sleep. Get a fresh start in the am.

I dropped my feet to the deck and Cutter stood with me. He caught me around my waist, hauling me forward and closing the foot or so gap between us. My hands went unbidden to the swell of his arms and I looked up at him questioningly.

"That, was a good first date," he murmured.

"You aren't getting any," I stated flatly.

"Just want my good night kiss," he breathed and his breath was warm against my lips. *Oh Hell yes!* My inner wanton sex fiend screamed while my brain tried valiantly to dissuade me with, *not a good idea Hope! Not a good idea!* But it was too late. Cutters lips touched mine, soft, so soft; so gentle. A query really, giving me ample time to shove him away, but I couldn't.

When I didn't shove him away he hauled me up tighter against his body and I deepened the kiss, flicking my tongue against his lower lip. I just had to know, had to have a taste to see if he tasted as phenomenal as I thought he would and *god*, yes he did! Salty and masculine, Cutter tasted of the ocean, like a fresh storm front moving in off the water. Crisp, like the wine we'd just drunk but also, just of *him*. I couldn't help the needy groan that escaped me as I practically melted in his embrace. Damn it. So not fair.

His hand swept up my body and buried itself in the back of my hair, pressing me to him and I was okay with that. Somehow my hands had done some wandering of their own, cupping his bearded cheeks, thumbs stroking lightly across his cheekbones. He growled into my mouth, a deep, satisfied, and completely base sound that loosened things in my chest and made me, yes *me*, Hope Elizabeth Andrews, ever loving badass extraordinaire, swoon. I swooned. I motherfucking sighed out into his mouth and sagged slightly into his chest like some kind of goddamn Disney princess… and it felt so fucking good to do it.

I lost myself completely for a minute there and couldn't even blame the wine. I mean I'd only had one glass and no one could accuse me of being a light weight, no sir. Cutter's hand, the one that wasn't buried in my hair, drifted to the swell of my hip and pulled me just that slightest bit closer. He was so warm, his energy still and controlled as his lips moved over mine and our tongues twisted and explored. His kiss was sweet and demanding at the same time and there was something that was a complete turn on about that. I pressed my thighs together and raised myself up onto my toes before dropping flat footed to the deck and rocking back, gasping for air.

Cutter's hands were suddenly both in my hair, gently pushing it back from my face. He smiled like a teenage boy who'd just talked the head cheerleader into the backseat of his car. He smoothed his thumbs along my jaw, his fingertips slipping out of my hairline to rest on either side of my throat, my pulse jumping beneath them.

He looked over my face as if committing this moment, my expression, to the deepest recesses of his memory, cementing it there for the rest of his life. He shuddered as if waking from a dream and his smile softened to something more serious.

"Not every man out here is out to dick you over, Sweetheart. *I'm not out to dick you over*... sometimes you just gotta have a little faith," his smile slipped when I recoiled in horror.

Shit. He knew something! He knew something about Tonya Anon, the last person to see my sister Faith! And here I was, forgetting that he knew something and wouldn't tell me! So what the fuck was I doing playing tonsil hockey with the son of a bitch on his boat?

I snarled in disgust, more at myself than at him and leapt for the dock. I landed lightly on my feet, as I'd been trained to do, and strode away, and I kept walking until I hit beach, and I kept walking after that. Striding across the sand and away from Anders Cutter Martin. A man who was too easily making me forget myself and what was at stake.

Faith. That was the big fucking problem and why I was here. I didn't have Faith anymore. My sister was gone and I didn't know where, or how, or what'd happened and I wasn't giving up until I knew all of those things and then some and had taken it out on every last motherfucker who'd had a hand in her disappearance.

God *damn it*, I had been stupid back there. I picked up my pace, the sand soft beneath my feet... Fuck! I'd forgotten my favorite heels, just fucking perfect.

CHAPTER 6
Cutter

"What did I say?" I called to Hope's retreating back but she was striding away like a fire had been lit under her shapely ass. I blinked and shook my head, marveling. That was *not* the reaction I typically got from women when I turned on the charm. I replayed what I'd said in my head over and over again.

"Not every man out here is out to dick you over, Sweetheart. I'm not out to dick you over... sometimes you just gotta have a little faith..."

I didn't get it. Something about it had her reeling back like I'd backhanded her straight in the mouth.

I couldn't help but smile, her mouth had been red, lips swollen from my kiss, from my teeth sinking gently into that lush bottom lip of hers. She'd tasted like candy and damn did I want more of that. I reached into my shorts and stroked my erection. What? It wasn't like there was anyone out here to watch me and if they were, fuck, that made them the pervert not me. I wrapped my hand around the neck of the wine bottle and drank straight from it.

I really wanted to know what had set her off but there wasn't any way to find out tonight. I went to head below decks and tripped. Hope's fancy strappy sandal heels. I smiled. Well at least I had an excuse to see her again. I wondered vaguely if she was going to come back for them. I brought them down below with me, just in case it decided to rain, and dropped them in front of the couch.

With a heavy sigh I finished off the wine and tossed the empty bottle in the recycling under the galley's small sink. With a stretch I trudged to the bow and dropped my shorts. I hung my cut on the hook inside the door and crawled up into bed. I lay on my back, hands under my head, haunted by calculating deep brown eyes and

Hope's lovely smile, when she gave it. The feel of her lips on mine, tongues touching; her fingertips on my face... Aw fuck.

I took my cock in hand and started jerking it. There wasn't any way sleep was gonna happen until I did something about it. The girl was phenomenal, there was no denying that. She had looks but didn't rely on them and I liked that about her. She had brains under that beauty and it'd been a long damned time since fireworks had gone off with a kiss but man, *she could kiss*.

I was a steel rod in my fist and I couldn't help it. I closed my eyes and fantasized about her. About those long toned legs around my hips. I wanted to fuck little Miss Hope against the nearest wall. Drive into her until she came around my cock and spilled all of her secrets and told me her story. Just the thought of her head tipped back, the long line of her lovely throat bared to me as feral sounds poured from it... Jesus. I came in record time. Fuck I wanted to know what she had going on.

I lay panting, staring at the ceiling of my bunk, listening to the water lap against the hull, listening to my breathing slow, and the blood rush in my ears and didn't feel a damned bit better for the orgasm I'd just had.

"Fuck," I muttered into the dark. How did I let this bitch under my skin? Better question was, how was I going to play this? Keep my club safe *and* get the girl. I wasn't looking to fall in love or nothing. Last time I'd pulled that shit had ended in disaster for me. I turned my head and looked at the photo of Li'l Bit. Her green eyes vacant and distant, deep lines of sorrow etched into her face as she stared off into space. Fucking tragic and beautiful at the same time. The kind of image that reaches into your chest and squeezes your heart. I felt a pang of wistful regret and with a sigh got up to clean myself up before my come had a chance to drip onto the sheets.

I'd waited, been there for her and during the height of her grief she'd come to me for comfort and like the selfish asshole I am, I took full advantage of the situation. I know for a fact Reave didn't hold it against me. I mean fuck, he was gone *six months* or more. I knew that L'il Bit felt a whole lot of guilt for it though, and that part is what made *me* feel guilty. Not that I'd done it, but that she bore the burden of it. I switched on a cold shower and stepped under the spray, rinsing off, lathering up and rinsing off again.

I didn't think I would ever let myself get over it. I still wasn't over it, over her... but I had to admit, Hope was providing a nice distraction for the moment. Only thing she was missing was the damsel in distress routine. I *loved* being the big damn hero but at the same time, it was refreshing that Hope was solid and didn't need saving. In fact she didn't have a single damned vulnerability that I could see. I shut off the tap and dried off on the way back to bed.

Didn't have a clue what was going to happen or where shit was gonna lead, the only thing I knew for sure is I needed to protect my club. But I was the kind of guy that liked his beer and drank it too, so I would see what I could do about having the best of both worlds. I stared at the ceiling for a long time, wide awake, my mind turning over the possibilities and roving down every avenue. Last thing I thought of before I finally crashed was, whether I should wait on Hope to come to me like some kind of feral cat, or if I should go to her. Maybe I should leave it up to fate? The town was small enough, I'd be bound to see her again at some point.

Yeah. I'd give it a day or two and see what turned up. That's what I'd do.

CHAPTER 7
Hope

I lay in the hammock on the beach between two palm trees, soaking up the sun. It'd been two days since the disaster on Cutter's boat and I'd had zero luck with the rest of the town on locating any information on Tonya. I'd canvased the entire damn place. Even went so far as to go door to door. Nothing. Zip. Zero. Nada. No one had either seen her, or would admit to seeing her. All roads to Tonya Anon led straight to The Kraken MC's door.

I needed a time out. To relax, sure, but mostly to think. How the fuck was I going to get those happy bastards to cooperate? So here I was, taking my time out, lazing in the sun and working on my tan. They had about six of these Hammocks all in a row between palm trees just sitting on the beach for anyone to use and so I took advantage. The warmth of the sun soaking into my skin made me drowsy, and I didn't pay much mind to the first touch on the instep of my right foot. Another came, just above it on my ankle, then another on my shin. I opened my eyes and tensed, staring wide eyed from behind my big, bug eyed, sunglass lenses.

Cutter knelt beside my hammock and placed another gentle butterfly kiss up higher on my shin from the last. I watched him curiously for a minute. He smiled, no, *grinned* and it was one of those secret little boy smiles that immediately made me wet. Fuck. So not fair, the kind of effect he had on me. He pressed a kiss to my knee, all the while his gaze locked with mine and even though I ached to have him keep going, I mean shit, it felt really damn good, I had to open my mouth and break the spell.

"What are you doing?" I demanded and arched one brow, putting on my resting bitch face.

"Seducing you, is it working?" he asked.

I laughed, then stated dryly, "Not really," when what I really meant to say was, *incredibly well, please continue.* Guess Cutter had some ESP going for him, because he pressed another kiss to my knee, then above my knee and I think I stopped breathing because the playfulness was bleeding out of his eyes and the heat index in them was rising, turning them molten.

"What 'cha thinking, Sweetheart?" he asked and his voice was low and as sultry as the air around us.

I opened my mouth to speak but was cut off by a nearby shout, "Cutter! You comin' man!?"

I tipped my face in the direction of the shout slightly but something flashed in Cutter's gaze and I couldn't tear mine away from his if I wanted to. My heart rate had picked up some time ago and thrummed in my chest and the side of my neck. I was turned on, I was riding that fine edge of adrenaline and it felt pretty good, I'm not even going to lie.

"Come with us," Cutter said and the grin was back.

"Where?" I asked, realizing quickly that the only way to what I sought was through the MC and the best way to them was through the man kneeling in the soft sand by my hip.

"Bowling," he said with that dazzling smile of his.

"Bowling?" I asked incredulous. Somehow I did not picture a bunch of badass bikers bowling. I thought about it and nope, never not once ever crossed my mind.

"Bowling," he stood in one fluid movement and it clicked, why I thought he was so fucking hot. Cutter moved with purpose in everything that he did. He was a trained Marine. Cutter was *dangerous* but his affable personality let you forget that. I gave him a calculating look.

"Have to change unless bikini bowling is in these days, in which case, I don't care I'm still changing."

"Seriously, dude? What's the hold up?" A woman trudged across the sand towards us, shorts and a silver bikini top, she was spectacularly tattooed across her chest and down one arm. The other arm appearing to be a work in progress, her leg also a work in progress, the flowers and butterflies climbing to her knee.

"Hossler, meet Hope. We're waiting on her to grab a change of clothes and she's coming with us," Cutter said.

"Really?" Hoss said dryly and looked me over as if she were assessing a new threat to her territory that she hadn't realized existed until just right then.

"Really," I said standing up and gathering my towel and beach tote.

Hossler rolled her pretty blue eyes, "Whatever, just hurry the fuck up already!" she said and turned to walk back towards the boulevard and the line of bikes there.

"Peace offering, Sweetheart," Cutter said, drawing my attention from the curious woman.

"What?" I asked and he held up my heels.

"Not sure what it was I said to offend, but I apologize." The charm was back and I smirked.

"Dial it down a notch, Casanova. It wasn't you, it was me," I said and took the proffered heels.

Cutter put both hands over his heart and looked pained before saying, "Damn, not even on the second date and I'm getting the 'it's me' speech? That's got to be some kind of record!" I laughed softly and smiled. I bit my lower lip and nodded slowly.

"Place I'm staying at is two blocks up, where you want to meet me?" I asked.

"Meet you right out front, Darlin'," he winked at me and I rolled my eyes and shook my head and moved in that direction. Quick rinse, change of clothes and let my hair down and I would be ready to go inside ten minutes. I began walking in that direction.

"Mm mm mm," I heard from beside me and I glanced over, "Mighty fine ass you got there, Baby."

I raised an eyebrow at the older biker and I gave him a slight once over, "Nothing to see here, so I'm moving on," I stated dryly and I knew it came out unfriendly. I meant it to. He was the same guy that'd reluctantly let me into The Plank my second day here, the day I'd met Cutter. He spit on the ground.

"You'd never have it so good," he said and grabbed his crotch.

"Tiny! That's enough man, Hope here is our guest and we don't treat our guests like that. You picking up what I'm putting down?" Cutter called from up the sidewalk.

"Yes, Captain!" Tiny grated. I gave Tiny my most winning smile.

"Nice to meet you too, Tiny," I said and made my way up to my B&B, an odd mixture of pleased and put out that Cutter had come to my defense. I mean shit, I could take care of myself! I didn't need anyone looking out for me, but I had to admit, it was nice all the same. Maybe I was just getting tired. My mood was decidedly dejected at having reached yet another dead end in Faith's case, but I had to admit to a certain amount of lift going on here. Cutter wasn't pissed, he was providing me an in and I was going to take it. If I had to sleep with him to get him to tell me, then I'd do it. If I did and he still wouldn't well, *then* I would beat his ass... or try to.

I cleaned up and slipped on a white summer dress with black accents along the top. Really, the straps were black along with the top along where my breasts would be if I had more of them. A thin black bow made of satin ribbon as thin as the spaghetti straps holding the dress up completed the look. I shrugged my feet into my white flip flops and hung my white concealed weapons purse off my shoulder. I whipped through a refresher on my makeup, threw on some clear lip gloss, smiled at myself in the mirror and let down my hair. Whipping a quick brush through it, it fell around my face and shoulders in beach waves. Fitting.

I swiped my bangs across my forehead and tucked them behind my ear before throwing on my sunglasses and locking up. I tossed my keys in the top of my bag and went out front. Stopping short at the smiling Kraken President on the back of a glossy orange and white Indian. He smiled broadly at me.

"You got health insurance with you?" he asked. I frowned.

"What?"

"Health insurance," he repeated.

"Yeah, why?" I asked.

"Florida helmet laws, Sweetheart, you gotta be at least 21 years of age and have at least ten thousand dollars in health insurance coverage to operate or ride on a bike without a helmet."

"No shit?" I asked. That sounded totally stupid but at the same time, kind of awesome.

"No shit."

I shrugged and got on behind him without missing a beat and he started her up. It was definitely a different sound than my baby gave off.

"Done this before, huh?" he called out over the growl of the engine.

"A time or two," I said, unwilling to admit that I wasn't used to being a passenger.

"Well hang on, Sweetheart," he said grinning and I wrapped my arms around him and he put us in motion.

There was seriously something different about riding with no helmet. The wind in my hair, the feeling akin to falling knowing there was no safety net… it was exhilarating. He was showing off a little but that was fine. I would too if I had a machine like his. I made sure to stay snug up against him, partially because he felt good and partially because short skirts traveling into the wind with no panties was a recipe for disaster. I hugged my arm in close to my body, crushing my purse to me, the hard outline of the gun digging in reassuringly.

We got on the highway and the air whipped past, rushing along my skin, filling me up and blowing out the back, taking all the stress and frustration and hopelessness with it. Cutter was warm, and solid and though I couldn't see his eyes from the wraparound sunglasses he was sporting, I could see his face in the side view mirror and the little smile that tinged his lips. I couldn't help but feel the little caress of one of my own on my lips which immediately took me back to the sensation of his mouth on mine. Of his trim beard burning my cheek, his strong jaw beneath my fingertips.

If I were less of a badass I would have swooned again, instead I leaned forward and called out, "Well your chances of getting in my pants are improving!"

Cutter laughed, "Is that so?" he yelled back over his shoulder.

"It could happen," I yelled over the cacophony of wind and traffic. Cutter's smile turned into a grin and he took the next exit.

We'd been travelling maybe fifteen or twenty minutes by now.

We didn't have to go far off the highway to reach the bowling alley. Like so many of them this place looked as dilapidated as they got and there were several bikes and a Jeep or two parked out front. A man in one of the Kraken leather vests took a cigarette out of his mouth and exhaled. He was blond, like light blond, almost white and his hair stood stiff but at the same time soft looking off his scalp in an almost-fro. Like dandelion fluff.

"Captain's here!" he shouted into the dark, cave like atmosphere of the bowling alley behind him. Cheers and applause drifted out of the darkened door way. Cutter put down the kickstand to his bike and shut it off. I climbed off carefully and managed to preserve my modesty… you know… if I had any.

Inside was dark and hot, like it didn't have any air conditioning hot. I blinked and realized what light there was came from those camp lanterns, their hiss loud in the dark, the white hot light glowing from them like captive stars.

"Are we trespassing?" I asked with a laugh.

"We do what we want, Princess," the blonde woman from earlier called out. I glanced at Cutter and realized by his guarded look, that this was some kind of a test.

"It's hot as fuck in here, anybody have a cold beer?" I asked, raising a brow. I was rewarded by a secret smile from Cutter and a cheer or two from some of the guys and a couple of girls.

A cold bottle was thrust into my hand and a younger guy wearing a vest that had no emblem on the back, the bottom rocker reading 'prospect' went jogging down the lane to set up empty bottles for pins. He stayed down the lane and off to the side and Cutter came up behind me, his breath almost cooler on my shoulder than the ambient air, which was saying something.

"Ladies first," he murmured and pressed his lips against the back of my shoulder, just to the side of my dress strap. I shivered and it had nothing to do with the temperature in the room, which really was just this side of Hades' balls.

I threw my hair up off my neck into a messy bun using the hair elastic I kept at the ready around my wrist. I set my purse to the side on a dusty chair and took the proffered bowling ball someone had found, from the man offering it. He wasn't bad to look at either. Tall and slender but not without his own strength, he was blond too, shoulder length and sported a goatee, his blue eyes cynical. The name tag on his vest said 'Marlin' and below that Vice President. Interesting.

I handed Marlin my beer, vowed not to drink from it again after I took it back, and tried to keep a watch on him out of the corner of my eye as I lined up. I took my slight running start and let the ball go, it rolled through the grit on the lane and demolished all but two of the bottles. Cheers went up. The prospect cursed and went after the ball and rolled it back to me down the gutter.

Music was started out of an old boom box and we bowled. Cutter sucked at it, and in a total role reversal, I found myself pressed to his back showing him how to do it right. The touches lingered, the glances held weight and we did this careful dance around each other that was equal parts flirtation and trying to get to the bottom of one versus the other. We flirted *hard* and I learned names and listened to stories.

"Hey, Hope! Where you going?" Radar called. We'd been here a couple of hours and I'd had more than one beer. Marlin had started drinking my original without thinking about it so I'd gotten another for myself.

"If they haven't shut off the water yet, then the bathrooms might still work!" I called back, and purse over my shoulder I went looking for it. As luck would have it, the water hadn't been shut off and there were still paper towels! Score.

As I came out of the bathroom, he caught me slightly off guard, but not enough to warrant me fighting back. His energy wasn't malicious, I don't know how I can explain it but when someone comes at you with mal-intent; it feels different than what this was. As I came out of the bathroom, Cutter was just suddenly there, pressing his body the length of mine, driving me back into the wall. I gasped and his mouth was on mine and my fingers wound into his hair which was falling out of its ponytail.

God damn it! This man could kiss. He devoured me from the

mouth down, my blood thrummed with alcohol and lust, no I wasn't impaired, just pleasantly buzzed. His hands slid over my body through the thin dress and I pushed my hands under his shirt. He groaned into my mouth and I sighed with contentment. He broke the kiss first and leaned back with that debonair grin plastered to his face.

"Been wanting to do that for a couple of days," he said.

"Why'd you stop?" I asked coquettishly and his grin broadened.

"If I'm going to take you, it sure as hell ain't going to be in some grungy defunct bowling alley," he stated and his tone held a finality to it that made me think a little more of him.

"Kiss me again," I demanded.

Cutter raised his eyebrows, "You like it when I kiss you, Sweetheart?"

"No, not at all, now shut up and do it again."

I pulled his mouth back down to mine, tugging on his leather vest to do it. Cutter smiled against my lips and flicked his tongue against my bottom one. I opened for him and he kissed me, his mouth warm, his taste overlaid by the crisp hoppy flavor of the beer we'd been drinking. He sank his teeth gently into my lower lip and I groaned. Things much lower in my body began to throb with need and I marveled once more at the attraction.

I had never had such a visceral reaction to a man and it was interesting to me. It was also extremely frustrating knowing that he was deliberately withholding the information I *needed* to find the last woman to see my sister. I pushed back, breathless, and realized that his palm rested warm on the outside of one of my thighs up under my skirt which caused me to shudder. God I was horny but my hormones needed to take a back seat. I stiffened in his hold and he smiled down at me, almost a little sadly.

"Shh, easy girl. Nothin' ain't gonna happen that you don't wanna have happen," he murmured and the tone and delivery he used just turned me on that much more.

Cutter put my leg down which had been raised up over one of his hips, the scorching length of his erection pressing against me through the denim of his soft, broken in jeans, left my mound feeling almost bruised with the force with which he'd been pressed against me. It was a delicious feeling, I'm not going to lie. For a girl that could most definitely handle her own, it was a rare thing for me to find a man who could man handle me, but I suspected Cutter was up to the job. I liked that. I liked that a lot.

"That's the problem, I want it to happen but it can't," I murmured and met his eyes with steely resolve.

Cutter had both palms pressed flat to the wall to either side of my head, my body bracketed in, trapped. Any other female and it probably would have been intimidating as hell but I wasn't just any female. I was me, with some of the finest hand to hand combat training the world over locked in my brain, muscles and joints. So no, I wasn't intimidated or afraid but a big part of that was the way that Cutter looked at me. He searched my face carefully, as if doing so could and would, divine every last little secret my heart held.

"You've been knocked down, dragged out, put through the wringer and don't trust no one as a result," he said finally and sighed, his tone liberally dosed with regret.

"You say that with some serious conviction," I put on a musing tone as I said it, more curious to see what he would do. It was kind of unnerving how he managed to pick up on things so easily. Okay, for me, it was *really* unnerving. I wasn't sure I liked it.

"Look at you, hiding behind your high walls. You're like a concrete maze, Darlin'. Just when I think I got you figured out, the maze changes and I'm right back to square one," he leaned in as if doing a push up against the wall and whispered the last against my ear, his breath fanning and sending a pleasurable little rush down the side of my neck, "You trust me a little, I'll trust you…"

He pushed back and his warm brown eyes searched mine. I let go of his leather vest with my left hand and held the inside of my left wrist in front of his face. His eyes refocused on the writing there and followed the sweeping lines.

"Virtue," he read, "Gonna have to fill me in, Beautiful. I'm not picking up what you're putting down."

I licked my lips which were suddenly very dry and swallowed a couple of times. It was hard to think with him so close, smelling so good; like clean saltwater and ocean breeze.

"I have two sisters, Faith and Charity... One is missing. The girl I am looking for was the last person to see her." I relented. Cutter stared at my face, hard. The lines of his own collapsing into neutrality.

"Wait here," he said and kissed me one last time roughly. He pushed back up off the wall, away from me, before stalking around the corner and back into the bowling alley.

"Council!" he barked, "Outside *now!*"

Uh-oh. Looks like I just opened up a can of whoop ass on somebody. I almost felt bad about that. The guys that formed the leadership of the club weren't half bad, that I could tell. I pushed off the wall and closed my eyes. With a groan, I fell back against it and leaned on it hard. What the fuck did I just do?

CHAPTER 8
Cutter

The boys were all silent, and like me, none of them were happy. I wanted to tell her, but the ramifications of that would be far reaching for my club, so I had to put it to a vote. The council stood around me at the far end of the lot and mulled over the implications.

"Tiny's got our nuts in a fucking vice," Nothing growled.

"Too fucking right. Wish the happy bastard would just fucking retire already," Radar kicked a rock across the worn out asphalt of the parking lot.

"We can't tell her anything, not until we know she's not going to flip out. We need a full club meeting, make sure every damn one of us is on the same page," Marlin said judiciously.

Pyro huffed a laugh and I looked at my best friend, "Play time is over. I'll get everyone over to The Plank where we can put it to a vote. I'm sorry, Brother," he said to me, "I don't see this going any but one way. She's connected to the cops. She'll fucking fry us."

"You don't know that," I said and scowled at my best buddy.

"We don't know that she won't, so put your resting bitch face on ice there, Captain," Atlas said. I sighed.

"Round 'em up. Have Hossler take Hope back to town. I want this shit settled in house and everyone on the same page."

My proclamation was met with a bunch of 'Aye, aye, Captain's,' and the boys drifted off in the direction of the bowling alley. It was Marlin who stayed behind. He put his hand on my shoulder and sighed.

"Man, I'm sorry, I know you like her. Haven't seen you this engaged since L'il Bit went home with her man," he patted me roughly on the shoulder twice but my gaze was fixed across the lot on Hope who was looking coolly back at me, her deep brown eyes calculating and curious. She knew something was up. I hadn't exactly bothered to hide it.

"C'mon Honey, Captain wants you to ride with me and I could use some girl power for a minute after hanging around with these assholes," I heard Hossler tell her. Hope hitched her purse higher on her shoulder and slid her sunglasses on her face.

"I'm down like four flat tires," she said to Hoss and got up into the passenger seat of Hossler's old '85 Land Rover Defender. The thing was ancient, the paint oxidized and rusted in places but there was no denying its reliability. Didn't break down often, and when it did, Hoss usually fixed it herself. Hope would be safe enough.

I froze and went back over my last thought... Hope was a big fucking girl who could handle herself. What was I fucking worried about? I thought about it, couldn't quantify it, so I got on my bike and rode for The Plank.

Midway down the highway it dawned on me. That night on my boat, we kissed and I'd told her that I wasn't out to dick her over, that she just needed to have some faith. I think I'd just figured out which one of her sisters was missing. I ground my teeth, I wanted to beat the motherfucking brakes off Tiny for bringing this all down on our heads. This was a right cluster fuck, and I didn't see any way out of it where I had a shot at Hope. Which that was a damned shame. I really liked the girl. Something about her felt different, like she was the moon affecting my tide. I felt pulled in her direction and wasn't it just my fucking luck? I find a chick who is single, who I like and who has been a challenge this far and the whole thing we've got going on between each other is nothing but a pack of lies and half-truths.

I spent the rest of the ride trying to figure out how to convince my crew that Hope wasn't a threat and to tell her what we could to hopefully help her find her sister. I had a couple of possible avenues to pursue that didn't involve my club, but it damned sure came close. I backed in next to Marlin who shot me a sympathetic look before getting off his bike and heading inside. I spent a moment longer shutting her down and collecting my thoughts before heading inside myself. I went straight to the back and took my seat, the rest of the club, and I do mean *everyone*, pulled up chairs expectantly.

"Hey, Trike! Close up and lock the doors, wait outside!" I yelled. The prospect did as he was told and closed up the bar, taking up post outside. I looked over my guys and shook my head. I wanted to help her, but it was up to my club...

"Why'd you bring us here, Captain?" Stoker asked. A tall, beefy motherfucker, Stoker was the lead singer for some band and looked every bit the rocker and metal head that he was. Long dyed black hair, kohl lined eyes and a deep dark stare, he looked like fucking Dracula or some shit, which is where he got his road name, after the dude that wrote that shit.

"We're dipped in shit, that's why," I said with a sigh.

"This have to do with the girl that Hope chick is looking for?" Lightning asked.

"Yeah, Hope ain't going to give up boys. The Suicide Kings' bitch was the last person to see Hope's sister before she disappeared."

I looked at a lot of troubled and impassive faces while they mulled this information over and waited, with a sinking feeling, for the questions to start.

"So don't tell her nothin'," Tiny said with a shrug.

"Shut the fuck up," Atlas barked, "If it wasn't for you going off on your own fucking program we wouldn't have this problem."

"Man, this sucks; I kind of like Hope," Radar said. There were grunts and nods of agreement from the fellas that had been at the bowling alley.

I let the dilemma sink in and tried to judge what my crew was thinking by their faces. It was a rough mix. Hope had personality and the dudes that'd been at the bowling alley had gotten to see it. She was witty, sarcastic and a riot to be around. She was also pretty damn solid from what I could tell. Her looks just sealed the deal.

"What're our options, Captain?" Nothing asked.

"Depends boys. This affects the club no matter which way you look at it... Really it comes down on if you think we can trust her or not." It was an unknown quantity, trusting Hope.

"She works with the cops, man. We can't tell her shit!" Atlas said.

"What if we didn't tell her anything?" Beast asked. He was an older dude, like Tiny, in his fifties, bald with a mostly gray trucker 'stache. He was carrying a gut on him but he was as his name implied in a fight. A total beast.

I shook my head, "She's in it to win it and she's got a scent. She isn't going to give it up unless she gets answers."

"So take the bitch out."

Silence, almost as one the rest of the crew turned towards Tiny, incredulous. Marlin was the one who finally spoke.

"Tiny, you dumb fuck. Have you not been listening to a word that's been said? She works with *the cops*. She'd be *missed* and none of this would be happening if it weren't for you in the first place. If you'd done what you were fucking told, and had taken the first bitch home. So dude, do us all a fucking favor and shut your god damn hole for the remainder of this meeting." My VP and Tiny locked stares for several tense minutes before, as expected Tiny got up.

"Man, fuck you!" he declared and stormed out. A collective sigh ran through the rest of my men.

"Fine Tiny a hundred bucks for the disrespect to a senior officer." I told Nothing, it was the heaviest fine I could assess according to our by-laws, which was unfortunate. Nothing was already writing it down on one of his little notepads he always had tucked away somewhere, nodding at what I'd said as I'd said it.

"Anybody else got any bright ideas about doing something so monumentally stupid?" Marlin asked. As expected no one spoke up.

"Way I see it, we can lie to her and send her chasing her tail, which I do not recommend because all she's going to do is come back here pissed off with the fucking cops... Jesus Christ what has he gotten us into? This is a capital offense man!" Atlas scrubbed his face with his hands and sat back in his seat.

"We tell the truth? She goes to the cops, we lie? She goes to the cops... What the fuck are we going to do?" Pyro asked no one in particular.

"We do a little of both," I said with a heavy heart, this sucked man. This was not what we were about. We weren't into drugs, and we sure as fuck weren't into killing people. Our illegal activity was more along the lines of tomb raiding some of the wrecks around here, of smuggling Cuban cigars, and if we were really strapped? Smuggling some fucking Cubans. We did *not* kill people, that hadn't done any fucking thing to us, let alone young girls.

"Captain?" someone said snapping me out of wherever I'd been.

"Yeah?"

"How are we going to do that?" Stoker asked.

"We tell her we dropped the girl off in Tallahassee and I call in a favor to the SHMC." I said. Some looks were traded.

"I need a vote boys. Is this an amenable compromise?" I asked.

We voted, it was decided. I texted Hossler to see where she and Hope were at and nodded. I had a place to start.

CHAPTER 9
Hope

Hossler wasn't bad company, in fact, she was pretty kick ass. I'd asked her what her function was within the club and she'd laughed.

"I don't know," she'd said with a gusty sigh, "I had an Ol' Man but he skipped town and left me taking care of our kids all on my own. I guess I was liked enough by the club. Cutter helps out when my business is down and I fool around with the guys some, I mean I'm a mother – I'm not dead!" We laughed and she went on, "The club is like a family. They look out for their own and I was a patched member's Ol' Lady. They ever catch up to him they're gonna beat his ass and take his patch but they aren't bad guys. The sins of my man didn't rub off on me or my kids. Cutter made things clear," she sniffed.

"What about you? You got any kids?" she inquired. I leaned back in the passenger seat and sighed.

"No! No, no, no. I had a tubal last year. No kids are happening here," I said and stared out the window.

"Why not?" It was the natural evolution of the conversation but I didn't want to answer it so I changed the subject.

"You said when your business was slow, Cutter helps you; what do you do?"

Hossler laughed, "I breed snakes."

I gave her a flat look, the kind that said 'please tell me you're joking' and she laughed a little more.

"What kind of snakes?"

"Constricters, Pythons and a few Boa's. Rats too, gotta feed them somehow," she gave an indelicate one shouldered shrug.

"Holy crap, you're serious," I said.

"As a heart attack, Baby," she said with a wink.

"That's so… cool," I said surprised. Snakes didn't affect me one way or the other. I didn't hate them, but I didn't like them either. I guess I was just sort of meh about them.

We spent the ride laughing and talking about the general retardation of the male half of our species, the rest of the way back to Ft. Royal. The whole way, my mind kept whirring and clicking away, wondering what had put Cutter's panties in such a bunch and shot him out of the bowling alley like he'd gone out of a cannon. He fucking knew something about Tonya. I knew that much, saw the lie in his eyes every time he denied it. Felt it in his stiff posture every time his lips met mine. The fierce attraction we felt for one another wouldn't sway him from protecting his club, but what did they need protection from?

The implications laid in front of me by his actions weren't good. I didn't figure Cutter for a killer, he felt more like a lover than a fighter, but looks could be deceiving. Oh, I knew he could kill, that he had killed, I still had my military connections and read what I could out of his jacket. There had been a lot of redacted shit in there but there had also been a lot left readable and what had been left was almost as useful as what hadn't been; all of it spelled out clearly that Cutter was one dangerous SOB that I shouldn't try to tangle with, and who I wouldn't ordinarily take on but, *Faith*.

"I'm sorry, what?" I asked. Hossler was looking at me, blue eyes wide with that look that screamed, *weren't you listening to a thing I just said?*

"Can I ask you a pretty personal question?" she asked.

"Sorry, yeah go ahead."

"You fuck him yet?"

I blinked, "Who Cutter?"

"No, the Pope! Uh, yeah, the Captain."

"Why have you?"

"Once upon a time."

"Interesting." I pondered that.

"You going to answer the question?"

"Oh, no."

She rolled her eyes exasperated, "No, you're not going to answer or no, you haven't fucked him?" she asked.

I gave her my trademark, sarcastic coy little smile and looked at her demurely through my lashes. She looked at me, eyes narrowed and tried to decide if I was fucking with her which I was, I smiled at her. I liked her, so I answered honestly.

"No," I said.

She nodded thoughtfully, "My unsolicited advice, Darlin'?" I cocked my head to the side.

"Don't. Cutter likes a challenge, to conquer, and once he's done that? He loses interest, fast. I like you, you're pretty badass and can hold your own with this pack of jokers. I would hate to see you doing the walk of shame out of town like all the others."

I sighed and dug through my purse for my pack of gum. "I thought he wasn't the love 'em and leave 'em type," I said.

"That what he told you?" she asked. I unwrapped a stick of gum and just looked at her, shoving it past my lips, the cool minty flavor scrubbing the inside of my mouth clean.

She snorted, "It is, isn't it? Well he wasn't *exactly*, lying. Cutter doesn't lie. He just doesn't tell the truth either." I raised an eyebrow at that.

"He doesn't ever love them, he just fucks them, then leaves them, or really just sends them on their way. Except for Li'l Bit. She got him but good," she smiled and it held a flicker of savage glee that was quickly overtaken by lines of regret that morphed into a shadow of anger, all within like a three second span. It was actually kind of fascinating to watch.

"I sense there's a story and a half there," I said and tried to sound casual.

"You'd be right," she said, but much to my disappointment didn't expand on anything, instead she changed the subject. We spoke amicably the rest of the trip into town, but my wheels were turning. Mostly on Cutter's reaction at the bowling alley. It was telling and it didn't tell me anything I wanted to hear. I had a seriously sinking feeling and I really didn't want what my gut was telling me to be true.

Hossler dropped me off where I was staying and waved through the open window of the beastly Land Rover.

"Beach party tonight, you should come! Just look for the

bonfire!" she called and pulled around the circular drive and out onto the street. I stared after her thinking hard, before going up to my room. I showered and changed into some white shorts and a light, peach tank top made out of silk. The dress needed to be washed, the back smudged with dust from the wall Cutter had pressed me to in the bowling alley. I swept my long hair up into a tight bun and wrapped it in a hair tie before tucking my bangs across my forehead and behind one ear.

I was just finishing putting on my face when my phone started ringing. I looked at it. Unknown caller. I answered it anyways, "This is Hope…"

"Hey Sweetheart," Cutter's voice purred through the line.

"How'd you get this number?"

"I got my ways," he said and I found myself nodding even though he couldn't see it.

"Uh huh… So what happens now?" I asked.

"Hossler tell you about the bonfire?"

"Yeah."

"Come see me," he intoned.

"You going to feed me some more lies? A bunch of half-truths?" I asked. I didn't want to aggravate him but I was tired of spinning my wheels in the soft sand of Ft. Royal, Florida. This wasn't a game. This was my sister and I wanted her back.

"I'm going to tell you what I can, Darlin', but I've got to think of my club," he said and his voice was raw and honest.

"Bros before ho's huh?" I asked and snorted derisively.

"Not to put too fine a point on it," he said and he didn't sound happy about it which earned him a few points in my book.

"Why the change of heart, Cutter?" I asked softly.

"I'm not a bad guy Hope, and I meant it about wanting to get to know you," he said, voice low and heated in all the right ways to send my body into a fit of wanting. Damn he was good.

"See you tonight," he murmured into the phone with that smooth velvet undertone and he hung up. I stood with my phone to my ear for several moments after he'd severed the call, my mind working overtime.

Too many games. Too many feints and jabs. That too-familiar sinking feeling took up residence beneath my breastbone again but Cutter sounded so damned sincere, I wanted to believe him. I really did. Either way I didn't have a choice. I would go. I would see what was what and I would do what I'd been doing for the last, shit; almost two years. I would hang onto the hope I would see my sister again, and I wouldn't lose faith. Either one of them.

I slid my phone into the pocket for it in my purse and stared at the white leather and rhinestones, picturing the very black revolver in its depths. Dusk was only a couple of hours off and I would hopefully have *some* kind of an answer. Something to go on... I chewed my bottom lip.

I got the genuine feeling that Cutter wanted to help me. I also got the feeling he was hiding things from me. I didn't like either, I wanted answers and I was going to get them. I snatched my purse off the bed and slung it over my shoulder. The bag rode high under my arm and the weight to it was a comforting thing. I went out the front and started walking. I needed something to eat, to fuel my body and mind and to kill the fading buzz from the beers at the bowling alley.

I slipped into a beach front fish bar and had some fish and chips, watching the smiling, laughing tourists walk by in the fading sunlight. I washed down my food with water and a squeeze of lemon, letting my mind blank for a bit. I didn't want to think. The same thoughts just kept chasing each other in circles and drove me nuts anyways.

Finally, the sun hanging low in the sky, painting the sand in fire and blood, I rose, and with my mood darkening with the skies, I made my way towards the beach. I slipped off my flip flops and tucked them into my purse before looking left and then right. To the right, in the distance, towards Cutter's marina where his boat was moored, a pyramid of wood smoked, light glimmering between the pieces as it caught fire. There were several people already gathered and I made my way down the beach, trudging through the soft, dry sand in their direction.

"Hey, Hope! Glad you could make it!" Hossler called out and I gave her a thin smile.

"Always, Chica," I said but didn't miss the wary looks from some of the men.

"Back again, Cap'ain's cock must be made outta gold or something," Tiny muttered. I eyed him speculatively. He was three sheets to the wind already and raised a flask to his lips taking a generous swig. I ignored him. Whatever his damage was, it wasn't related to me and I wasn't going to rise to the bait.

"Hey, Sweetheart..." I turned and eyed Cutter speculatively.

"Hey," I answered and he held out his hand to me. Tiny snorted and I frowned. I took Cutter's hand and he tucked mine in the crook of his arm and led me around the fire. He sat with his back to a fallen log and I sat beside him.

"I like this," he said and trailed a finger over the silk of my tank.

"Thanks, but I have to admit, I'm getting kind of tired of dancing around the elephant in the room," I said. He nodded and Tiny who had moved inside earshot barked a laugh.

"He ain't gonna tell you what you want to hear, Girl."

"Tiny..." the warning in Cutter's voice was clear and my patience frayed that much more. I got to my feet and Cutter muttered a curse under his breath.

"Look, I don't give two shits what any of you are into. That's your fucking business, I just want to find Tonya, so how about we cut the bullshit and get down to business. Is it money you want?" I demanded and stared Cutter down.

He looked resigned, his expression holding an undertone of sorrow. Tiny started laughing like it was the funniest goddamn thing he'd ever heard and I frowned. The conversations around us had died and the atmosphere grew tense. I looked back and forth between Tiny and Cutter and realized there was some inner turmoil going on, something removed from me but connected to me all the same. Problem was I didn't give two fucks, I just wanted to find Tonya and by default my sister.

"Look, we met the girl you're looking for last year, we was asked to bring her back to Tallahassee, I told my boys to take care of her..."

"We took care of her alright," Tiny said with a leer and gave Cutter a half assed drunken salute. The look Cutter was giving Tiny was one of pure fury and he was getting a lot of unfriendly looks from the rest of The Kraken too.

That sinking feeling returned and my mouth went dry. I wasn't stupid. The women that had been around the fire started drifting back, edging outside the firelight.

"Tiny, shut your fucking hole, Man!" Atlas, the club's Secretary looked murderous, his arms held out from his sides loose, feet shoulder width apart in a brawler's stance. So far everyone's attention was on Cutter and Tiny.

"I ain't gotta shut nothin'! Fuck you fucking fucks, Man!" Tiny swayed on his feet and I met his eyes with mine. One of my commanding officers back in the day had once told me something that surfaced now. He'd said, *"Don't ever forget what someone says to you while they're drunk, because drunk words are sober thoughts..."*

Tiny's mouth thinned down into a malicious smile and he spilled my worst fear across the sand at me...

"Bitch you're looking for is dead, Cunt. Captain ordered me to do it, too."

"Tiny, you fucking son of a bitch," Marlin, the Vice President of The Kraken was suddenly there, roughing Tiny up, shoving him, male voices clamored, shouting obscenities and about betrayal and I didn't care about any of it.

Tonya was dead. My last hope of finding Faith, the final lead, after hundreds of exhausted bullshit leads... I felt tears well, hot and immediate as my frustration and anger crested. No one but Cutter was paying attention to me and even he looked at me with a pained expression.

"So it's true..." I said hollowly.

"It's not like he says, Sweetheart," I let my purse slip from my shoulder, the bag falling to the ground, the Ruger clutched in my hand. I leveled it right between Cutter's eyes.

"I think you'd better start talking. No more bullshit, I'm done playing nice," I said. Shouts, indistinct, the men around us went still, Cutter raised his hands in surrender and stood stalk still.

"Easy, Darlin'," he soothed.

"Nope, I tried it that way, you decided to dick me around, so now we're doing this my way. Start talking. Now!" my voice only moderately shook and the first twin sets of angry tears spilled scalding down my cheeks. *Faith...* I felt my sister slip away with Tiny's admission.

"We agreed to take the girl back to Tallahassee, I told Tiny and one of the prospects to fucking take care of her, meaning take her home..." Cutter took a step forward.

"You know, you don't really need to cock these like you see in the movies," I pulled back the hammer on the gun with a satisfying click, "Can't argue with the dramatic effect though, can you?" I asked. Cutter's eyes narrowed but he stopped advancing.

"Right," he studied my face and I caught motion out of the corner of my eye.

"One more step and I will fucking shoot him," I intoned dispassionately.

"Easy, Sweetheart, Tiny's right, Tonya *is* dead but she was living with a crew up north, The Suicide Kings, now that club is no more but one of their girls is living with a crew that we happen to be friendly with. Put that down, let's talk, I want to help you Baby, and that's the God's honest truth... look me in the eye and see if I'm lyin'."

I met his gaze and saw the truth in his eyes but something Hossler said earlier came back to me. Cutter didn't lie but he didn't tell the truth either. He inclined his chin and I realized too late one of his men was coming up on me. I whirled, Cutter lunged and damned if he didn't disarm me with my own fucking maneuver.

Oh hell no!

But it was on, and there were more of them than there was of me. I needed to concentrate. I sidestepped and the man who'd lunged for me, passed me by.

"You don't want to do this," I said.

"You're right, Sweetheart, I don't but you didn't leave me or my men much choice now did you?" Cutter asked ominously.

No, I guess I hadn't. I'd started this, and now it was time to finish it. Wouldn't be my first time out numbered and it probably wouldn't be my last. I shifted my balance and put the fire at my back. I was as ready as I was ever going to be.

CHAPTER 10
Cutter

"Don't hurt her, just subdue her," I ordered and I could tell by the fire and steel in her eyes she didn't like the sound of that one bit.

"Can't do this just you and me?" she taunted.

"Oh, we're going to be one on one soon enough," I told her with a grin. Damn but she had a fire inside.

"We going to stand here talking about this all night or are you going to bring it, boys?"

Pyro lunged and Hope laid his ass out face down in the sand, her long limbs delivering a punishing kick to the balls that had him bending forward and cupping his junk. Balanced to perfection she delivered a kick to the back of my best buddy's head and he went down for the count. She was a force of nature, and I didn't want any more of my boys hurt. Atlas and Nothing were tied up with keeping Tiny subdued and I jerked my chin at Marlin, glancing at our former SAA and Pyro.

"You sure, Captain?" he asked, amusement tinging his tone.

"Just do as you're told on this one, please?" I shot back. Marlin nodded and put a hand on top of the bandana covering his shaggy blonde head.

I didn't want to hurt her but if she wanted to throw down like a dude, then me and my boys would treat her like one. We didn't tend to hit women. It was one thing to belt one in the mouth if she got mouthy but that was as far as that fucking went.

Hope was sizing me up, determination seeding and taking root in her dark and lovely eyes. I feinted and went in. She threw a kick to my ribs but I blocked it. Still, she jarred my shoulder a good one, girl wasn't playing and neither could I. I needed to get her on the ground. I'd have the upper hand if I had her on the ground. I'd watched all of her videos, had an idea of what I was up against and was counting on the fact that she didn't know me. Still, she had some skills hidden in her back pocket and so she landed a blow or two that fucking counted, one of them opening up a small cut above my eye.

We went at it solid for who knew how long until both of us were squared off, chests heaving. Sweat glimmered on her chest and darkened the silk of her tank at her back. She twisted and I lunged and got my arms around her and with a lightning quick speed she was off the ground, those long legs of hers going around my head and neck. I got my arm up and between them just in time to keep her from choking me off, her dark eyes flared venomous but it was too late.

I had the upper hand and by upper hand I meant the strength and wherewithal to end this shit and end it now. I was glad we were in the sand for what I knew I had to do next. I slammed her bodily down onto it, fucking hard too. I had to, to knock the wind clean out of her, which I did. Hope making a satisfying woosh, at least to me, as the air left her body in a rush. She tensed in my arms and I flipped her onto her stomach as she tried to drag air into her lungs but her body wasn't having any of it, not yet.

"Easy, Sweetheart," I grated and whipped my belt out of its loops. I bound her arms above the elbows and reefed back on them, binding them tight.

"Marlin!" I called when she kicked out. Her heel connected with my back where I sat on the backs of her thighs. It fuckin' hurt but not bad enough to make me let go. Not by a long shot. Girl was fucking dangerous. I liked that. I liked that a lot.

Marlin bound her ankles for me and I got off her ordering him, "Get her up," he lifted her and she spat at me, struggling in his grip, glaring at me murderously.

"C'mon Baby, lets you and me have a talk," I said and put my shoulder to her midriff and hauled her up like a sack of grain. Hope squawked her protest and I slapped her on her ass. She was fucking turning me on.

"Marlin, Radar, take care of Tiny, Hope and I will be on my boat if you need us."

"The hell we will you son of a bitch! Put me down!"

"Cool it, Sweetheart, we're going to have ourselves a little talk." I marched in the direction of my boat, Hope wiggling and struggling the whole way, cussing my ass out with some pretty inventive shit.

"Such a dirty mouth," I said grinning. I could feel the aches starting to set in and wasn't too happy about that, but as rough as I was going to feel come morning I was betting Hope would be feeling it too. Now *that* I did feel bad about. I really did.

I walked up the length of my dock and set her on her feet, she promptly spit in my face. I closed my eyes and wiped it away, counting slowly inside my head. I tolerated a lot of shit, disrespect pissed me the fuck off though.

"Untie me you son of a bitch," she seethed.

"Not until we talk; now, if I undo your feet you gonna climb aboard yourself?"

"Fuck you!"

"Okay, have it your way, Beautiful," I ducked and put her back up over my shoulder and leapt up onto my deck, it was awkward as fuck but it hurt her more than it hurt me, my shoulder digging into the soft of her belly. Wouldn't be surprised if she were bruised all to hell from the ride. I took her below deck and set her down on the couch. She gasped and let out a breath.

"You okay?"

"No," she glowered at me and I fixed her with a look. She searched my face, the fire of her anger dying down, transforming into concern.

"What happens now?" she demanded.

"You calm the fuck down, I look after you some, and we talk," I told her and tucked her bangs back behind her ear. She was a mess. A spot of blood decorating the corner of her mouth, a bruise starting to flower along her jaw. I didn't even remember hitting her there.

"Stay here," I murmured and she snorted indelicately. I got up and went to the galley sink and wet a clean dish rag and brought it back.

"You gonna let me do this?" I asked and she nodded cautiously. I dabbed at the corner of her mouth and she flinched at first before leaning into the cool cloth signifying I should go ahead. I cleaned her up and she calmed down some.

"What happens now?" she repeated, softer than before.

"You going to fight me if I untie you?" I asked.

"Maybe," she shot back.

"Then we talk like this." I stood up and tossed the rag back into the sink. Hope's gaze burning a hole right through me where I stood. God, after a good fight with her trussed up like that...

"Keep looking at me that way, Darlin', I'm going to bend you over and fuck you." She gasped and her brow crushed down into a frown but not before I caught the desire in her eyes. My cock throbbed in my shorts.

"Tell me about your sister," I demanded.

"Why?" she demanded right back.

"Because I meant it, Sweetheart, I'm going to help you."

Hope looked up at me and we stared each other down, I waited her out, my patience dwindling while she decided for herself how this was going to go.

"Why?" she asked again, her voice much less certain, her vulnerability peeking through. Fuck. I got that much harder in my shorts. I was such a fucking sucker for a damsel in distress and Hope was quickly adding it to her alluring mix of beauty, brains and strength.

"Good question," I said and leaned forward, putting my lips against hers. She froze, hardening up beneath me, body stiff and unyielding. Maybe I had been wrong, maybe she wasn't as attracted as I was, just when I was about to pull back she opened to me, her tongue tentatively flicking against my lower lip. I drew back just a touch, speaking against her mouth,

"We going to do this?" I growled.

"Yeah," she answered breathlessly.

"And then?"

"Then you're going to do what you said, you're going to help me," she said. Good. She believed me, even better, she was calm now and it seemed, like me, desire was simmering in her veins too.

"You try to hurt me, Hope..." she looked at me expectantly, keen intelligence sparkling in her eyes, "I'm going to hurt you back, and worse, you get me?"

She inhaled sharply and nodded slowly, I leaned forward and kissed her gently and she kissed me back, tentatively at first. She was still bound, and I had every intention of letting her go, *after* I could be sure she was really on board with this.

"You okay?" I asked her, voice steady.

"Untie me," she breathed against my mouth.

"How'd we go from fighting to fucking?" I asked, I needed to know.

"You aren't turned on?"

"Yep, definitely turned on," I said.

"You mean it, what you said about helping me? About that lead up north?" she asked and her voice was strained, raw even. I drew back and looked her in the eyes.

"I mean it, Hope. I'm fucking sorry as hell for what Tiny did. We don't fucking roll like that."

"You'll make the call, first thing?" she asked.

"You want me to make it now?" I asked softly. Her breath caught and she nodded slowly.

"Stay here," I got up and went to my office in the stern, returning with my laptop. I set it up on the coffee table.

"Untie me?" she asked and I looked back over my shoulder.

"You gonna behave?"

"You're going to make the call right?" she asked.

"Yes." I knelt down by the couch and went for the bindings around her ankles and loosened them, her skin silky and smooth beneath my fingers as I eased the leather of Marlin's belt off from around her limbs. I massaged the indentations left behind by the belt and Hope sighed out in relief. Her eyes were closed as she concentrated on the feel of my hands on her and I liked that about her.

"Okay, Sweetheart, take it easy. I'm gonna trust you first this time," I helped her to sit up and sat behind her, my legs bracketing her hips as I undid the belt binding her arms sharply behind her. The leather gave with a little sigh and Hope groaned. I massaged the feeling back into her arms and drew her back against my chest, pressing my lips to the side of her neck. She shuddered.

"Make the call," she whispered and I leaned forward, bringing up Skype. I tapped the screen and the laptop started making the call to Data, the Sacred Hearts computer whizz and Secretary. His face came up and so did ours in a smaller screen in the corner. The black curtains were drawn behind the man and he eyed Hope cautiously. He didn't know her and this was highly irregular but fuck it. She'd been through enough.

"What the hell happened to you two?" Data asked.

"Philosophical differences," I grunted.

"Uh huh. To what do I owe the pleasure, Man?"

"Thirteen and his Ol' Lady around?"

"Can't say that they are, Cutter man, what's up? Usually you ask after Reave and Doll, what do you want with Thirteen and Dani?"

I put my arms around Hope who was holding her breath, I could feel her stillness and I smiled, and I knew it was sad. I spelled it out for Data and he nodded thoughtfully. He turned in his desk chair and twitched back the curtain and hollered out into the common room. Dragon appeared a minute later and I reiterated the mess in my lap.

"I'll call Thirteen. Not sure what Dani can tell you, but I'm sure if she can help she will. Can you ring us back sometime after noon tomorrow?"

"Can and will do, my friend. I owe you." Dragon snorted and called bullshit.

"With as much as you've done for me and mine, this ain't nothin'. Call us back on this thing tomorrow, noon-ish. Data will be here waiting."

Hope found her voice, "Thank you," she said.

"Don't thank me, Darlin', that's all Dani, I hope she can help you," he said.

"Thanks, Brother," I said and he nodded.

"Want I should give Reave and Doll a shout to come in here?"

"No thanks man, I gotta get going for now, get us both cleaned up."

Dragon's dark eyes roved the screen on his end of things, "What the hell happened to you two, anyways?" he asked.

"Philosophical differences," Hope repeated and I looked at her, she looked back and shrugged. Dragon chuckled.

"Okay, whatever you say. Tomorrow then."

"Tomorrow," I affirmed and Data ended the call. Hope sat very still between my thighs, my arms around her, holding her hands with my own; my palms resting against the backs of her hands, my fingers fitted in the spaces between hers like they were meant to be there. I sighed and nuzzled the side of her neck, placing a kiss behind her ear. Hope shivered and rested her head back against my shoulder so she could look up at me.

"I want to help you," I murmured, voice a little rough with my physical need at this point.

"I don't understand," she said softly.

"I like you, Hope."

"I shoved a gun in your face and threatened to blow your head off," she said dryly.

"I know, it was hot."

She broke into one of her rare smiles, and laughed a little, "Yeah?"

"Yeah."

"What happens now?" she asked.

"Now I finish what I started on the beach and you're going to let me," I said gravely.

"Oh? What's that?" she asked. I smiled darkly.

"Gonna finish owning you, Sweetheart," she shivered at my words and the sensation of her body shuddering against mine was out of this world. It was only going to get better.

"Stand up," I ordered.

"If I don't?"

"Then I make you, I'm not going to be denied any longer, Babe. You and I have danced around this enough. Now get up and march. Bow of the boat, now."

"Aye, aye, Captain," she breathed and stood up.

Nice.

CHAPTER 11
Hope

I must be nuttier than a goddamn fruit cake but I believed Cutter, what's more, as much as it shouldn't have, his getting the upper hand out there, holding me down, tying my ass up, *owning my ass* into next week, turned me the fuck on. I stood up and he let me. I walked towards the bow of the boat not really knowing what to expect.

I was all mixed up and inside out, so many things happening in rapid fire succession had me twisted up in knots. To have my last and only hope of finding my sister snatched away followed by having that hope returned, even if it was just a glimmer at this point… I closed my eyes as Cutter's hands fell onto my shoulders, kneading sore muscles.

"Easy, Darlin'; we ain't gotta do this right now if you ain't up to it," he said. I swallowed and melted a little bit more that he was giving me an out.

"Emotions running a little high; huh Baby?" he asked me, voice husky, patient and kind. I nodded. That was putting it fucking mildly. He was close to me, right on my six as I moved up the narrow hall. I jumped slightly as his hands found the hips of my shorts. He grasped the hem of my peach silk tank and lifted. I raised my arms and let him take it. He gave an appreciative hum as I lowered my arms, and I felt his gaze like a weighted thing as it swept down my back.

"Stop," he ordered just before I reached the two steps at the end of the hall. His bed was flush against the door, except it was more like a cabinet door than a door into a room. I waited and he reached past me with his leather vest and hung it just inside the bedroom door, off of some invisible hook there.

I closed my eyes and listened to him take off his shirt and drop it to the floor. The warm cotton of the tee coming to rest against my left ankle and on top of my foot. He stepped into me. Close. So close. His body heat warming my back though he wasn't touching me quite yet.

"Rough bother you?"

I smiled, "No."

He caressed my hips, his thumbs digging into my lower back, kneading, massaging for a moment before he pulled me back against his chest.

"Kiss me," he demanded and I obediently tipped my head back while he palmed one of my non-existent breasts and claimed my mouth with his.

The kiss was hot and fierce and the press of his erection into my ass left me breathless with wanting. He pinched my nipple and I gasped into his mouth, his tongue plunging further into mine as he worked the button and zip on the front of my shorts, shoving them down in front, his fingers grazing my bare sex. God that felt good.

He growled into my mouth when he found my pussy wet and ready for him. Not like I could help it. Alpha males like him, strong enough to subdue me, smart enough to out maneuver me, they were rare and hard to come by, and I had been attracted to Cutter from the get go.

His hands left me and I whimpered in protest which soon turned into a moan of want and need when I heard his zipper go and his shorts drop to the floor. His hands returned and smoothed up my back, around my ribs, over my stomach and chest as he felt me up. God he had nice hands. Big and strong, long fingered and calloused. One palmed the outside of my hip while the other gripped the back of my neck.

"Take down your hair, Sweetheart," and his voice was as sultry as the deepening night around us. I took it down and let it envelop the hand at the back of my neck. His fingers disappeared into it and he gripped the back of my hair in a hold designed for control with just the barest edge of pain. I gasped and he urged me up to the top step.

"You on the pill?" he demanded.

"Tubal ligation."

He didn't even pause, he stepped up behind me and shoved his cock between my ass cheeks.

"I'm going to fuck you bareback," he declared, but paused, letting me have my say.

"You only live once," I said, my pussy clenching with want and need. God I wanted skin on skin with this man.

"What are you waiting for, Cutter?" I demanded and I swear I could hear the grin before he kicked my feet apart and slammed me face down into the soft mattress. I gasped and he shoved into me, hard.

I cried out as he filled me, stretching me almost to the point of pain but he didn't stop or slow down and I *really* fucking liked that about him.

"Harder!" I cried and his hand tightened in my hair, his arm pressed down on my back and his hand rose from my hip. His palm crashed down onto my right ass cheek and I yowled in pleasure, my sopping cunt pressing down around his invading cock.

"I'm going to give it to you the way *I* want to give it to you, you lost your fucking say the second you pointed that gun in my face."

Oh my fucking God that was hot, I arched, grabbing fistfuls of sheet and pressed back onto him, clenching down on him at the same time. His thrusting slowed as it became harder to work his way in and out of me.

"God*damn* you're fucking tight," he uttered, voice strained.

He let go of my hair and smoothed a hand down my spine as he went for a grip on my other hip. Fingers digging with near bruising force he held me, pressing into me deep and deeper until he bottomed out and that fucking *hurt* in all the right ways. So good, so deep, he filled me out and pushed my limits, and started that slow and exquisitely torturous build in my womb.

"Oh God! Cutter, you feel so good!" I bit my lower lip, grasping it between my teeth as he rode me.

"You going to come?" he demanded.

"Yes!"

"Good."

It was a rare thing for me, coming without the benefit of having my clit stimulated but Cutter had found the right combination. He rode over my g-spot, touched that place deep inside me, stimulated all the right places both physically and intellectually and I had about died and gone to heaven as a result. Each forward thrust of his hips was punctuated by a feral, feminine cry, spilling from my mouth, coloring the air with my desire and lust and I loved it. Couldn't get enough of it. I was close, just so freaking *close*.

Cutter's voice broke through, "Come on, Baby, just a little bit more, tighten up for me….Yeah, that's it! That's a good girl, come on, Sweetheart, give it to me, YES!"

I came, exploding all around him and over him, my arms giving out, which I don't even remember them holding me up off the bed. I collapsed against the crisp cotton sheets and Cutter kept his rhythm, stroking deep, a little slower than before but still just as intense as my cunt quivered around his shaft.

"Oh God!" I gasped.

"Nope, just me, Sweetheart; not done with you yet either," he pulled out of me and his arm snaked beneath me, his palm pressed between my tits as he bent over me, his chest pressing to my back. He straightened, taking me with him and held me panting and trembling against his chest for a moment.

"Up into the bed, lay on your back," he ordered and my knees were so weak it took me a couple of tries to comply. He climbed in after me and settled back between my thighs. I was so incredibly wet. Wetter than I ever remember being before in my life. Cutter gazed down at me, solid, in control, assessing me before nodding to himself and introducing his cock back into my pussy.

I arched off the bed and he hooked my legs over his arms, palms flat to the mattress, driving into me deep, the angle different but no less erotic, no less arousing than before. It was like he touched all the places he'd missed in our initial coupling.

"Tease your clit," he ordered and I un-fisted the bottom sheet, letting my right hand drift that direction. I kept my eyes closed and reveled in the sensations he wrought.

"I said touch yourself," his voice was rough and demanding and sent an all new thrill across my nerves, I opened my eyes and the intensity of his gaze stole my breath away. His eyes were lovely, dark and deep, and that darkness had nothing to do with the color. I grazed my sensitive nub with gentle fingertips and gasped, my pussy spasming around his dick where he was buried balls deep.

"Hmmm, oh yeah, do it again." Cutter's eyes drifted shut and he turned his head, savoring the sound of my cry as I did it again. It was almost too much but I didn't want to stop. No, not at all. It felt so good, *he* felt so good. He resorted to these deep, short little thrusts that made my toes curl and my eyes roll back in my head.

I was close, so very close, just that little bit more... and *oh god*... I came screaming his name, back arching so completely off the bed I was sure I would permanently damage something. That I would snap in two and would never be able to walk again and I didn't even care.

Cutter's arms left from behind my knees and curved beneath my back, gathering me to him while he still rode deep inside my body. He kissed my chest, between my small breasts, to my throat, before placing a gentle chaste kiss on my chin. I cupped his face with gentle hands when his lips met mine. His beard tickling my palms as we kissed languorously, so slowly, the gentleness a shocking change from our rough exchange of earlier.

He moved slowly and carefully inside me now, while I trembled uncontrollably in his arms, coming back down slowly from the stratosphere where he'd launched me. He smoothed my hair back from my face and captured my gaze with his.

"Easy, Sweetheart, I've got you," he whispered and emotion welled within me as blood welled from a cut, spilling out of my soul and welling slightly in my eyes. Ah, fuck, it wasn't supposed to be like this. It was supposed to be a hot fuck and nothing more, I wasn't supposed to *feel* anything but physically good... what the fuck was Cutter *doing* to me?

"Shh, I'm right here," his voice was soothing, tone sympathetic – no, empathetic and I swallowed hard, forcing down the confusion and myriad emotions struggling to keep them in check, to not feel what was going on. He kissed me, soft, gentle pecks of his lips on mine, hips lazily moving between my thighs. I twined my legs around him and rode on the gentle current of pleasure he sent thrumming through my core and he smiled down at me and it was probably the most beautiful and intimate smile any man had ever given me.

My heart did a series of back flips in my chest, fluttering erratically and I think, for the first time that I could ever remember doing it, I fell a little in love.

"You good, Sweetheart?" he asked me and I nodded and again with the smile that made my heart stutter in my chest.

"K, hang on to me," he ordered gently. I twined my arms around his shoulders obediently and trusted that he had me as he took me through yet another orgasm, only this one was much less fierce, a sweeping, gentle thing that left me limp with total satisfaction. He leaned down and kissed me again and I was vaguely aware of him twitching his last inside me which set off a whole 'nother set of aftershocks through me.

I lay gasping in Cutter's bed, carefully bracketed by his muscular body and I felt… safe. Cared for… it was strange, unique. I was used to being in control of myself and all of my faculties and somehow, someway, Cutter had stripped me of them all. Left me bare and raw and vulnerable beneath him, and instead of lording that fact over me, he protected me. Held me in the palms of his hands, soothed me, kissed me and silently promised to use the power he held over me now for good rather than evil purposes and I think that's where I lost it completely.

Relief flooded out from the center of my being so strong, so absolute at being able to let go… to be able to trust and I had no fucking idea why I even did, just something about him, some sublevel vibe told me I could and right now I was going with it. I needed to go with it or I was going to implode.

"Shh, it's okay, I've got you, Sweetheart. You just go ahead and let it out," he murmured, and so I did.

CHAPTER 12
Cutter

She had me, hook line and sinker the moment she trembled beneath me and hitched out that broken little sob. Tough as she was, the girl had a lot going on inside and I was feeling a lot of things in that moment. Chiefly, that'd I'd brought it out in her, broken her, cracked her wide and sent all of these emotions tumbling out and now it was my duty to put her back together again. I didn't see it as a long haul project, not with Hope. No she would cry, she would sleep, and she would be fine again. She was a tough cookie. What surprised me was how much that disappointed me.

I really liked her, she felt fucking amazing, and I wanted more. A lot more. I smoothed her hair from her damp cheeks, peppered her face with a bunch of damn butterfly kisses and just let her be what she needed to be. A woman finally setting a burden down, sharing the load.

Her arms twined around me so sweetly and she held herself close to my body and I gave her shelter there. It felt damn good to be needed, but not only needed, *allowed* to help. Hope let me in and god damn that felt so *good* after months of sex and loving someone and being held forever at arm's length... not that I faulted Li'l Bit for any of that... it just was what it was.

I closed my eyes and breathed Hope in and banished all thought of Hayden Michaels from my heart and mind. It wasn't fair to go there with the woman in my arms, here and now. So I shut out Li'l Bit's small frame and haunted green eyes and focused on Hope, and the relief and other mixed up soup of emotions pouring from her. I shifted into a better position to hold her and made soothing noises, rocking her gently until she quieted and her deep and even breathing let me know she was down for the count.

She felt so good, a solid weight against my chest, filling out my arms and it didn't take much or very long for me to fall into a deep and satisfying sleep of my own. By the time the thump and scrape up on deck woke me up, the sun was streaming bright and strong through the portholes and Hope was stiff in my arms, listening just as I was. A series of raps above deck and I relaxed.

"It's cool, Sweetheart, just some of my men, probably making sure you haven't killed me." Hope tipped her chin against my chest, rolling her head back on my shoulder to look at me. I drew her hand to my mouth where it'd been resting on my chest and gently kissed her fingertips.

Her eyes drifted shut at the minute touch and I smiled, still a touch raw but she'd be boot strapping herself in no time as soon as…

"Yo, Captain!" Marlin called from just inside the door below decks.

"Yeah! We're good, Brother," I called back, "Give us a sec!"

Hope pushed off of my chest and sat up, I popped open a cabinet door and pulled down one of my tees for her and she arched a brow before taking it.

"Neon orange is so my color," she remarked sardonically.

"Beggars can't be choosers, Baby," I teased, "Your clothes are out there with them."

She rolled her eyes and pulled it over her head and I really liked her in my shirt. I slid to the end of the bed and stood up.

"Aw Christ, man! Put on some fucking clothes," Pyro griped.

"My boat my rules, no one said you had to look," I pulled on my pair of shorts from the night before and asked, "What time is it?"

"Just after eleven, you got somewhere you have to be?"

"After a fashion," I went up my short, narrow hall, making a pit stop in my water closet before hitting the living room. Hope was leaning against the wood paneling by the water closet door when I came out, a slightly amused look on her face before she ducked in to use it herself. Pyro's sour expression made me chuckle.

"Didn't expect her to hand you your ass last night did you?" I asked.

"Nope," he said plaintively.

"Going to be any bad blood, man?" I asked.

"Nope, she got me fair and square and hasn't said a word about it, I'm good so long as she doesn't make fun."

"Afraid she's going to bruise your ego more than your melon?" Marlin asked from the couch, booted foot propped next to my open but dark laptop.

"Boots off my table," I said interrupting whatever Pyro was going to smart back. Hope appeared in the mouth of my narrow hall, long legs crossed at the ankle as she leaned, arms crossed, against the wall. Her face was impassive but I had her number now, she was waiting to see how things were going to play out.

"Leave it to you, Dude," Pyro said, flopping down on the other end of the couch and looking Hope over appreciatively. She inclined her head in his direction but remained neutral. Nice to know she could take a dude checking her out as a compliment; but I still wanted to slap my buddy upside the head for doing it. That was my woman, and no, I didn't even question the possessive jealousy swirling in my veins. Nor was I going to be a brutish cave-douche about it either. Hope told me to fuck off? Off is the general direction in which I would fuck. Still, the way her deep dark eyes swept over me spoke of two things, one, she wasn't done with me yet and two, she was uncertain. Both could be addressed later.

Right now, Marlin was speaking to Hope, "You know we don't take kindly to anybody pointing guns in one of our brother's faces, we take even less kindly to you pointing one in the Captain's face," he said coolly, but the edge of hostility in his blue eyes was pretty fucking unmistakable. I wanted to step in front of Hope, protect her, but I locked that instinct right in its box. My girl could handle her own.

"Sorry about that," she said but her tone said she was anything but. She was giving Marlin a solid calculating once over. Marlin was doing the same to her. I had to admit she looked good wearing just my shirt, with the wild freshly fucked look going on that I'd put on her. She had a pretty solid bruise at the corner of her mouth, blossoming in sickly brown and purple along her delicate jaw from where I'd clipped her the night before. I grimaced inwardly, I didn't like that one bit but it couldn't be avoided.

"Uh huh," Marlin's eyes traveled from Hope to me, "Only you can have a woman pointing a gun in your face one minute and screaming your name the next," he said and it almost sounded like he was complaining. I grinned at my second in command.

"That's just great," Hope griped and her posture was markedly stiffer than it had been the moment before.

"Sorry, Sweetheart, you pointed a gun in our Captain's face, the man don't go nowhere without some kind of shadow otherwise what kind of club would we be?" Marlin arched his eyebrows but Hope kept him fixed with that neutral look of hers.

"Man, she don't know shit else about how a club operates," Pyro said with surprise.

"What was your first clue?" she asked.

"That dumb assed expression you got on your face," Pyro growled back.

"Uh huh," Hope raised one eyebrow and pushed off from the wall, she wandered over to my recliner and dropped into it, slouching, her gorgeous long legs stretched out in front of her but artfully splayed, knees together, none the less. I wanted to put Pyro's eyes back in his skull backwards for the lingering look he gave them.

"Out," I ordered my men, both of them looked up at me sharply.

"Captain?" Marlin queried.

"Seriously, Hope and I got some business with the SHMC up north, fill you boys in after, go back to The Plank."

"Whoa, ain't happening, Cap. We'll be up on deck but fuck that! We aren't leaving you alone with an unknown quantity." Pyro shot Hope a dirty look. Hope stuck her tongue out at him.

"Yer an unknown quantity," she said like a petulant child and Marlin and I both cracked a smile and slight laugh. It was cute as hell. Pyro even smiled, caught off guard.

"Look chick, no offense but you got some moves, and you used them against us," Pyro said.

"None taken and I know, and I did, I was there... I got a little... upset," she had the grace to look embarrassed.

"Yeah, about that, what's the friggin' deal?" Marlin asked.

"The Plank. Later. Go," I demanded and the guys got up reluctantly.

"We'll be on deck," Marlin said, taking Pyro's side, "Got some clothes coming for the minx," he sniffed.

"Awesome," Hope muttered but didn't sound exactly happy about it.

"That Ruger the only thing you were packing? Best tell us now, Radar is going to find if you got anything else," Marlin's tone was dark.

"In case you hadn't noticed, I don't exactly need a gun to be dangerous," she said and topped the statement off with a nonchalant shrug, "But yeah, that was the only weapon I had and I'd like it back at some point."

"Maybe if you're a good girl and we decide we can trust you," Pyro said. Hope flipped him off and he laughed.

"She's got spunk, good luck with that buddy," my best friend told me. I arched a brow and remained silent but I'm sure my expression said it all, *get the fuck out*.

Marlin and Pyro went above deck and a second later we heard the drone of Marlin's voice on his cell. Hope and I exchanged a look and she gave me another little shrug.

"Let's make this call," I stated dryly but couldn't help but smile. She really wasn't concerned, in fact she was as relaxed as could be. Tough as nails or had a death wish, this one.

She got to her feet and came to me and looked up the scant inch or two that separated us in height.

"Thanks," she murmured and tipped her face up to mine for a kiss. I pulled her the rest of the way against me by her hips and kissed her slow and deep. She drew back and her expression was haunted, fearful, but not for herself. Her gaze was distant, her heart and mind wherever her missing sister was, dead or alive. I sighed silently.

"Come on, let's see what kind of answers we can get you," I murmured and she nodded, troubled. Sometimes it was better not knowing, but when you *had* to know... I knew that feeling too.

I dropped onto the center cushion of my brown leather couch and pulled her down between my knees, circling her waist with my arms. She settled into my lap and I brought up the laptop screen, signed in and put the Skype call through. It was a little early but the screen popped up immediately onto Dani and Thirteen. The small woman perched in her man's lap, wide blue eyes filling up the screen as she leaned back, almost a mirror for me and Hope.

Thirteen's eyes skated over Hope then me before he spoke, "Dragon said it was important. What's up, Man?"

I sketched out what was what and Dani and Thirteen both went very quiet, Thirteen searching his girl's face. She shifted uncomfortably in his lap and chewed her bottom lip, the wheels turning in her head.

"Please, anything, even if you don't think it's important it could mean the world... just whatever you can remember about her, about where she came from..." Hope was desperate and her desperation was showing in her pleading tone.

Dani sighed, "I don't know what happened to Tonya, but I remember her. She was a social climber of the worst order. A total bottom feeder. She latched onto The Suicide Kings to run from some other bad situation. Thought they would protect her," Dani snorted with derision, "She just leapt out of the fire into the frying pan, the Kings were a step up from whatever she was running from, but not by much."

Hope was tense in my arms, "Do you know what she was running from?"

Dani shook her head, "Not what they were into, no... but I know they were Russian. Mob maybe? I don't know, she let slip one name when she was drunk, Ivan something, I really can't remember the last name. Said she'd like to see Ivan get through The Kings if he ever came looking."

Dani looked off to the side, her eyes glazing and gaze distant, she was clearly trying, she finally shook her head as if waking from a particularly horrible dream and gave Hope a sympathetic look.

"Tonya was not good people, she was hooked on drugs, a scammer, selfish and cruel. She wouldn't hesitate to throw one of the other girls up under the bus if it got her one step closer to whatever goal she had in mind. All I know is she came from New Orleans and she was running from some guy named Ivan because of something stupid she did to cross him. I wish I could be of more help, I really do."

"Thank you, Dani. It's something where there was nothing I guess," Hope said but I could tell by the fine tremble in her hands she was having a tough time not breaking something. She was holding it together but I had a feeling something needed to give, and I was a shit for thinking it, but I was sort of half hoping it would be another wild and angry fuck.

We ended the call on an amicable note and Hope's shoulders dropped, "Shit… another lead and probably another fucking dead end," she sighed and I shook her a bit. She put her hands over mine.

"You don't know that yet, Darlin'. Let's go talk to the guys and see what we can come up with. I got shit to deal with in-house."

"Tiny?" she asked.

"Sorry, Sweetheart, you don't get to know that. That's club business," I told her. She nodded.

"Kick him in the balls at least once for me," she said, "Guy is a prick," she rose off my lap and stretched, "Where're my clothes?" she asked.

"Right here," Marlin ducked below deck and tossed a backpack at her feet, she stooped and picked it up looking inside.

"Thanks, I think," she frowned, "You pick this?"

"No, Radar did, why?"

"Radar sucks at women's fashion," she stated dryly.

"Fuck you, Princess!" Radar called from above deck. Hope rolled her eyes and went for the water closet.

"I'm showering," she said and I nodded.

"Go right ahead, Sweetheart; mi es tu castillo," she ducked backwards out of the water closet and looked me over, apparently impressed that I'd said it right. Goddamn she was fine. She arched one dark eyebrow, blew me a kiss and shut the door behind her firing up the narrow shower.

"Above deck," I said and followed Marlin up.

"Where is he?" I asked.

"In the Glades where we keep them kinds of things," Radar said low and dark.

"Anything else we should know about Miss Thang down there?" Pyro asked.

Radar looked me over, and I looked right back, hard.

"Spill it man," I demanded.

"She seems to be on the up and up, her sister went missing almost two years ago. She had a bunch of files back at her room, bitch travels light. What clothes she did have fit in a back pack and her purse along with the files. Went through her phone, took a minute to crack it but Atlas got it. She's got a whole lot of law enforcement contacts…"

"Sort of have to, it's part of the job," her voice startled all three of us, she looked us all over in turn, "You want to know anything, all you've got to do is ask." Jesus, she showered like a dude. Get in, get out; get on with it. I had to like that!

"You a cop?" Radar asked her point blank.

"Nope, all I do is teach them not to kill whoever they're arresting. Army gave me a particular skillset, Junior. You can't fault a girl for putting it to use. Plus, I figured it might help me find my sister somehow, someway, that's about the extent of that." Hope gave Radar a cool and appraising look. The gloves were off apparently, there wasn't no lie in her face, her posture was guarded, but I think that was because with a rough lot like my boys she was expecting more violence.

"I just want to find Faith, I don't give a fuck what you do or what you're into. I just want to find my sister, or at least what happened to her," she said. Radar nodded slowly.

"We ain't bad guys," Marlin said softly.

"Tell that to the bitch who last saw my sister," she wasn't going to give any quarter there and I didn't blame her. Hell if it was a female close to me, like Li'l Bit or even Li'ler Bit, I would tear the Earth and sky apart right alongside their men to find them. I mean shit, what if it were Hoss? She's got three kids counting on her…

I shook my head, "That wasn't something any of us condoned, Sweetheart."

"We'll have to agree to disagree on that one, Baby Cakes. Your man that did it was walking around and doing just fine when I got here," she leveled me with an accusing glare and I couldn't argue with her logic, even if it was totally civilian. She didn't understand our ways and the crash course in the MC life would have to come later, right now the rest of the boys were waiting. It seemed Radar thought now was the time though, he started in on her first lesson.

"You don't get it, Princess. Good, bad, or indifferent, Tiny is a brother and we protect our own, even when they do extremely stupid shit," Radar crossed his arms and stared her down. Hope gave him a bored look.

"Right, okay, I'm not going to pretend to get it, guess I just have to know one thing, am I supposed to be some kind of prisoner or something retarded like that because I know too much?" she asked, but she was asking me, her gaze fixed firmly on my face. I grinned wide.

"You going to the cops?" I asked.

"No."

"Your word on that?"

"Yes."

"Then for now, we're straight," I palmed the back of my neck and pulled on it trying to ease some of the tension there.

"Just like that?" she asked.

"Just like that," I affirmed. She narrowed her eyes and I could see the questions dancing inside that pretty little skull of hers. She pulled her wet hair over her shoulder and braided it. She was dressed in what the boys had brought her, some flowery strapless dress that hung to her feet. It didn't look like something she would wear and in fact looked like she had to safety pin it some.

"Where the hell did you get that thing?" I asked Radar, he shrugged.

"It's my oldest kid's," he grated. His oldest kid was his 17 year old daughter. Dude was forty-three.

"Good to know, now where are *my* clothes?" Hope asked sweetly but her expression was sour as all get out.

"Moved your shit from The Nautilus to our safe house, it'll all be there when you get there," Pyro said. Hope's expression darkened but then turned thoughtful.

"My, how heavy handed of you. I thought I wasn't a prisoner."

"You're not, but as of now, I guess you're our guest," Marlin supplied.

"You touch my bike?" she asked.

"It's at the safe house too, took it there myself. Nice little pasta rocket you got there," Radar said. Hope looked positively mutinous at that.

"Hey," I said and she turned back to me. "What'd I tell you?" I meant last night and she knew it, she didn't blush but the memory of it slid behind her eyes. She looked at me thoughtfully.

"You've told me a lot of things, but I guess I'm picking up what you're putting down. So what happens now?" she shifted on her feet, nerves putting her into a bit of a fighter's stance. I smiled at her.

"We take you to the safe house, and then I go deal with some shit," I said. She searched my face and nodded slowly.

"It's going to have to do for now. I need to come up with a game plan on what to do, where to go from here," she said.

I felt like telling her she wasn't going anywhere without me, but it wasn't my place to say, not yet anyways. I'd remind her that I'd promised I was going to help her find her sister after I dealt with cleaning house.

"Right this way, Darlin'," Pyro said and held out his arm, he and I traded a look and I gritted my teeth. Bastard was doing it just to get my damned goat. Hope looked from one to the other of us.

"I think I got it," she said and leapt lightly to the dock, "Which one of you jokers has my phone?" she asked.

Nope. She wasn't going to give any quarter and the emotional storm of last night was over as far as I could tell. I smiled on the inside, a self-indulgent little smile. The chase was still on, and the carefully considering look she was giving me said she wanted me to chase her. Game on, Sweetheart. Game fucking on.

CHAPTER 13
Hope

"You know this is kind of bullshit," I was sulking, but only mildly. Cutter's chuckle thrummed through his back and into my chest where I was pressed tight against him. He pulled up in front of a modern looking house, a real nice place that looked like it belonged on the front cover of Better Homes & Gardens.

"I won't be too long, Sweetheart. You and I have some things to talk about."

Wasn't that the ever loving truth? He shut off the bike and I got off of it, hiking the bag made out of old fishing net higher onto my shoulder. It had my shorts and tank from last night in it. Cutter slipped my phone out of his vest's inside pocket and handed it to me. I palmed it and looked over the driveway.

My baby was indeed parked in the shade of a couple of palms in the front of the house, off to the side. The place was a two story monstrosity with wide stone steps out front and by the looks of things, sat right on the beach. We were a bit far out from town for a normal person to walk it but I wasn't your average Joe, plus I had my bike. They didn't know about the hidden key.

"So you leaving me here by myself?" I asked, not quite believing that I wasn't some kind of prisoner or something. Not like they could hold me if they wanted to. I was pretty sure out of all of them that Cutter was the only one that could give me a run for my money. The rest could probably hold their own against anyone else, I was just far too trained for them to handle me one on one... Two on one might even be a stretch for them to be honest. It took Cutter to bring me down the night before and I was still deliciously sore from how that'd turned out. I still had some mixed feelings about that, but for now the good outweighed the bad.

"Sweetheart, look at me?" he said softly and I did because he asked and because he was treating me with more respect than I probably deserved. His eyes were a brown with deeper flecks of bronze to them. Lighter than mine but no less deep. He invaded my personal space so beautifully and brought his forehead down to mine while his boys looked on from a short distance away.

"You're not a prisoner, not like we could hold you if you got determined anyways and I don't want to see any of my guys hurt. Likewise, I don't want to see you hurt either but things have gotta happen in a certain order here, you feel me?" he asked. I nodded, mouth suddenly inoperable due to his proximity. I wanted him to kiss me. I wanted to disappear into Cutter's arms and never come up for air again. I wanted to forget, briefly, like he'd made me forget last night. Faith...

I closed my eyes and breathed out and somehow knew that he knew. He wrapped me up in his embrace and hugged me as I nodded my understanding even though I didn't get it, I understood protocol and apparently his merry band of misfits had protocols in spades.

"Gimme a few hours, I'll come back here and we'll talk, figure out our next move. Okay?"

Our next move... I liked the sound of that. It was the sound of not being alone anymore and as much as I didn't want to admit it, I was tired. Really tired of carrying this fucked up burden all by myself. But it was my cross to bear, no one else's.

"Why are you helping me?" I asked and leveled him with a steady gaze.

"I'm not a bad dude, Baby. Maybe I wanna prove that to you," he murmured. I scoffed a little.

"You don't give a fuck what people think," I stated judiciously.

"Maybe not, Darlin' but for some reason, I care about what *you* think," he winked at me and slipped from my grasp taking a step back. His buddies looks of mistrust were burning me up where I stood and I felt a little bad about that, but not bad enough to really care all that much. After all, one or some of these assholes killed my only lead, even though from what the Dani girl had said, she wasn't someone really to be mourned over which was its own particular kind of awful and sad when you thought about it.

"Just do whatever you have to do and get your ass back here," I grumbled.

Cutter laughed, "Yes ma'am!" he shot me a smart salute and got back on his bike. I watched them leave and went into the house.

It was cool inside, the air conditioning running strong and a welcome respite from the oppressive heat and humidity outside. I set myself to exploring, mostly in an effort to track down my belongings. I found them in the master suite upstairs. They'd just shoved everything in a giant ass cardboard box and put it on the bed. It was all here though. Clean, dirty, didn't matter, it was just in one giant jumble, my few paper files and tablet on the bottom under my emptied backpack and riding boots.

I sighed and spent the next thirty minutes sorting everything out. Once everything was in neat little OCD piles, I put all my dirty clothes back into the box a la laundry basket, and started a hunt for a washer and dryer. Might as well get something accomplished if I was going to be waiting for hours.

I stripped out of the god awful, oversized dress meant for someone with actual tits and dropped it in with the rest of my shit. I had two loads to do, both small but one was reserved for my delicate clothing of which I had plenty. Delicate material took up a whole lot less room in a pack and when you lived off the back of a bike like I had been doing, the more delicate the material, the more of a wardrobe you could carry.

I had a storage unit in Cali that had my cold weather gear and furniture and such in it, but it had been a minute since I'd needed any of it. One of the joys of working for yourself was choosing where to go when. I hated the cold. I worshiped the day star passionately, and stuck to warm, sunny climates as much as I could.

I returned to the master suite bare assed and didn't even care. I mean I was here alone, so fuck it, right? I sat down heavily on the bed and powered up my phone and tablet and went through them. I had to hand it to The Kraken, for being a bunch of seemingly low-brow Neanderthal biker thugs, they were thorough. They'd been through all my shit backwards and forwards. Surprisingly I didn't care about that so much. All they found was what I'd been telling Cutter this entire time.

I was looking for Tonya Anon in hopes that she would lead me to my sister. I really could give two fucks about what these happy bastards were into. They didn't need to know that I knew about a few of their extracurricular activities. I mean seriously, who gave a shit about Cuban cigars and bootlegging moonshine? I'm sure they were in to more than just that, they were playing their cards too close to the vest, but from everything I could tell? They didn't do guns, they didn't do sex workers, and they didn't do hardcore drugs. Compared to most other motorcycle gangs, these guys were pious little angels. I had to smile on the inside, because compared to most women, I was better trained and smarter than carrying the information I had on them anywhere other than in my brain.

I finished taking stock of everything and was pretty surprised to find that everything, including my fully loaded Ruger, was accounted for. Only thing missing was a wayward eyeliner pencil which upon further digging, I found in the bottom of my purse.

"What is your guys' deal?" I muttered under my breath. The short answer? They didn't see me as a threat, and they were right, I wasn't. Everything about their behavior up to this point screamed that they were trying to cover their ass and protect their own and I could appreciate that. Wasn't that exactly what I was doing when it came to Faith and Charity?

Charity... it'd been a few days since I last checked in. I picked up my phone which had three percent battery and plugged it in. I rooted around for my toiletries and decided on a proper shower. I'd wanted to catch them off guard earlier so I'd just done a quick rinse.

I spent a long while under the spray of the bigger house shower and let the massaging showerhead beat my sore muscles into submission. I let my mind drift and sighed out when it invariably ended up on the more intimate moments of the night before. Cutter was quite possibly the most amazing lover I had ever been with and I would be a fucking liar if I said I didn't want more. I lightly banged my forehead against the shower wall.

I fucking hated this shit. Feeling all over the map and out of control was so not my usual thing. I needed to get my shit together and fast. I shut off the tap and dried off, wrapping a towel around me. I looked around and jackpot, found a hair dryer. Most hotels and B&B's had them. Score that this place had one too. I dried my hair, found some clean clothes, grateful that I was washing. I was seriously scraping the bottom of the barrel when it came to wearable outfits.

I switched the laundry and got the second load going and by the time I got back to the master suite my phone had enough of a charge to call my littlest sister. It rang, and rang, and rang and rang before kicking over to voicemail. I groaned just before it beeped.

"Blossom! It's Buttercup, call me back," I sighed loudly, "I'm still in Florida and I'm on to a different lead, I'll fill you in later. Love you, bye." I hung up and tossed the phone, charging cable still solid, onto the nightstand. I scrubbed my makeup free face with my hands and spent my time whiling away the next few hours finishing up my laundry and scouring my files for any mention of an 'Ivan' anywhere and going over everything New Orleans related.

"Fuck, fuck, fuck, fuck, fuck!" I exclaimed and flopped back onto the bed when I came up empty on both fronts.

"Thought you had enough but I'm certainly willing to oblige."

Cutter crossed the carpet, and flopped down on the bed beside me, propping his head on his arms. I turned my head and looked at him huffing out a loud exaggerated breath.

"You look like you've had a hell of a day," I said dryly. He shrugged laconically and reached an arm across my middle.

"Could have been worse. House is clean, we took out the trash, doesn't get the dirt out of our souls though," I searched his face and nodded slowly.

"I'm sorry," I said and I was, whatever he'd been out doing had obviously taken a toll on him and his.

"How about you?" he asked.

"Been over everything, twice. Nothing. Not a God damned thing points to anybody named Ivan," I scrubbed my face with my hands again and Cutter slipped his hand beneath the hem of my tee, giving us skin on skin contact. His hand was warm in the air conditioned coolness of the house and I couldn't tell him how much I relished the skin on skin contact.

"Where do we go from here?" I asked.

"Depends, Darlin'. What context? You talkin' about you and me or you talking about the search for your girl?" he asked.

"Both, really..."

"Well, I think both of us need to eat some food, take a deep breath, and figure it out a moment at a time. I want to help you. I promised you I would help you and I meant it. I like you, Hope. You're sassy and give me a run for my money. I think I've needed that," he gave me that panty scorching grin of his and I felt an answering throb in my cunt. Damn it. Wasn't fair how fucking sexy he was.

"Something to eat sounds good," I conceded.

"The way you're looking at me, Sweetheart, I should probably say I'm not on the menu..." he said but we were both drawing nearer to one another.

"Sure about that, Slick?"

"Nope, not at all," and we kissed. My blood caught fire and my hands gripped his face between them of their own volition. Then it was a whole lot of me pushing his leather vest off his shoulders and scrambling at the catch on his jeans, which is about when it struck me, he was wearing jeans and heavy boots, not exactly beach gear. I put it from my mind as we worked each other out of our clothes.

Everything of mine had been neatly put away in my pack, which I just about always had my gear stowed at a moment's notice, in case I had to bounce. My tablet and phone were both plugged in and chilling on the nightstand, my purse and my paper files ended up sloshing to the floor in our heated frenzy to get naked. I pushed him back into the bed and straddled his hips, lowering myself onto him.

Oh my God he felt amazing. He looked up at me with lust filled eyes and pressed his thumb against my lips, I sucked his thumb into my mouth, biting it gently as I ground down onto his cock. He was seated in me as deep as he could go and I fucking loved it. He let me have my way, didn't order me to ride him harder or faster, but rather just took his time and let me do what I wanted. I liked that, I liked that a lot, that he was secure enough to let me have control this time around.

"Make me come," I ordered him and he smiled with savagery. He drew his thumb away from my mouth and used my own saliva as lube to tease my clit. Fuck he was hot.

I threw my head back, my hair grazing the tops of his thighs and I listened to him suck in a sharp breath. I rolled my hips and watched his eyes drift shut, as he concentrated, his head tilting as if listening to music only he could hear.

"Fuck yeah, Baby, like that – just like that…" he breathed and I squeezed down on him. I loved that I could do this, make him feel good, make me feel good, it'd been too damned long. What's more, back then, it'd just been sex… I couldn't deny that whatever we were doing, last night or today, that it was definitely something *more* than just sex. There was weight and emotion behind joining with Cutter, I just was hesitant to put any labels onto something so new.

"Oh God yeah, right there, mmhmm!" I encouraged when he stroked my clit just right. I clamped down on his cock with my pussy just a little bit harder and bent forward to claim his mouth in a kiss. His free hand tangled in my hair, holding it gently back from our faces as we made out and I spiraled that much higher, coiled that much tighter. I couldn't exactly kiss him and ride him at the same time so he picked up my slack with some controlled and steady thrusting as he did what I commanded and made me come.

I splintered apart, gently at first, but the orgasm was like a freight train, lumbering into view, until suddenly it was just there, blasting past you, blowing through you, until with an inarticulate cry into Cutter's mouth and a jerk of my hips he knew he'd completed his task. Too much, too sensitive, he removed his thumb and took his hand from my hair and gripping my hips held me in place so he could fuck me and take his own satisfaction.

As far as that went, it didn't take too long for him to come either. The sex of today, as compared to last night ended up being a quickie and I think we were both alright with that because as I lay panting across his chest, both of our stomachs growled in unison.

We laughed and he swatted me playfully and painlessly on the ass to get up. I reared up and shivered with delight as he slipped from me, when I looked again he was looking up the length of my body in wonder.

"Come down here and kiss me one more time?" he asked softly. I bent at the waist and complied, placing my lips gently against his.

"God you're gorgeous," he breathed against my mouth and his words gave me a rush of pleasure.

"Thank you, you're not half bad yourself," I said, voice husky.

"Come on, let me treat you to some dinner and we'll figure out where to go from there," he murmured.

"Sounds good," I breathed.

It did, it really did…

CHAPTER 14
Cutter

Tiny was gator food. It had to happen. He'd betrayed us, put our entire club at Hope's mercy and that was just fucking unacceptable. We'd tried, man. Treated him like a brother far longer than he'd deserved to be one, and after last night, it had been no surprise that it'd been a unanimous vote for Tiny to meet Davey Jones up close and personal.

I looked Hope over as she typed into the fancy tablet she owned. She was in my shirt and nothing else while I stood in just my jeans and cut in the kitchen preparing us a meal. She was beautiful, despite the slight frown of concentration marring her face.

"What're you doing?" I asked softly, she smiled, a gentle curve of her luscious mouth and answered me without looking up at me.

"Why do you need to ask me? Your boys will tell you soon enough, or did you think I would miss the tracking software ghosting everything I typed?" She leveled me with a clear and steady look that said nothing and everything.

"Clever girl," I said and checked the fish under the broiler.

"It's cool, I get it," she said softly and I believed that she did, "No lies, no half-truths Cutter. I just want to find my little sister."

"I know Baby, and I really want to help you find her."

"But?" she asked.

"No buts, I want to help you find her, I just want to make sure my club, my brothers are safe too," she gripped the seat of her chair between those long legs of hers and leaned forward.

"Cuban cigars, moonshine and what else?" she asked softly. I froze and cocked my head to the side. Moment of truth, it seemed she knew some things. I didn't know how or from where but if she held some truths... Fuck. Fuck, fuck, fuck.

"I want to tell you but it goes against our code, Darlin', nothin' heavy. I can tell you that much. We don't traffic in girls, or hard drugs. Me and my boys are clean from any of the really dirty shit. Next school shooting you see on the news, I can confidently say me and my boys had no hand in it. You get me?" She searched my face and nodded carefully.

"I get you," she said solemnly, "And I'm sorry I pointed a gun in your face."

"They give it back to you?" I asked.

"Yes."

"Good, point it at me again it won't be just me fucking you and it won't be just your pussy," I told her and let that sink in.

"Right," she said with a frown, I could tell she was trying to figure out if I was serious. I smiled to myself. She was mine. I would never let my guys pull a train on her, not in a million fucking years, still, if it served as some incentive to keep her gun pointed away from my face, I was okay with that.

"You aren't serious, are you?" she asked finally and I chuckled.

"Usually I don't mind sharing, but for some reason, with you, I got a problem with that," I told her truthfully. She nodded carefully and I dished us up some food.

"Good to know," she murmured and pushed to her feet. She went to the fridge and brought out a bottle of white. I wished I could say it was interesting that she wasn't outwardly phased or outraged by a threat of rape but she'd been in the military and threats of that nature, hell, *follow through*, wasn't an uncommon practice.

"You okay?" I asked.

"Hmm? Yeah, why?" she asked.

"Suddenly feeling a little guilty for that asshole remark," I told her.

She set the bottle and glasses on the counter and came to me, pulling me into her by the belt loops on my jeans. I put my hands on her shoulders and looked down the couple of inches into her dark and lovely eyes.

"I'd knee you in the balls if it made you feel better but I'm going to need them later," she murmured demurely and I chuckled darkly.

"Run for my money," I uttered and kissed her softly, she bit my bottom lip playfully and I went from zero to hard in point three seconds.

"I'm hungry," she whispered against my mouth, punctuating the statement with a chaste kiss before stepping back.

"Dinner is served as soon as you sit your ass down at the table and pour us some wine," I told her. She smiled coyly over her shoulder and took the bottle and glasses she'd scared up to the table, pouring two generous glassfuls.

I brought the food over and we sat in silence, eating quietly, savoring our dinner. It was nice not having to fill the silence with inane chatter. Nicer still that she rose and did the dishes with me at the sink. Dishes done and put away I took her hand and linked my fingers with hers, leading her to the living room couch. We took our wine with us and sank into the leather, cooled by the house's AC.

"Tell me about yourself," I murmured.

"Not much to tell, really… My mother had me young, she was sixteen… then she had Faith when I was ten and Charity when I was 12," she fell silent and I could tell that this was going to be a painful story for her.

"What about your dad?" I asked, low and careful.

"Took mom's virginity, left her pregnant, and bounced, I never knew him. Only picture I saw was out of the high school yearbook. Mom never talked about him really, I don't even have his last name. My mom put hers on the birth certificate. I'm not entirely sure the encounter was consensual if you catch my drift. Any time it came up she would just shut down, I'm not sure he even knows I exist." I pulled her back against my chest and she took a large swallow of her wine.

"I'm sorry…"

"Don't be, you can't miss what you never had in the first place. I mean, am I right?" she laid her head back against my chest and I nodded slowly.

"I guess."

"Anyways, mom met Dirk when I was eight or nine and they got hitched. A couple of years later she had Faith, then a year and a half, two years after that there was Charity. Dirk started drinking or drugging or both and Mom ditched his ass by the time Char was two and it was just the four of us. She hooked back up with him off and on while the girls grew up until I was around fourteen, then she lost him for good." She was quiet for a minute, sipping her wine thoughtfully, before she roused herself to continue.

"Then Mom got sick when I was sixteen. She died the day after my eighteenth birthday. Thank God she managed to hang on that long, otherwise Dirk may have gotten Faith and Char and that was going to happen over my dead body. It was a fight and a half for custody as it was... I enlisted, Grammy helped out as much as she could 'til I got through basic and the rest is sort of history," she said.

"How old were the girls when your mom died?" I wanted to check my math.

"Eight and six, I went from big sister to sister-mom overnight," she sighed and sagged into my chest a little, "Not like I would trade it for anything, I love my Bubbles and Blossom to death," she smiled.

"Bubbles and Blossom?" I asked choking on a laugh.

"Yep and I'm Buttercup!" I couldn't see her face, just the top of her head with how we were laying but I could hear the grin in her voice.

"How the fuck you figure?" I asked.

"Haven't you ever heard of the Power Puff Girls?" she asked.

"No, what's a Power Puff Girl?"

"Oh my God!" she sat bolt upright and turned, "This set up have Netflix?" she asked waving her hand at the television and entertainment center.

"Uhhh I think so, I don't really pay attention to that kind of crap."

Next thing I know, Hope is working remotes like a pro and I'm watching some retarded kid's cartoon about three little girl super heroes, laughing my ass off at the green one's attitude problem, which I guess was Buttercup.

"The girls loved this," she said, "Want to watch another one?"

I gazed at her and it hit me just how rough her situation was, both then and now...

"Maybe later," I grazed her cheek with my thumb and she switched off the TV and whatever else she had running.

"Why are you looking at me that way?" she asked softly and looked uncomfortable.

"You're kind of amazing, you know that?"

She shook her head, "If I were amazing, I never would have lost Faith in the first place. Charity wouldn't be out her closest sister, and I wouldn't feel like such a fucking failure," she said unhappily.

I looked her over. I had a feeling that she was leaving a lot of shit out about her situation growing up. Like why, as young as she appeared to be, she would have done such a major surgery to prevent any pregnancy. I wanted to ask, but I kept my mouth shut. It was none of my business what she did with her body, really, and it wasn't like I was complaining. Kids weren't any part of my future plans, not leading this outlaw life of mine.

"What?" she demanded when I'd been staring a touch too long.

"You've had it rough, haven't you, Darlin'?" I asked gently.

"Rather not talk about it anymore," she said.

"Fair enough, what would you rather talk about?" I asked gently.

She stood up and straddled my lap looking down into my face, studying it for a while, the hour was growing late and her eyes slipped shut. She sighed out...

"How do you think this is going to end?" she asked quietly.

"Does it have to?" I asked, pitching my voice low.

"Eventually. Everything has to end," she murmured.

"Yeah, but we don't have to think about that today, or tomorrow or even the next day. Why not just enjoy the ride, Sweetheart?" I asked.

"Not sure I've ever been able to. Everything seems to have a timestamp on it for me. An expiration date. It's just the way it's always been."

I smoothed my hands up under my shirt along her satiny skin, she was warm and alive beneath my palms and I smiled a whimsical, crooked smile at her.

"Sure, yeah, okay…" I said without much conviction, I didn't want to argue or fight with her, I just wanted the tension to ease out of her posture and for her to just fucking relax for a minute.

She slowly lowered her face towards mine, her hands smoothing over my chest, I grew hard with the anticipation of her lips meeting mine. She was so fiery, so determined. Strong and hardened by life's circumstances but at the same time, soft and yielding under my touch. She aroused me in so many ways, physically, intellectually, and yes, even the beginnings of emotionally.

Her lips hovered a fraction of an inch above mine, her breath warm, fanning across my lips sending a shot of adrenaline straight to my heart, causing it to swell in my chest and her fucking phone rang. She smiled, lips curving gently and murmured, "Hold that thought," before pushing off of me and to her feet.

I was gonna die.

She padded to the dining table and scooped up her phone, her eyes glued on me and answered it without looking…

"About time you called me back, Blossom," she said grinning but then I saw the easy smile slide right off her face.

What the fuck?

CHAPTER 15
Hope

"Hope Andrews?" a male voice, thick with a southern accent, rolled out of my earpiece at me.

"Yes, sorry, I answered without looking, I was expecting my sister to call. What can I do for you...?" I left the question open ended in anticipation that he would tell me his name.

"Yes, Ma'am. This is Detective Atchison of the Plaquemines Parish Sherriff's Department over here in Louisiana," he said.

"Well Detective Atchison, what can I do for you?" I asked. It was around five o'clock here, but only four in Louisiana so it wasn't outside the realm of possibility that he was calling me for a consult.

Cutter was looking at me, his expression carefully neutral as I slipped into my more professional role of Hope Andrews, Defense Contractor. I went to him and straddled his hips again, a ghost of a smile on my lips which sloughed right off when Detective Atchison started speaking again.

"Well Ma'am, I think it's more what I can do for you. You see we're holding your sister, Faith Dobbins on a charge of prostitution, she was brought in early this morning and when we put her name and prints through the system it hit over in New Orleans. Now it took a minute for them to contact us down here, but the Detective I talked to, Detective Thibault, you know that name?" he asked.

"Yes, I trained his department and he was the Detective assigned to my sister's case when she went missing." My voice sounded hollow, distant, I couldn't believe this was happening, I mean was this really happening!? Cutter's hands were riding over his stolen shirt, smoothing up and down over my hips, as I held myself ridged above him. I locked eyes with him and compassion and support radiated off of him in waves.

"Well Detective Thibault said I should contact you, so that's what I'm doing. Your sister has yet to be arraigned but typically this being a misdemeanor and her first offense she'll probably be held on about a thousand dollars bond, you can bail her out…" his voice droned as what he was saying finally hit home.

Faith. Arrested… *arrested for prostitution.* What the hell?

"No, no! No… please, can you keep her there? I'm about twelve hours away. I'll leave now. I'll ride in. I can be there by morning, just can you keep her there?" I asked and I knew I sounded desperate.

"Well she's here until she's arraigned and if no one posts her bail, yeah," he said.

"Okay, I'm coming, I'm on my way, what's the address?"

Cutter worked his phone out of his hip pocket and opened the notepad app and took the address down as I repeated it. He stared me in the eyes with a grim resolve and mouthed at me *I'm with you…* I nodded slowly and was surprised at the relief that brought me. I blinked and spoke with the Detective a little more and by the time I hung up Cutter was in the midst of his own call.

He gave my ass a short smack indicating I needed to get up and I bolted to my feet. He stood and I tuned in to what he was saying.

"Then take a fucking vote on who's with me but I'm going, Man; so you'd better have a wrecking crew ready and get Atlas on finding out who holds the territory. I'll call 'em from the road if I have to. Hope and I are leavin' inside the hour."

I swallowed hard, amazed that he would do that for me… that he really was a man of his word. He'd promised, but in my life and my world, promises didn't mean diddly squat.

"Right, meet us at the safe house then," he tilted the phone away from his mouth and addressed me, "I gotta run to the boat, grab some shit, you gonna be ready when I get back?" he demanded. I nodded.

"You take off without us, I'm not only going to chase you down, I'm going to own your ass again when I catch up to you," he threatened with a wink. I smiled, warmth suffusing me.

"Hurry the fuck up then, I'll be dressed and ready to ride by the time you get back."

He nodded and went for his leather vest, which for some bizarre reason he called it a cut, and pulled it off the back of the kitchen chair. He talked into the phone, mostly making noncommittal noises or grunts of agreement. I stripped his shirt over my head and handed it to him. He winked and shoved it in his back pocket before he stuffed his feet in his boots.

I went for the master suite upstairs and my gear, fear and wonder, anger and confusion, spurring me on. Faith. Prostitution. Fuck she'd never left Louisiana! What the fuck had she gotten herself into?

I stopped inside the door to the master suite and listened to Cutter's bike roar into the distance. I turned my wrist into the light coming from the bathroom and caressed over the writing there with my thumb. *Virtue*... All three of us girls had them done on Charity's eighteenth birthday, it was what my mother had named us after. Hope, Faith, and Charity, the three virtues of legend.

I stared at the ceiling and blinked back the tears that were threatening as the implications of that phone call hit home. *Faith was alive.* My little sister was alive and hurting and into God knew what. I sniffed, spurned back into action. My little sister was alive and ass deep in alligators and sinking fast and I needed to do what I set out to do from the very beginning. I needed to save her. So it was time to man up rather than bitch out. I had a long ride in front of me. I ducked into the shower, washed quickly and got out, pulling my hair back, and up into a tight bun at the back of my head that would be comfortable under my helmet.

I dressed to ride in my gear and was grateful I'd pretty much packed my shit. By the time I was sitting in the living room, lacing up my boots, the first bikes started to rumble up the street outside. I wondered vaguely how many would be coming. Who would want to stand with the woman, who not twenty-four hours before, pointed a gun in their leader's face.

I tucked the Ruger into the small of my back up under my jacket into its inner pants holster and shoved my purse into the top of my pack, cinching the drawstrings tight and closing the flap. The front door to the house opened and a few of Cutter's men came in.

"Hear we're going to the great state of Louisiana!" one of them said, a man I recognized but I didn't know his name.

"Chill out, Lightning. We don't know what's what until the rest of the guys get here. Just because we voted it don't mean we're clear to go, you know that." The man who spoke was an older guy, fifties maybe, bald and built with a graying trucker's 'stache.

"Hope," I said to the older man giving him a chin lift. He grinned at me.

"Beast," he said back.

"No offense, Beast, Lighting… but that's my sister. I'm going with or without you guys."

"Calm your tits, Sugar; just certain requirements have to be met. We don't live in your civilian world 'n you don't live in ours."

I eyed Beast carefully and bit my bottom lip, worrying it carefully in thought. This was Cutter's world and rather than get butt twisted and piss these guys off more, I decided I'd bite.

"Can you explain it to me?" I asked and Beast's grin grew larger.

"You see states, counties, cities… we see territories. New Orleans and its outlying parishes is Voodoo Bastard territory. Now our territory, Kraken territory is small by comparison. We never wanted a big national charter like the Sacred Hearts have. You know who I'm talking about with them, right?"

I nodded.

"Right, well The Kraken just hold Ft. Royal and about five miles in any direction of it. We don't want more 'n that. Where we're heading is another MC's territory. MC's operate on respect first and foremost and part of that is you don't go tromping onto the next dude's territory without giving them a heads up, or in certain cases askin' permission. Now our fearless leaders are working on that as we speak. You'll find Cutter's got one hell of a loyal crew. Captain barely had to ask and we all signed up for this shit." That set me back on my heels, these guys barely knew me and what they'd seen of me, well I'd been mostly a bitch since I'd hit town…

"Why're you helping me?" I asked quietly.

Lightning flashed a grin at me, his light green eyes luminous. He was handsome in his own right, just young for my tastes. Mid-twenties maybe and wiry with short cropped light brown hair. It was he who answered me, "'Cause, you've made the Captain smile again," he told me which was one of the fucking weirdest and most cryptic things for him to say but I didn't have time to ask because here came Marlin and Pyro, Radar and I think Atlas with Cutter coming in behind them. All of them carried packs or gear.

"Hey," I said by way of greeting.

"Awright listen up!" Cutter barked as even more of his men came in behind him, "We're headed to New Orleans, Pyro has our route planned and Atlas has made contact with the brotherhood in control of the territory out there. They're expecting us. Pyro, brief us, Man. We ain't got any time to waste." Cutter looked at me as he delivered his last and I gave him a slight nod.

"Okay, we're taking the I-75 North to the I-10 West, you stay in formation. Get your pockets full of change, we're going to be hitting some toll booths. It's gonna be around a 10 hour ride, we're going straight through, that's Captain's orders so if any of you want or need to puss out, do it now. We're going to stop and fuel on the way out of town. Grab an energy drink if you need to. Trike is going to be following us up in the crash truck, Beast, you're our tailgunner," Beast gave a snappy little salute at that, "Hope, you're riding up front with the Pres since you're A, fucking him and B, don't know what the hell you're doing with a crew." Pyro gave me a tight lipped little smile and I raised my eyebrows a little.

"Jealous?" I asked with a wink. Pyro grinned.

"Ask me in front of my Ol' Lady I'll deny it but hell yes. Your ass is fine," he shot back. Cutter smacked him lightly upside the head and scowled at him. Pyro laughed.

"Atlas," Cutter intoned.

"Right," Atlas cleared his throat, "We've got clear passage through Voodoo Bastard territory and as long as we stick to the big slab we're clear through all the territories leading up to theirs. You fuckers better have your bikes in working order, there ain't going to be any unplanned fuel stops. We should be good to go once we get on the road. You need to stop you know the signal."

"Yell if you need to, Sweetheart," Cutter told me. I was actually kind of surprised at how well organized and efficient these guys sounded for looking as hodge podge, rough and slapped together as they did, they seemed to have this shit down to a science.

Atlas and Pyro rattled off some other miscellaneous information and we all pulled on packs, cinching straps and making sure clasps and buckles were secure. I picked up my helmet and fell into step just behind Cutter, going for my bike. I put my helmet on, not caring to ride without it, mostly because my bike didn't really have a place to stow it. Cutter gave me a side long look with a little smile as I climbed astride my baby.

"We gotta get you a real bike," he said. I fired up with the sharp growl and whine unique to Ducati sport bikes and smiled.

"I like my bike just fine," I said.

"No accounting for taste, Sweetheart, but I sure do like you on the back of mine," I grinned secretly, my mouth hidden behind my helmet's face mask and snapped down my tinted visor.

Cutter waved me up on his left and Marlin took to his right. I'd never ridden in a procession so large. I'd occasionally fall in with one or two other riders heading in the same direction while out on the interstate or highway, but I'd never been in more than a pack of four or five at the most. This was different. There was something base and almost tribal about it and I could tell my presence among them weirded a few of the guys out. I think it was both that I was a woman and that I was riding and it definitely didn't help that I was riding a bike that was completely out of form from the rest of theirs. I imagined they had a rule for everything and what sorts of bikes were permissible within the club was one of them.

The roar and pulse of the bike's engines was deafening, I tucked my earbuds in up under my helmet and plugged the wire into my phone which I zipped into a pocket in the upper arm of my jacket. My music played, Cutter gave a hand signal and we poured out of the drive and onto the street. An old U-Haul box truck falling in behind us. It was going to be a long ride.

CHAPTER 16
Cutter

Hope was holding up like a champion, there were times she would edge a little far up and I would have to throw her a hand signal but I got it. It was her sister. Hell, I had a brother, we didn't speak but if it'd been him, I would want to get to him at break neck speeds myself. She'd been antsy at the first stop to top off our tanks. There were only so many pumps at the station and it'd taken two rounds to get all the bikes topped off and the crash truck too. She'd filled up, all the while bouncing on the balls of her feet ready to just fucking *go*.

The first pit stop we'd made she'd gone into the women's restroom, returned to her bike and fired it right back up. She wasn't speaking to anyone, didn't even pop off her helmet. She was brooding and I didn't blame her. She and her sisters were close, which meant one thing and one thing only. Whatever her girl Faith was into, it wasn't something she wanted to be doin' and she wasn't in any position to get away or call for help or she damn sure would have done it by now.

It was creeping up on six-thirty in the am when we pulled off the exit of the I-10 West and dropped down into the outskirts of the city. I checked my rearview and followed Pyro's hand gestures, making turns and wending through some quiet, busted ass, hoods. Some of the buildings around these parts were nothing but the cement slab of a foundation. Houses taken out by Hurricane Katrina and just never rebuilt.

It was a fuckin' shame too. Those white slabs gleaming in the dark reminded me of the flat markers in modern cemeteries and with the destruction that storm caused, I probably wasn't far off the mark. Hope edged up next to me and looked over, her face hidden behind the gleaming carapace of her ultra-modern helmet. I gave her a reassuring nod and when she dropped back just behind me to my left. It was kind of nice we were in tune enough after such a short time that we could pick up words and intent without ever having to speak. Her little move had spoken to me clearly, *are we close?* All it took was a slight inclination of my head to reassure her that yes, we were close.

I didn't think I had to be nervous about her and the meet and greet with this new MC, but she *had* pointed a gun in my face the last time she got worked up. I sighed, we'd deal with it if and when it came up. I glanced back and Pyro gave me the signal that it was the next driveway on the left.

It was a fenced in lot, one of them chain link fences topped with barbed wire with the plastic privacy slats in them. The slats were gray but some enterprising street artist had gotten to them with their spray cans. What resulted wasn't any half assed gang graffiti though. No, they'd done quite the mural of the MC's colors on there. A skull grinned out at us from an angle, one of those round eye piece things, like Mr. Peanut sported, crammed into its eye socket, magnifying the eyeball behind it which was green. The Skull wore a purple top hat and in gold letters *The Voodoo Bastards* was proclaimed loud and proud.

Not very subtle, but if you had the reputation and the balls to back it, you didn't need subtle. I pulled into the lot with my guys and my woman ranging out behind me. There were five or six bikes backed against the cinderblock building, by the single door. I chose to back us into the open area on the left.

At the sound of the bikes, three men came out the front door. Probably their wrecking crew, to scope us out. Didn't blame them one bit. I shut off my bike and put down my kickstand and a fourth man exited the club house. A big dude, bulky and solid.

"What the fuck you riding, Boy?" he demanded, eyes fixed on Hope who was standing beside my bike, I smiled and she looked down at me, face still masked by her helmet. I shrugged and popped my chinstrap. She shrugged back and went for hers.

She pulled off her helmet and her hair had come unpinned during the ride, tumbling almost artfully down around her shoulders, her bangs flopping into her eyes. She stuck out her luscious bottom lip and blew, her bangs flying up out of her dark eyes and fixed the men of the Voodoo Bastards with a curious look.

"One, I'm not a boy, and two, she's a 2013 Ducati Diavel and I love her," she flashed the boys her cheeky grin and I chuckled.

The man who'd spoken from the back huffed a laugh and pushed through his guys, "Well, I'll be damned. What's your name, Darlin'?" he asked her and she pulled off her gloves while she calculated what she could and couldn't get away with. I could see her doing the math and it was hot as fuck.

"Hope," she said and stuck out her hand to shake. The big dude took it and turned it and bowed gallantly brushing it with a kiss.

"Well Hope, welcome to my humble abode, I'm Ruth. My boys call me Ruthie but only the ladies are allowed to call me Baby Ruth." He gave her a roguish smile.

So this was the President of the Voodoo Bastards. Interesting. I got off my bike and left my helmet on the seat.

"You Cutter?" he asked, turning his attention to me.

"That I am," I said and stuck out my hand.

He shook it and asked, "You do that?" and indicated with a nod of his head the bruise on Hope's jaw.

"Unfortunately," I intoned and made my regret clear.

"If it makes you feel any better I *did* point a gun in his face. Not sure you can provoke a man much more," she told him.

"Is that right?" he asked, "Well, come on in, we got some cots set up so y'all can grab a little sleep. I'd really like to hear the whole story on why it is that you're here, in the meantime please accept our hospitality."

Hope gave him a wan smile, "Much appreciated," she said, "But if it's all the same I would really like to go get my sister. Happy to tell you whatever you want to know and then some *after* I've got her."

Ruth looked over to Hope and glanced her up and down before saying slowly, "Nah Darlin', I feel you… you know where you're going?" he asked.

"Plaquemines Parish Sherriff's Department, I have the address right here," she reached for a pocket in the upper arm of her jacket but Ruth waved her off.

"Naw, Darlin', it ain't nothin' but a thirty minute ride from here, we'll show yah, you sure you're up to it though?"

"Yep, I'm not waiting another minute to get my sister. I'm sorry but I can't... I know you boys are used to doing things in a certain order or a certain way but I've got to go get her," she was looking at me as she spoke and her expression spoke volumes. She was so very apologetic with her eyes but her desperation had me mounting my bike.

"Lightning! Radar!" I barked, "You're with us."

There was no way I was letting her go with anyone without me by her side, whether she could take care of herself or not. Atlas and Lightning were the most rested out of the guys that'd come with us.

"Hex, La Croix, mount up, Boys. Let's take the lady where she wants to go," Ruth winked at me and I nodded in return. This was going to cost me and mine a pretty penny but it didn't matter much. Most of it was coming out of my pocket and cuts of our smuggling operation. I went into my saddlebag and pulled out the box of Cubans and handed them to Ruth. He smiled broadly and lifted the lid on the cigar box, eyes alight.

"Why thank you kindly, Cutter," he said with a wink and called out, "Collier!"

A prospect came jogging out of the building and after relieving the box of Cubans of one of the cigars he handed it to the man.

"Put these in my office and get these men settled and comfortable. You get me?"

"Yes, Sir, right away. Anything else?" he asked.

"Girls up?"

"Not yet, Sir."

"Well, get 'em up and ready to suck some dick, looks like some of these fellas could use it, go on now," he waved the prospect off and I straddled my bike, Hope was astride hers and had mouthed 'thank you' at me while whipping that long hair of hers into a French braid and tying it off with a band from around her wrist. Her face was now hidden behind the emotionless black facemask of her helmet.

"Fall back where he tells you," I told her and she nodded.

Ruth got on his bike, a fat purple gold and black Harley, and fired it up. His two boys, Hex and La Croix followed suit. Hex didn't seem so bad, a regular looking blue collar Joe but La Croix, he was a scary looking mother fucker. The kind of scary you didn't want to encounter in a back alley late at night. Big, bald and mean looking with a set of blue tribal tattoos across his scalp, he wore his cut over a tee with the sleeves ripped off.

His arms crawled with some scary badass ink in twin full sleeves and his eyes were hidden by a pair of wrap around black sunglasses. He had no flash on his cut denoting office so I was betting that La Croix here was Ruthie's enforcer. Hell, he had 'enforcer' traced all over him. From the set of his shoulders to the jut of his jaw, everything about him screamed that if you crossed him he'd just straight up fuckin' kill you.

Ruth got his bike going and I sat my helmet on my head and buckled up. He put his brain bucket on after tying a purple bandanna over his shaved scalp and put on a pair of clear lenses to protect his eyes. I was sporting a pair of yellow shooter's glasses myself. As the two presidents, we would ride even. That was a given.

"Hey Darlin'!" he called to Hope, she nodded in his direction to indicate she'd heard, "Why don't you ride behind me?" he asked with a wink and she nodded again. I threw hand gestures at Lightning and Radar, my Enforcer and SAA, and they fell in where indicated. Ruth looked impressed and with a nod indicating our readiness, we rode out.

I'd be lying if I said I didn't check on Hope like every three seconds the whole way there. She was tense and there was a lot riding on this for her. I just wondered where it all would lead. For her, for her sister, and yeah even for me. I guess we would just have to see.

CHAPTER 17
Hope

I was exhausted. It was pushing twenty-four hours since I last slept, and I knew for Cutter it had been the same. I kept my eyes fixed on the road ahead but they kept straying ahead and to the right of me, to the sun shining down on Cutter's back, turning the orange threads of the kraken dragging the broken ship beneath the waves bright. I knew I was breaking down, that the tired was catching up to me when I found myself wishing we could just stop for a minute so Cutter could pull me into the shelter of his arms.

I was afraid of what, or who, I would find wearing my sister's skin. *Prostitution...* The word rattled ugly in my head, a whisper from the pervading darkness at the edge of my being that was constantly threatening to swallow me whole if I would let it. The darkness that had, apparently, snatched my sister right out from under me, rolled her, swallowed her whole and dragged her under completely.

It wouldn't keep her, I wouldn't let it. There was no way I could let it. As soon as we came up within sight distance of the Sherriff's office sign, I showed these guys just why it was I loved my baby. With a sharp, angry whine I gunned her, and shot out from around Ruth, passing him by as if he and Cutter both were standing still. I caught a glimmer of dissatisfaction on both of their faces and saw Cutter shake his head ruefully and shout something to Ruth in my rearview but I would deal with whatever it was later. Right now I was throwing down the kickstand to my bike and striding to the door, pulling my helmet off as I went.

I bee lined for the sheriff's office lobby, my heart hammering in my chest, crawling up into my throat as I breezed through the front door and right up to the glassed in front counter. I set my helmet down on the ledge in front of the old school partition and waited for the deputy behind the desk to acknowledge my existence, vaguely aware of Cutter, Lightning, and Radar hovering in my background by the glass doors I'd just come through. I glanced back over my shoulder and Cutter gave me a nod of support.

Baby Ruth and his two men sat and stood around the bikes in the early morning sunshine, smoking and shooting the shit. I didn't blame them for not coming in, I doubted they were on the level where the cops were concerned. I swallowed and my impatience mounted as the deputy behind the glass continued to ignore me. Finally, with a gusty sigh, he looked up.

"What can I help you with miss?" he asked and I wanted to throat punch him for the bored tone he used with me. I smiled bravely instead, to hide my irritation and voice surprisingly steady, for how I felt like I was going to fall apart, told him why I was here.

"Yes, you have my sister, Faith Dobbins in custody. I've come to bail her out," he turned back to his computer screen like he hadn't heard me even though I knew he had.

"Let's see... let's see... Dobbins... Dobbins... Oh yep, looks like you're too late, her boyfriend and his lawyer bailed her out something like two hours ago." My stomach bottomed out, my heart dropping clean through it.

"What are you talking about?" my voice sounded shocked and hollow and I caught Cutter and his boys going still, their reflection in the glass just losing all movement as if a predator had just gone by, except that I knew the predator was me and what they were really afraid of was me losing my shit.

They were right to be afraid, because all the strings holding my emotions in check had been frayed by twelve plus hours on the road coupled with two years of fervent looking only to reach this time, this place, right here and right now to be told that I'd lost Faith all over again...

That I'd missed her by two fucking hours!? When they knew I was coming!? Oh hell no!

"Answer me you son of a bitch!" I grated, my fury bubbling to the surface, "What are you fucking talking about she's been bailed out!?"

"I suggest you adjust your tone, Missy," the Deputy narrowed his beady hazel eyes and I lost it, I hit the glass that separated us with the heel of my hand hard enough that my skin split and left behind a smear of blood. The Deputy jumped and had the grace to at least look a little scared as the blood thrummed through my veins, I could feel my face flushing, my temples throbbing in time with my heart beat.

"Where is she!? Who took my sister!? Who bailed her out!?" I demanded, a buzzing like an angry swarm of bees filling my ears. I felt Cutter coming up behind me saw his reflection nearing, but held my ground.

"Answer me!" I snapped.

"I don't have to tell you that, what's more I won't tell you that. You should ask your sister," he sneered from behind the safety of his glass and I hooked a fist into it, the glass spider webbing and cracking, Cutter was suddenly there, arms hooking under my arms, hands locking behind my head in a Full Nelson as I thrashed.

"Nope, come on Baby Doll, time to take a breather!" he said in my ear, then shot back over his shoulder, "Lightning, Radar, see what you can find out please while I take my girl here for a time out."

Cutter dragged me out into the muggy heat of the Louisiana morning and turned me loose. I stumbled and rounded and threw a wild punch out of pure fucking anger and adrenaline which he easily evaded which just seemed to piss me off more, so the punch turned into a backwards elbow strike which he blocked followed by another hold, this one better than the last but much more primitive. He wrapped his arms around me from behind, pinning my arms to my sides and I just doubled over and screamed my fury and injustice into the bright, sunny, and overly cheerful morning air. Birds fell silent, Ruth and his boys who had been laughing at the spectacle I'd been making, had the smiles wiped right off their faces.

I sagged in Cutter's grip and he lowered me gently to my knees, to the cement as I sucked in enough air to let out another outraged scream.

"Jesus Christ her sister fucking die or something!?" one of Ruth's men, the skinnier one, demanded taking a drag off his cigarette.

"Shut the fuck up Hex," Ruth ordered, a sympathetic look flickering across his face before it was swallowed by his stoicism.

"Shh, it's okay Baby, I got you," Cutter's voice was warm against my ear as he pulled me tight, back into his body and rocked me.

"Not again, I was so close! So close! I can't do this anymore!" I whined and okay, after two years and the week I'd just had, I sort of snapped in two and was having a fucking melt down. But after eighteen years of being sister-mom and fucking up so badly, I figured hey, I'd earned this, I would pull myself up by the boot straps after it, put on my fucking big girl panties and go find my fucking sister.

At least that was what Cutter murmured in my ear, and damned if he wasn't right. I listened to him, to what he was saying, taking his orders and grabbing onto them with both hands. I let Cutter become my anchor, holding me firmly on the ground when all I wanted to do was explode into the ether and just give up.

"Good, good, deep easy breaths, Darlin'. I need you to hold it together, I need you to think; what's more, Faith needs those things from you." I nodded numbly and sniffed. Cutter turned me to face him and when he was sure I wasn't going to hit him or do anything else dangerous he smoothed my tears away with his thumbs and kissed my forehead. My eyes drifted shut at the reverent touch I was sure I didn't deserve.

The front door to the police station grated and Lightning and Radar came out. Lightning carried my helmet in one hand and neither one of them looked happy. Two deputies came out with them and stopped a ways up the walk, letting Lightning and Radar finish the trip towards us physically unescorted.

"Come on Hope, we gotta get moving before they arrest you," Lightning grated and handed down my helmet.

"They give you anything?" Cutter asked helping me to my feet.

"Not a damn thing," Radar said and spit on the ground.

"Let's get a move on, Darlin', before Tweedle Dee and Tweedle Dum get any ideas about that luscious ass of yours," Ruth said and puffed on his cigar. Grinning around it, he shot the two deputies a one fingered salute.

"Might have gotten some answers if she didn't throw such a damn tantrum! Also might've got some if she kept better company," the deputy on the right commented. He was tall with a deep brown mustache and curly brown hair. I cocked my head to the side and hoped and prayed that this office would contact me for work. That way I could tell their superiors to fuck right off and why.

Instead of popping off again I thrust my helmet on my head, Cutter escorting me to my bike. I climbed on, starting her up.

"You good to ride?" he asked me and I jerked my head in a nod. I wasn't really, but I had to be.

"C'mon y'all. You need some food and rest before you do anything else," Ruth said but he was looking at me. I couldn't say I disagreed.

We rode back to his compound and the further we got from the Sherriff's department, the worse I felt for my outburst. God I was just failing Faith and fucking up left and right. It was only a matter of time before I failed Char too... hell, I was already failing Char too if we were keeping serious score. I'd lost her big sister, and let her slip through my fingers yet again.

I beat myself up the whole way back to the Voodoo Bastards compound but at the same time, I was also already devising a way around the fucktards at the Plaquemine's Parish Sherriff's office. I shut off my bike and put down the kickstand startled to realize I didn't really remember the ride back here. I'd been lost in thought the whole way and just sort of on auto pilot. Fucking dangerous. I sat astride my bike staring at the tank and the still and silent gauges while Cutter pulled off my helmet.

"Shit, Babe. I hate seein' you like this," he said, tone heavy with something akin to regret.

"I'm going to find her," I said, "And I'm going to kill whoever has her. Do you understand what I'm saying?" I asked and my voice sounded bitter, hollow and scary, a foreign facsimile of what my voice should be. The woman speaking right now was dispassionate and full of discord.

"Come on Hope, come with me; come sleep with me. We'll deal with all of this after we've had a few hours," Cutter tugged on my hands and I was puppet to his master and glided to my feet as if pulled by invisible strings. He led me from behind, his hands on my shoulders as he urged me into the cooler twilight of the Voodoo Bastard's club.

It looked like any ol' bar with couches and the like here and there. Gaming tables for blackjack and poker, a pool table, hell I think there was even a roulette wheel... It was all sort of a blur. Cutter led me to a row of cots where some of his men were already wracked out. He sat me on the edge of one and I collapsed, staring at his handsome face as he set to work pulling off my boots.

I looked on, almost detached as he worked first one then the other off my feet. He put his hands on my knees and captured my eyes with his, sighing out. I leaned forward and kissed him. I had no words right now to express how grateful I was that he was here with me, helping me, and so I kissed him. A gentle press of lips full of reverence and just everything I had in me that I couldn't say right then. Partially because there were eyes on us in the form of some of the Voodoo Bastards, and partially because I was a little scared of what I was feeling. It was just too soon and so big and I didn't know what to do with it.

"Hmm," Cutter made the sound and flashed me a brief smile, while he unzipped my jacket and peeled it off of me, carefully stripping me of enough to be comfortable but not so much I should be worried. Not that I really was. The guys wouldn't have much left to beat once I got done with any would-be attackers myself.

I glanced over and caught some of the Kraken watching me and their president, brows furrowed with concern as Radar and Lightning spoke with their brothers in low careful tones. Some of those looks shifted from concern, to sympathy, to anger, on my behalf and I appreciated them for it.

Cutter's hands smoothed beneath my white baby doll tee along my ribs curving around my back. He rested his chin on my chest and looked up into my eyes as he popped the clasp on my bra, dragging his hands back across my skin until I shuddered. He peeled the offending straps down one arm before pulling the entire contraption out the other sleeve. I smiled at him and he smiled down at me, swinging my legs up and drawing the blanket up over me. I was down to my tee and panties and I didn't even remember him pulling my riding pants off. Damn.

He didn't waste any time stripping down to bare feet and just his jeans. He shoved his cot right up against mine and lay down on his side facing me. We clasped hands between us and he pressed a reverent kiss to my swelling knuckles. I blinked. What had I punched? Oh! Right. The glass.

A bag of ice settled onto my hand and I startled, Ruth smiled down at me from over my shoulder. I blinked.

"Sleep, Darlin'. This whole mess will be here to sort out in a few hours," he wandered away and it was just me and Cutter despite how surrounded we were by the men of both MC's.

"I promised I'd help you find her, Sweetheart. I meant it, I'll be right here. Try and get some sleep."

CHAPTER 18
Cutter

Her sleep was uneasy. I woke before her to it being dark outside. Some of the guys were up quietly playing cards with some of the other MC, nervously shifting eyes looking us over from time to time. I slipped my hand out of hers. Someone had taken the bag of ice a while ago. I'd woken up for that, but went right back out.

I smoothed some wayward tendrils of her deep chestnut hair away from her open mouth as she slept on and got up to take a piss. Ruth was waiting outside the bathroom and gave me a chin lift. Right. Detailed explanation was owed. I followed him back to his office, which I think was also their chapel and he shut the door. He took a seat at the head of his table and motioned with his hand. I dropped into the proffered seat and he lit up the stub of a Cuban I think he'd been working on most of the day.

"Mighty fine," he commented and I smiled.

"Don't smoke 'em myself."

"That's a damn shame man, you don't know what you're missing," he said. We enjoyed a moment of comfortable silence before we got down to it.

"You gotta fill me in, Man. What's up with your little Darlin' out there?"

I sighed, "I'm a sucker for a damsel in distress."

Ruth snorted and laughed out loud, "Seems to me you got yourself one hell of a wild cat out there. So what's doin'? How did you and yours get mixed up in all of this?"

So I explained, every damn bit of it. Me and mine had voted on it and decided it was only fair seeing as we were crashing on Ruth's turf so hard and so fast and the guy was being so stand up about it.

I told him about the SHMC Lake Run debacle and Ruth shook his head, "That's a damn fuckin' shame right there. Now-a-days any 'ol jackass with a Harley and a notion makes up a club, pulling all manner of bullshit ideas out of the ether. Most of these dumb fuckers don't know the first thing about what it is to be a part of a brotherhood."

"Preachin' to the fuckin' choir, Man," I said and heaved a heavy sigh. "Had some trouble with that m'self, a dude by the name of Tiny. Inherited him along with the patch, part of the old guard…" I launched into the next part of the story about how Tiny took it upon himself to off Tonya and how Hope showed up a little under two years later, just last week looking for her and why.

"Hell, not sure I can entirely blame you for wantin' to help there brother, a fine piece of ass like that walked into my place, I'd want to know what's what too, damn shame – "

He didn't finish what he was saying, a crash, some breaking glass, objects scattering across the cement floor out front and what's more; several outraged shouts of surprise from both my men and his. Ruth and I both were on our feet and moving as one to the chapel door. Ruth thundered up the hall in front of me, shorter than me by a lot, his presence crackled like a thunderhead. We poured out into the main room by the bar to see cots overturned, and Hope on the ground. She had one of the Voodoo bastards between her legs, choking the shit out of him. I laughed, she had more than that, she was about to rip the poor bastard's arm out of its socket.

Ruth squatted down by his man and tsked shaking his head, "What'd you do to piss off the lady, Rusty?" he asked his man. Rusty let out a strangled gurgle in response.

"Radar!" He was my man in charge of security, he'd better have a fuckin' answer for me.

"Aye, Captain?"

"Report."

"I was takin' a piss, Sir," he said plainly unhappy. I looked Hope in the eyes and met cold dark fury.

"Can you fill me in, Sweetheart?"

"Stop struggling or I'm going to break it!" she snarled at the man in her grip and wrenched down on him tighter with her legs, Rusty's feet went to kicking and Ruth laughed.

"Let 'im up, Darlin', you're going to choke him to death," he chuckled and stood up himself. I like that Hope looked to me for confirmation before doing anything. I gave her a nod and quicker than light she'd shoved Rusty away from her and had lightly and silently gotten to her feet. She stood staring down those long, toned legs at the man writhing on the floor, sucking in air.

"Woke up with his hands where they didn't belong," she said darkly.

"Is that right?" Ruth asked.

Hope came to me and tucked herself into my side, shuddering with revulsion. She wasn't hurt that I could tell but some injuries, no matter how capable or strong you are, aren't physical things. Especially for a woman.

"Where was his hands?" I asked.

"Down her panties, wasn't they?" one of the Voodoo Bastards asked. Ruth looked murderous, like off the fucking charts pissed.

"That true, Boy? You better answer me truthful now," he said. Rusty was still trying to suck in air and was coughing miserably but he nodded.

"Uh huh, and anyone care to tell me *why* Rusty's hands were in our guest's panties?" Ruth demanded. The big one, La Croix, was looking at Hope like she'd done something fascinating. My arms were already around her but I gave her shoulder a little squeeze and tucked her closer into my side. Her face was carefully schooled neutral but she was staring stoically at Rusty. I could see her wheels turning but had no idea what she was thinking.

La Croix stepped up and bent down, speaking in barely there tones to Ruth who nodded along to whatever was being said, his expression a mix of incredulous and furious. He stared down at Rusty and cocked his head to the side.

"Boy, you know that deserves an ass whoopin', now you're half way there, and seeing as it's the lady you trespassed against... Darlin', what would you like me to do to him?"

Hope looked to Ruth and without missing a beat said, "Break his damn hand."

A bunch of the men sucked in a breath and one of them murmured, "Damn that's a cold piece."

Her reaction told me everything I needed to know, though. He'd touched her. There. There wasn't anything 'close' about it. This was no near miss. He'd violated my woman.

"Mind if I do the honors?" I asked Ruth.

"Naw Man, you go right ahead."

I let Hope go and sat, pulling on my boots beneath my jeans, taking my time. I went to where Rusty lay on the floor.

"Radar, Atlas..." My men dove on top of Rusty who started fighting. Radar got a hold of the man's wrist and pulled his arm out, flattening his hand against the cement floor. I didn't think about what I was doing. I just did. I slammed the heel of my boot on his splayed hand and the fucker howled. Bones crunched satisfactorily and I stepped off.

"Let him up," I said and the man clutched his busted hand to his chest.

"Good enough?" I asked her. Hope nodded, her dark eyes slightly haunted but only if you knew what to look for.

"I need a fucking shower," she grated and snatched up her back pack.

"Through there, to the left," Ruth said a look of amusement on his face. I followed her and shut us into the bathroom and she started up the shower.

She turned around and with a furious look in her eyes came at me, I braced and she was up, in my arms. My hands found her ass while her legs went around my hips and her mouth crashed into mine.

"Cod, I know this is fucked up but I need you to fuck me," she said against my mouth.

"What happened?" I demanded.

"Woke up with his fingers against my cunt, fishing to get inside." I gritted my teeth, clenching my jaw for a moment.

"Should have broken his arm too, Baby. I'm sorry I left you," I whispered.

"Don't be, as you can see, I can take care of myself but if you really want to take care of me stop talking and start fucking, I want you there. I want only you there."

Fuck that was hot.

"Down, down, down," I ordered and she slid to the floor with an unhappy noise. I whisked her panties down her legs and her shirt off from over her head the same time I struggled to kick out of my boots. I got them off, but had to let her go to pull them off hopping on one foot. She laughed at me and I had to laugh a little too. I knew I looked ridiculous but I didn't fucking care if it put a smile on her lips after that.

She went for my belt and my jeans before I could and I stood there and watched her undress me, smoothing my hands over her shoulders. God damn I wanted inside of her. I wanted to erase every bit of the presence of that cock sucker and to give Hope what she asked for. She was back up, those legs wrapped fine around my hips, her arms around my shoulders and I pressed her back against the wall.

I slid against her, my cock slicking through her folds only once or twice before finding purchase. I sank into her gratefully and loved how her head tipped back, a sultry moan climbing out of her throat as if I pushed it from her. I sank into her deep, and reveled in her heat. God damn she was so fucking perfect. She bit my bottom lip just until I grunted in protest, then she backed right off, smiling against my mouth.

"Hard, Cutter. I want to feel every inch of that cock, ride me you bastard!"

Damn she knew how to rile a man up with that dirty mouth of hers! I gave it to her, just how she'd asked for it, and vowed that one day we'd actually get to do foreplay. That someday I would get to take my fucking time with her. For now I was perfectly content to drive myself up into that hot, wet, tight; sweet pussy. I could fuck Hope like this for hours but with the way she tightened down on me, that wasn't going to be an option. I bowed my head and caressed the side of her throat with my lips, and murmured my encouragement.

I think she liked it when I urged her to come, that it turned her on and gave her that edge she needed to go over the cliff. I growled against the side of her neck and nipped her shoulder and she spasmed around me, her silken channel rippling around the head of my cock and it took everything I had in me *not* to fucking come right then and there like some teenage jackass.

"Oh God, Baby, you feel so fuckin' good, but you gotta fuckin' come for me or I'm gonna go and I'm gonna have to finish you another way…"

That did it, with a low moaning wail, Hope came like I'd flipped her fucking switch or something. She shuddered and trembled in my arms, her pussy convulsing around my shaft and *that* did *me* in. I came, deep inside of her, pressing her back against the tiles of the bathroom wall by the door to a rousing course of cheers from the main room.

"Fucking assholes," she panted against my shoulder. I laughed, and pulled back, she smiled up into my face and we kissed, probably one of the most perfect and meaningful meeting of souls I'd ever experienced in my life. I drew back to look at her one more time and she unwound her legs from my hips. I slid from her and she got her feet under her and we both sighed simultaneously. We shared a shaky laugh and she pulled me after her into the shower were we went at it all over again.

God yeah, I could get used to having Hope in my life. Now I just needed to figure out how to keep her once this was all over…

CHAPTER 19
Hope

I think that the boys were a little surprised when the badass militarized version of Hope came out of the bathroom behind Cutter. I'd forgone lighter, cooler clothes in favor of unrelieved black as utilitarian as it came. Black fitted tee over black 5.11 tactical pants tucked into black combat boots. My hair was drawn up and back into a severe bun and the only concession I'd made to being a woman was my makeup. A heavy smoky eye and some clear lip gloss. I looked like what I was. A defense contractor and a good one, which is what I needed.

"I'll be back," I murmured and kissed Cutter.

"I don't much like you going alone," he said and I nodded.

"I hear you, but you heard the deputy yesterday, I think I'll do better with this without the biker shadow."

"I don't disagree Sweetheart, still don't mean I have to like it."

I nodded and swung my jacket on, zipping it up. I was headed to the heart of the city, to the department I'd trained out of last year to see if I could get some answers from one of the detectives there.

"We'll be waiting," Cutter murmured, kissing me one last time at my bike. I started her up and checked my phone. Two missed calls from Charity. I would have to call her back later. I put on my helmet and with a final nod, pulled out into the street, my phone chirping turn by turn directions through my headphones.

My mind drifted, I missed Cutter already, which wow... desperate much Hope? Except it didn't feel like it. It felt as natural as breathing when I was with him, which was unnerving in its own way. It was like Cutter just got me like no one ever had before. Maybe it was both of us having spent time in the military? I didn't know. I didn't really want to pick it apart right now either. I shook myself as if waking from a dream and focused on getting myself to the police station.

It was a short ride, fifteen minutes or so, to the central precinct. I left my helmet with my bike and marched up the wide front step and into the building's interior. We were only an hour or two past sunset and normal business hours were just drawing to a close. I smiled at the officer behind the front desk, no glass partition here, and took a deep breath.

"Hi, is Detective Thibault in?" I asked. The officer eyed me carefully for a moment and nodded slowly.

"Tell 'im who's asking, Honey?" he asked, but I didn't take offense. The man behind the desk wrap looked like he was a week from retirement and the use of the word 'honey' came out natural, not condescending in the slightest. Kind, watery blue eyes looked me over from underneath a trim cut of silvery gray. He looked like he'd been partaking of too much of the good food the Quarter had to offer in the last couple of years, but looks could be deceiving. I bet dollars to doughnuts it would task him some, but that he would pass the physical requirements to keep his badge should they pop him with a random physical.

"Hope, Hope Andrews," I told him. He nodded carefully and picked up his desk phone, punching in an extension.

"Got a Hope Andrews at the desk here for you, Boy. What you want I should do?" he looked me over one more time and I gave him a slight, polite little smile all the while telling myself on the inside not to fucking blow it, to keep cooler than I had at the last station.

"Uh huh, whatever you say, Boss," he said and hung up the phone.

"Can you fill this out for me, Darlin'?" he asked, "And have you got a copy of your ID?" I nodded and smiled genuinely relieved when he passed me the visitor's form. I dug out my California driver's license and handed it to him and whisked through the form. He handed me a visitor's badge which I clipped to my jacket and he buzzed me through the heavy reinforced door, by his desk.

"Take the elevator, third floor, robbery is down and to the left," he said. Robbery, so they'd moved Thibault out of missing persons. I wondered when that'd happened and how he'd heard about Faith to tell Plaquemines to call me.

I followed the desk sergeant's directions and stepped out of an archway onto a cubicle farm. Thibault, a big, good 'ol boy Cajun with the accent to match stood up and waved me in his direction, his expression a little grim. Good. I didn't have to pretend anymore. I went and shook his hand before spilling myself into the seat by his desk.

"Girl, you sure know how t' piss them motherfuckers in Plaquemines off. What're you doin' runnin' with the Voodoo Bastards and the likes of Luis 'Baby Ruth' Caballero?" he said by way of greeting.

"I'm not. Technically, I'm running with The Kraken out of Ft. Royal, FL," I told him.

"Tomato, Tam-ah-to," he said. I smiled at him.

"I need your help," I said tiredly.

"Figured you might, surprised it took you this long to get here; I called them bastards over at Plaquemines as soon as I saw your sister's name come across the wire."

"They called me about seventeen hundred yesterday, Florida time," I said. Thibault swore, which told me all I needed to know about that.

"They wouldn't tell me anything Joe," I said in a harsh whisper, "Just that my sister's boyfriend and her lawyer bailed her out and took her home something like two hours before I got there and that she'd been picked up for prostitution."

Thibault was already clacking at the keys on his computer, he sniffed and cleared his throat and said kindly, "Girl, I'm sorry, I can't tell you anything either. Wait here, I need to take a piss... be back before you know it." He got up with a meaningful look in my direction and slid out of the cubicle, walking away. He cleared his throat loudly and I slid into his vacated seat.

I snapped several pictures of what he had up on his laptop's monitor before it could go dark, and read everything I could read before it did too. *Thank you Joe Thibault.* I sent up in silent prayer, hoping some power that be somewhere gave the man some much deserved Brownie Points for what he'd just given me.

My sister had been arrested as some part of a large scale prostitution ring out in St. Bernard's Parish, but that wasn't what it was… My stomach twisted as my eyes flew over her mugshot. Her hair was dark, but I don't think it was her hair, I think it was some kind of a wig. Her eyes were sunken and her cheeks hollow and her pupils were as big as saucers and she was painfully thin.

I slipped back into my seat when I heard Joe clear his throat up the aisle. He sat down and looked me over. I looked back and knew my expression was grim, haunted somehow.

"What the fuck, Joe?" I asked in a harsh whisper.

"Took police from the city and three different Parishes to deal with that mess, some dumb-assed frat boys from Seattle got theyself's mixed up with a drug runner's riverboat party. Their friend decided to get mixed up with a Quarter lap dancer. He was the smart one," Joe shook his head.

"Anyways, his dumb assed friends text the kid or some such, and he and the lap dancer decide it's time to go git 'em. They stumble on this prostitution deal, but it's not, it's much worse than that. A lot of these girls they got chained up like animals in storage lockers. Some of 'em was just *kids*, Hope. I ain't seen nothin' like it…"

I stared at Joe, just stared at him, "Joe, what happened to my sister?" I asked.

"Here's the thing Cheri, the foreign ones, they get the help. Sent back to family or wherever they come from, the local ones? From here? They usually get brought up on charges 'cause they say just about anything to keep theyself outta trouble. I'm sorry, Baby. I called as soon as I saw her name but Plaquemines got they own ideas and think they know it all."

Joe *looked* sorry too. I took a deep breath in through my nose and out through my mouth. I was going to kill someone. A lot of someones… and I didn't feel one iota of guilt for it.

"I've got to find her," I heard myself say. Joe nodded and put a hand on my shoulder.

"Be careful, Girl; they arrested some Russians involved in this shit and everyone 'round these parts knows, they is not to be messed with." I gave Thibault a hard look and he put up his hands. I nodded.

"Warning received loud and clear, Detective Thibault."

"Yeah, I just bet it is, you go do what you gotta do, Cherie; you just keep it on the down low. You got it?"

"I got it, thanks."

I pushed to my feet and said quietly, "Thank you."

"Don't thank me, Baby Girl. I know what I just done."

"And what is it you think you've done?" I asked.

"I just signed some men's death warrants, but Darlin'... I was there. I was there, Baby Girl, and I hope you find your sister, I hope you get her out and get 'em good. I ain't never gonna be able to close my eyes again and *not* see what I saw. I'm gettin' too old for this."

"You and me both," I murmured and we gave each other a crooked grin. Joe Thibault was entering into his fifties, he had about twenty years on me and I honestly didn't want to think too hard about what I would be like when I got to his age if I got much further into this. I was terrified of what I would find when I got to Faith, at the same time, after seeing her mugshot, I was terrified I wasn't going to make it in time.

I gave my visitor's badge back to the desk sergeant and took my unhappy ass outside where I took deep, cleansing breaths of river air. I straddled my bike and shot a text to Cutter and tried to call my littlest sister, Charity again. She answered.

"Hope?"

"Yeah, Blossom."

"Where are you?"

"New Orleans, listen Blossom, I've got a hard line on Bubbles but it isn't pretty..." I told Charity. I told her everything, it was our deal since Mom had died. We didn't keep shit from each other. No matter how ugly or fucked up.

"Find her, sis. Find her and bring her home no matter what shape she's in, and you call me. I'm packing a bag and having it ready. I'll be waiting," she said and I could hear the tears. Tears I refused to let fall. I held onto my rage with everything I had until it turned my heart into a pit of ice in my chest surrounded by fire in my veins.

"I love you, Charity," I said, well aware that what I was about to do was beyond dangerous. That my littlest sister might lose both me and Faith when the smoke had cleared. I swallowed hard.

"I love you too, you come back, the both of you."

"Do my best, I've got to go. I don't have any time to waste."

"Kay, be careful."

"As I ever am," I said and started up my bike. Charity laughed and I ended the call just as one from Cutter rang through.

"Where you at?" he asked before I could say hello.

"Headed back to you. Be there in fifteen."

"Make it ten."

"Copy that," I said and ended the call shoving my helmet on. I rode out and made it back in seven. We had work to do.

CHAPTER 20
Cutter

Ruth finished dealing with his man Rusty and the one that put Rusty up to it before Hex took Rusty to have his hand looked at and put in a cast. Fucking tool. I charged Pyro with getting us set up in a cheap motel down the road. My boys and me, we took a quick vote and they agreed, we could do without the Voodoo Bastard's hospitality. They were quickly coming around to Hope bein' one of us and I think they could tell, I wasn't about to let the wild cat go any time soon.

Still, I was afraid of runnin' out of loyalty before this was through. When I got the text from Hope and told the guys what was up, we'd all gone still. Marlin had been the one to speak first and when he did, it was sense; which is why he was my VP.

"Let's get the full story when she gets back and we'll go from there," he'd said and was met by nods of agreement from everyone including me. Hope pulled up inside ten minutes and I felt something akin to pride bloom in the center of my chest.

She marched into the place like she owned it, and there she was, my woman on fire again. Her eyes fell on me and she softened marginally.

"Who has my gun?" she asked and Radar handed it over, she tucked it into the back of her pants and came over to the table. Ruth wandered over.

"What're we looking at?" Marlin asked while she scrolled through her phone. She raised a finger.

"Where's my backpack?" she asked me. I went over to the pile of gear and brought it to her. She pulled out her tablet and brought up some pictures of a laptop screen.

"That's your sister?" Lightning asked.

"Not the way I remember her," Hope said and sounded resigned.

I glanced at Marlin who was studying the picture thoughtfully. He had some history with druggies and one glance told me that *now* this was hitting close to home for him.

"She's a junkie?" he asked.

"I don't know," she said and launched into her findings. Told us everything she'd learned from her detective friend.

"Sounds like baby sister landed smack dab in the middle of the Big Easy's underbelly and it swallowed her whole..." Ruth commented. He looked over the girl's picture, Faith's picture and sucked his teeth, "Damn shame," he muttered.

"She didn't get there by herself," Hope said with conviction and her dark eyes met mine, pleading. She didn't have to, I was committed.

"Okay, so how do we find her?" Atlas asked, "You get a name?"

"I did," Hope whisked her finger across the screen and the next picture was of some form up on the monitor. Under the heading of 'lawyer' there was a name.

"Walter Baines," I read aloud.

"I know that name," one of the Voodoo Bastards piped up.

Ruth waved him over, "Spit it out then, Saint. Damn, we ain't got all night, Man."

"Sorry, Ruthie. Back in the day he was a city defense guy. Then all of a sudden, he's private practice and shit. Word on the street says he went to work for the Russians." Saint and Ruth exchanged a meaningful look and Ruth got a slow, lazy grin. The smile of a predatory man onto a scent.

"That so? The Russian's mixed up in this?" he asked Hope and she met him with a somber and level gaze.

"Well, Ivan is a Russian name and that *is* who Tonya was talking about, and my source at the N.O. P. D. told me to watch my six; that the Russians were all over the bust in St. Bernard's Parish."

Ruth's expression turned calculating, "That wouldn't be Ivan Vassili, now would it, Darlin'?"

"Never got a last name," she said honestly.

"I'll be dipped in shit, your sister got mixed up with the wrong fucking people, Girl." It was La Croix who spoke this time. The most we'd heard out of him since we'd gotten here. Hope frowned as La Croix rubbed a hand back and forth over his tattooed scalp.

"What do you know that you aren't telling us?" I asked, steady.

"Crash course in local underworld politics..." Ruth said and poured himself a shot. He tossed it back and set the glass down with a clack on the table we were standing around.

"Few years back the Russians moved in, took over the skin trade. No one really had a corner on the market and no one really wanted to fuck with them, I mean, these was some nasty sons of bitches. Brutal fucks, and I can appreciate me some brutal bastards, just not when they start movin' out of skin and start poaching on our trades. You feel me?" I nodded, picking up what he was putting down... we had an ally in this. Maybe more than one if we played our cards right.

"Look, all I want is my sister, you can have whatever is left over after I put these rabid bastards down. I don't care." Hope looked at each of us in turn, defiant.

"Calm your tits, Sugar. I'm on your side," Ruth said with an easy smile, "You got yourself a solid lead with ol' Walter there. He's the bottom of the food chain, but he knows who and where to find someone higher up. Why don't we pay 'im a visit and see what he knows?"

"I thought you'd never ask," Hope said and I exchanged looks with my guys, most of whom were nodding slowly.

"We don't all need to go," I said, "Radar, Nothing, you're with me and Hope," I said. They nodded. Nothing put a cigarette between his lips and lit up.

"La Croix, Saint, with me," Ruth was all out smiles.

Hope strapped a knife to her outer thigh, and looked as lost inside her own head as I'd ever seen her. This was playing hell on her and it was plain for me to see. Her expression was dark, a little too neutral; hard and focused.

I sighed and caught her before she reached the door and pulled her into an alcove, just her and me. She melted into me a little but remained stiff in my arms. I tipped her chin up so I could meet her eyes and sighed.

"You doin' okay?" I asked her.

"I'm fine," she said with her lips but her eyes told me a different story, wild and too wide, she was desperate and freaking the fuck out inside. We were silent for just a fraction of a minute and she came clean.

"What if I'm too late?" she whispered and wouldn't look at me.

"Then we take every one of the bastards out, even if it takes years. We wreck 'em. It's as simple as that," I said with a shrug. She looked up at me.

"Didn't figure you for the 'vengeance will be mine' type."

"Ohhhh, you're still getting to know me, Sweetheart," I said with a low and dark chuckle.

"True enough," she murmured, voice sweet and husky.

"This is over, I'd really like to finish getting to know you," I told her honestly.

She bit her bottom lip and looked away from me, eyes gone distant as she imagined, at least I imagined, what could be.

"I'd like that, but there's no telling which way this is going to end, I..." I touched a finger to her lips.

"Then let's just keep doing what we're doing," I whispered.

"Which is?"

"Figuring it out as we go along, Sweetheart, we're just figuring it out as we go along."

She nodded and offered her lips for a kiss which I would be crazy not to take so I did. She pulled away first and I smiled and followed her out to where most of the guys were ready to roll.

"See you at the hotel, Captain," Marlin said and I nodded. We fell in and followed Ruth's man, Saint, to the lawyer's office which was in the Central Business District. We parked the bikes in an adjacent alley.

"La Croix, break anybody that touches 'em," Ruth told the big man, who grinned one of the toothiest, unfriendliest grins I'd ever seen on a man. Okay. Bikes were safe.

We fell in behind Hope who slipped into the lobby and went to the floor map. She found the suite of offices occupied by Walter Baines Criminal Defense Attorney and we took the stairs, noting the lack of cameras.

"Shady motherfucker right there. No cameras in the stairwells," Ruth commented quietly.

"Mm," I grunted non-committedly.

Hope slipped out into the hall and gave the all clear. If there were cameras, we couldn't see them. I opened the office door and she went through.

"Can I help you?" the lawyer asked when we bypassed the empty secretaries desk and went right on through into his office.

"You'd better hope so, Partner," Ruth said with a smile, "Otherwise the lady is gonna be pissed, and you *really* don't want to see what that looks like."

"Ruth…" Hope intoned, the warning not to play with the man clear in her tone. The lawyer laughed.

"Now what kind of a name is Ruth for a man?" he asked. Ruth's face collapsed into a scowl.

"Oh, now I *know* you ain't laughing at my name… Saint."

Saint closed the office door and stood in front of it, crossing his arms. Well shit. I exchanged a look with Radar and Nothing and they gave me barely perceptible nods before fixing their eyes on Hope.

"You bailed out a Faith Dobbins earlier today from the Plaquemines' Sherriff's office," she said and the Lawyer whipped his attention to her impassive face.

"Now where did you hear a thing like that?" he asked, a cocky grin spreading across his face. He crossed his arms, in his too expensive shirt that matched the gray too-expensive suit jacket hanging off the back of his chair. His tie tack glittered real gold in the diffuse light from the banker's lamp on his desk and Hope huffed a slight laugh. She perched on the edge of his desk and his vision trailed up her long legs. I glanced around and sure enough, everyone was wearing their gloves. My girl was smart.

She gave the lawyer an imperious look, "Doesn't matter how I know, just matters that I do… at least for you. My sources tell me you and her boyfriend bailed her out. I want his name, and I want an address where I can find them and you're going to give them to me."

The lawyer laughed and it was a big mistake because as bulky as Ruth was, he moved fuckin' fast. He was across the expensive looking carpet, lunged past Hope and had the lawyer slammed face down over his own desk.

"Want to know how I got my name motherfucker?" Ruth asked with a sick grin, "It's short for somethin', wanna guess what that it?" The lawyer bleated in fear as Ruth held him pinned and flattened his hand against the mahogany desk.

"Hey Darlin', you wanna hand me that letter opener?" he asked Hope. She paled slightly, a little sweat dewing her upper lip, but she had no other tell that she was uncomfortable. Her face as impassive as they got. She plucked the letter opener from the fancy holder where it rested with her leather clad fingers and handed it to Ruth by the blade, hilt first. He took it from her and smiled a rictus grin, giving her a nod of appreciation.

"Thank you kindly, now, bottom feeder – how about you tell the lady here what she wants to know? You do that, I'm only gonna hurt yah, I might not kill yah."

Baines started babbling, "I can't! You don't know what they'll do to me!"

"You ain't gotta be afraid of what they *could* do, you gotta be afraid of what I *will* do," Ruth snarled and started to drive the point of the letter opener into the back of the lawyer's hand. Hope, watched, mouth slightly parted her dark eyes fixed on the bead of blood welling around the gold letter opener's sharp tip.

"Oh shit! Oh shit! Oh shit, oh shit! You're crazy! You're fucking crazy!" The lawyer was afraid now. Ruth gave a nasty little smile.

"No, I'm fucking Ruthless," he said and drove the letter opener clean through the lawyer's hand. The man howled like a wounded animal and I almost felt sorry for the prick... who was I kidding? I watched the whole thing going down in front of me and the only thing I felt was worried for Hope, but she was taking this bit of ugly into her soul like a pro. Her soldier showing.

Hope slapped her hand down on the desk beside the lawyer's face, the sound reverberating through the office. The lawyer shut up, and whimpered, he was sweating and if I had to bet, his hand probably hurt like a bitch, but if he gave up what we needed, he might yet still be able to use it.

"Faith Dobbins…" Hope repeated imperiously.

"Okay! Okay!" The lawyer screamed, frantic, "She's one of Ivan's girls! Right? Right!?"

"Ivan who?"

"Vassili!" the man wailed, "You really don't know who you're fucking with, you don't have a clue!"

Hope pulled out her Ruger, checked the chambers and snapped it back into place, she put the gun against the lawyer's head and her expression even scared me.

"No, you have no idea who you're dealing with, Princess. I want an address, I want to know where they're keeping Faith. Do you understand me, Walter?"

The man's breath sawed in and out of his lungs, he was going to hyperventilate and he wasn't telling Hope what she wanted to hear. She shot me a wink and cocked the hammer back on the gun and Walter spilled his guts.

"Okay! Okay! I don't know where they keep the girls! I know where they score their drugs! The heroin! They pump the bitches full of it to keep them compliant! Dealer by the name of Gavrikov! The shit comes in over at the Port. The big one over on the East Bank, it comes in on the shipping containers. Gavrikov has a guy, goes and gets it. Drops it at a titty bar every Thursday night. A place in the Quarter, a place called Objections, that's all I know! That's all I know!"

Nothing was taking notes and nodded to Hope that he'd gotten everything. Hope nodded and her eyes met mine. They were raw, pain filled and I nodded slowly. I understood what hearing this bastard's spew was costing her. She tucked her Ruger away and the lawyer breathed out.

"Oh thank God!"

"No God here, Buddy; no God here… Get you gone Darlin', you and your boys. We'll meet up back at ground zero. You feel me?" Ruthless said and I knew exactly what he had planned. Hope faltered at first, uncertain, but then she stared down at the lawyer and her expression crystallized and hardened.

"Make it hurt and make it slow," she intoned and turned, striding past Saint who shot her a little salute, I was right on her heels, Radar and Nothing backing me up. The lawyer started screaming as we crashed through the door and into the stairwell. The door didn't shut out the screams fast enough and we slid out the lobby and onto the street, making our way to the alley, the terror and pain echoing inside our skulls. Each of us holding an expression of grim determination as we walked down the block, not one of us expressing any sorry for what Ruth and Saint might be putting that cocksucker through.

I met Hope's eyes as we got on our bikes, La Croix didn't comment except to say, "See y'all back at the club."

We hit the road, Hope riding even with me. We pulled up two by two to a stoplight and she reached out her hand. I took it, and we sat through the light, and just held hands. She needed the grounding and I could do that for her. I saw Nothing and Radar exchange a look in my side view mirror. Neither of them commented but their expressions were resigned. We lived this life. Had been living it for some time now. Our hands had been dirtied and washed clean so many times before, it wasn't even funny.

No matter how ballsy, how tough, Hope was… none of us liked seeing a woman dragged down to this. Into the seedy dirt alongside us. The light turned green, I gave Hope's hand a little squeeze, a reassuring shake and let go. Yeah, sure, the views of me and mine were sexist as fuck, but women of quality, women like Hope… man… she deserved better than this.

I think this was the realization, the conclusion, my boys had reached after seeing how she handled herself against Rusty. After she'd gone to talk with her detective friend, all conversation had turned to how to best help her after she'd rode off. Suddenly it was all about how to get her out of this city and back to Ft. Royal the fastest. It was one of those times that I realized that my brothers, each and every one of them, had my back and I was so damn grateful for that. That they had my back and because Hope was becoming important to me, they had hers by default.

We rode back to the Voodoo Bastard's house and Pyro met us outside the front door. As soon as we were off the bikes he reported, I liked that about my best friend, he never kept me waiting, be it club business or business back home with the maritime salvage.

"Got eight rooms rented at that fleabag Motel; just like you wanted, Captain. Some of us is gonna have to double up," he shot a quick glance between me and Hope, "But I don't think that's gonna be a hardship. Trike moved our gear along with Lightning, here's your key. You're room six." I took the key and shoved it down into my jeans pocket. Hope looked me over and lifted her shoulder in a shrug.

"Can't do shit else until tomorrow night and this drop happens," she said.

"True enough, Sweetheart. Gotta sleep sometime, right now, we need to eat."

She nodded and I dispatched Beast and Atlas to go scare us up some grub through any 'ol drive through. They took off and would bring it back to us here. The party was in full swing inside the club house. Drinking, some whoring, and a game of pool between Marlin and one of the Voodoo Bastards. Felt sorry for that fucker. Marlin was a shark.

I pulled Hope into my lap and palmed the inside of her thigh. Not missing a beat, she dipped her head and crushed her mouth to mine in a heated kiss. Fuck that girl could kiss. I felt my jeans begin to tent from the careful attentions of her mouth and just about lost my shit completely when the vibration of her moan trilled across my tongue where it wrapped around hers.

We took the opportunity to unwind and forget the nasty shit we left behind by just losing ourselves in each other's mouths. Kissing, making out like teenagers, until the fucking food arrived.

I was halfway through my second burger when Ruth walked in with La Croix behind him. He winked in mine and Hope's direction and shouted, "Sherelle! Where you at girl?"

A tiny slip of a girl in platform heels and a shiny silver mini-dress sashayed into sight. Her dark hair was pulled up into a French twist and though she wore a bit much in the way of eyeliner, she was a pretty little thing… My mind flashed back onto Li'l Bit for a second and I was surprised to find that the memory didn't hold as much bite, or sting as it once did. Not with Hope sitting beside me, looking at me curiously.

"She reminds you of the picture of the girl, the one in your bunk on your boat, doesn't she?" she asked.

Fucking insightful bitch. I chewed more slowly and considered her. She smirked.

"It's okay, I'm not jealous or anything crazy," she said, I opened my mouth to say something but we were both interrupted by a squeal and the crack of Ruth's hand on his girl's ass. He had her bent over the pool table, her dress riding high around her waist.

"Oh, gonna make you cry for me, Darlin'," he said with a savage grin and shoved into her ass dry. Sherelle writhed under him and gave a little broken sob. Her eyes watered and her mascara streaked and she closed her eyes as Ruth pumped in and out of her ass. My burger went forgotten in my hand.

"Wow," Hope remarked dryly.

"Boss always gets like that after a kill," Hex commented, "Sherelle lives for this shit; she knows her safe word. No worries, she's safe as can be."

Ruth's man pushed off from the armchair next to ours and joined the ring of spectators around the pool table, Marlin was putting up his cue stick shaking his head while Ruth ass-fucked the girl with no mercy. He certainly lived up to his name.

"We should come back tomorrow," Hope said judiciously.

"Right I'm with you, Babe." I gave her a little nudge and she stood up without much urging.

"Kraken!" I shouted over the din, "Return to base!" which for us was our hotel.

"See you tomorrow around noon!" Ruth hollered and I gave him a nod. His guys were laughing at us and I'm sure some of 'em were calling us pussies behind our backs but this shit just wasn't our scene, not with a lady present, which Hope *was*, despite her badassery.

She pulled another moment of it out when she called out to Ruth, "Hey Ruth! It all right if I leave my bike? Anybody fuck with it?"

"Go right ahead, Darlin'! Nobody better touch it or I'll. Have. Their. Ass!" he punctuated each of the last words of his declaration by reaming into his girl's ass with some particularly rough thrusts. She wailed and the sound was more pleasure than pain to me. I shook my head, to each their own, and raised my eyebrows.

"Come on," Hope said and we left out the front. She put her helmet on and got on behind me, without so much as a word, twining her arms around me, getting snug up against my back. I put my hand briefly over hers before riding out. Following the hand signals in my rearview to take me and mine to our home away from home.

I bid the guys goodnight and without a word, Hope ghosted along with me up to number six's door. I keyed it open and let her go first. She set her helmet on a table just inside the door. I flipped the switch on the wall, just inside and the bedside lamp came on and with a gentle shove, I sent the door swinging shut, closing out the outside world. It was just me and her and no one else… finally.

She looked at me, face expressionless which bled into somber and her eyes closed. A wave of exhaustion overtaking her.

"Can I ask you a favor?" she asked quietly.

"You can ask me anything, Sweetheart," I kept my voice pitched low, soothing and it did something to her. Her face screwed up, anguished, and she pinched the bridge of her nose and let out a broken little gasp. I shrugged out of my jacket and cut and tossed it onto the table and I went to her, pulling her gently into my arms. I tucked her head beneath my chin and held her close as she fell apart against me, petting her silken hair and making shushing noises above her head.

"I'm sorry," she warbled and I chuckled.

"Don't be," I whispered, "What did you want to ask me?"

"For this…"

"To hold you?" I asked.

"Yeah."

I chuckled, "Aw, Sweetheart, you ain't never got to ask me for this, I love holding you."

"Yeah?" she sniffed and wiped at her eyes and let out a shuddering sigh, relaxing into me.

"Yeah. Can I ask you something?"

"Sure…"

"You got a mind towards what comes next? After we get your sister?" I asked.

She let out a bitter, derisive little laugh and pulled back to look at me, "We don't even know if we *are* going to get my sister back."

I cupped her face with my hands and smoothed my thumbs through the moisture and makeup beneath her solid brown eyes. I searched her face and what I found there was twisted and tortured with guilt and so many other things, I sighed softly.

"We're going to get her back, Sweetheart. I believe it and you should too, but you gotta be ready for what comes next…"

"I guess I haven't thought that far ahead," her brow furrowed.

"Yeah, well I have. Come back to Florida with me. Your sister is gonna need time and a place to heal, people to look out for her. Let me give you that place at the very least… take all the time you and your family needs to heal." She searched my face for a solid minute.

"Why would you do that for me? You barely know me."

"True enough, but I like what I see and I'm enjoying the hell out of getting to know you. I like you, Hope. I want more of this. I want a lot of things from you."

"Like what?" she asked.

I smiled, "Like more of this," I kissed her lips lightly and pushed her jacket off her shoulders; she let it fall to the floor and swooned towards me. I untucked her shirt and smoothed my hands against her skin, "And more of this…" I whispered and she sighed.

Yeah… I wanted more and more of Hope until she had nothing left to give. I wanted all of her, and I wanted to keep all of her to myself. I felt like I'd met my match in Ms. Andrews and I wasn't about to let any of that go.

"What else do you want?" she asked her voice husky, low and sexy.

"I want you to let down your hair, I want to take all this off a piece at a time and I want to lay you back and kiss every inch of you, starting with your heart… if you'll let me."

She closed her eyes and savored my words and I could see that she desperately wanted what I was holding out in front of her. She nodded slowly and reached up, unpinning her hair, pulling the tie that held it tight in its bun.

"I want that," she whispered, "I really do…" her hair spiraled out and frothed around her face and I buried my hands in it, drawing her face up to mine. I kissed her, lingering, dark and deep and smiled against her mouth.

"Relax, Baby. Let me take care of you for tonight, okay?" I asked.

"Okay," she murmured so sultry and sweet. I drew her against my body and kissed her soulfully.

Okay.

CHAPTER 21
Hope

Cutter was warm in the air conditioned coolness of the cheap ass motel room. His lips moved carefully against mine and I couldn't help myself, I surrendered completely. Gave myself over to his care and let myself, my burdens, just everything go. It would all be there in the next hour, or the one after that or just whenever he got through with me, which a part of me hoped that he never would.

There was nothing I could do right now but wait. Wait for the hands on the clock to crawl around the dial, wait for day to break, the sun to crawl across the sky at its snail's pace, only to set again so that we could head for the titty bar, Objections. To flush out our rat so we could follow it back to its nest. So for now, the best thing I could possibly do, is at least try to unwind. To find a distraction so that the clock would wind down faster and put me that much closer to finding my sister.

"Hey," Cutter jostled me slightly in the circle of his arms, "Thought you said you were going to let me take care of you." He arched one brow and smiled at me, his teeth white in his neatly trimmed beard and I closed my eyes shoulders slumping.

"I'm sorry…"

His expression gentled and he touched a finger to my lips, "Don't be, just let me give you what you need, okay?"

"Okay," I agreed, once again.

I reached up, twining my arms around his neck and pulled the tie holding his ponytail careful to do it in such a way as to not pull against his scalp. He smiled at me through the curtain of his hair as I combed my fingers through it, parting it from in front of his face. It was much softer than it looked and felt good gliding through my fingers.

Cutter tugged gently on my tee and I let him take it. He whisked his own off from over his head and I took the time to really look at him, not just the chiseled, lean muscles and tan skin, but also at his tattoos. I trailed fingertips lightly down his ribs over the bright rendition of a pirate ship in full sail. He skirted to the side and laughed and it was one of the sexiest sounds I'd heard him make yet. His laughter lightened my mood just enough to keep the weight of it from pressing the air from my lungs completely.

I touched the scar where I was pretty sure he'd taken a bullet in front, just off to the side of the pirate ship and felt a pang of sorrow for him. I glanced up into his face, where he looked down at me, watching me, tranquil and impassive. He was letting me explore and I bet if I asked him, he would tell me the truth of it.

He must have seen the question in my eyes because he smiled with a hint of sadness at the memory and spoke it into air conditioned hush hanging between us.

"Got me just right, a gap in the body armor," he murmured and pressed my hand to his back and the scar of an exit wound, much bigger out the back, "Damn near lost the kidney but the docs, they saved it somehow. I was lucky."

"I was hit once too," I murmured, "Body armor did its job. I was the lucky one, just bruised all to hell for a really long time. Hit so hard I thought it'd bruised my soul..." I smiled but it was a bitter, broken thing.

"Was in transit, wasn't even in a declared hot zone. Had just finished training a unit of Iraqi men for their police. They didn't want to listen to me, of course... They were more inclined to listen after that firefight. Only one I've ever been in. My friend, mentor, Andres... he didn't make it. He took one to the face." I bowed my head. I hadn't told anyone but the councilors and the superiors who'd I'd had to debrief about the incident after the fact. Cutter pulled me into him and kissed me again, a finer, gentler thing filled with our mutual sorrow and regret.

I'd never been with someone who had been there, either. Who knew just what it was to go through something like that, to lose someone dear in the blink of an eye... The kiss deepened and Cutter's hands traveled to my ass urging me to jump up, to wend my legs around his hips. I took the invitation. I loved how he'd so easily fucked me against the wall earlier. I was a real fan of down, dirty sex, when the situation called for it, but this time, I don't know... this time called for something else.

He took me to the bed, and laid me down gently, tapping the outside of my thigh to indicate I needed to let him go. Which, duh, too much in the way of pants and boots to properly get it on this way. He surprised me though, kissing down my neck, down my body, leaving blooms of heat and desire in the wake of the seeds he planted with gentle touches of his lips. He straightened and put one thigh forward. My legs hung off the bed from the knee down and with his gaze firmly fixed on mine he lifted one and planted the sole of my boot against his thigh.

With a gentle smile curving his lips he dragged his eyes down my body leaving a heated blush across my skin wherever his gaze fell before he carefully worked the knots in my laces free, deliberately taking his time, easing them through the eyelets until the leather casing had loosened enough to easily slip my foot free.

He set the boot neatly at the foot of the bed and with a devilish little grin, stripped me of my sock and pressed thumbs to the center of my arch on the underside of my foot. I fell back flat against the cheap mattress and bedspread and groaned my appreciation. That felt *so* good, and the more he kneaded and rubbed the more I sank back into the bed and a relaxed state of bliss. Bastard! He sure had my number. He finished with the first foot and repeated the process with the second and I became putty in his hands. There was no denying it. Cutter had some smooth fucking moves, and I was down to let him try every last one of them on me.

"Help me out, Sweetheart," he whispered and I smiled at him, he had his fingers hooked into the waistband of my black cargo pants, and had already made quick work of the belt and button fly. I arched my hips and he drew them off, down my legs, and the look in his eyes as they trailed over the skin revealed by the black cloth heated my blood to a pleasant simmer.

I lay in bra and panties and he ordered me, voice roughened by sex and need, "Scoot up, lay on your stomach."

I did what he wanted and he unhooked my bra, I took my arms from the straps and he whisked it away as I settled back down onto my stomach.

"Don't move," he ordered and I had no intentions of it. Rather I lay, head turned to one side and closed my eyes. I had a feeling that the foot rub was just a preview of coming attractions and I was right. After a moment of him rooting through his saddle bags he came back to me. He stripped my panties down my legs and straddled the backs of my thighs, the hair on his legs prickling my skin. I smiled. He'd lost his jeans. I liked that, I liked that a lot.

I hummed in deep pleasure as his hands, coated in oil; caressed my back, lightly at first before he started really digging in, finding those nodes of knotted muscle and easing them free with gentle and consistent pressure. He chuckled as I absolutely melted underneath him, the tension easing out of my body degree by degree until I was all but boneless beneath him.

"What'd you think about what went on back at the club?" he asked softly.

"What, about the chick getting drilled in the ass?"

He laughed out loud, "I like how you just let it all hang out."

"Do I look like Willy Wonka to you?" he laughed again and god it was sexy. I couldn't help but smile and laugh a little too.

"Uh, that would be a no, why?"

"Because unlike that bitch I don't sugar coat nothin'," I said.

"Look at you all west coast gangsta." I could hear the smile in his voice and his hands hadn't quit their kneading so I knew I was on safe ground. God it was hot that he would play with me and that he would laugh at my crude jokes and didn't seem to want me any less. Still saw me as a woman, as a lady…

"You going to answer the question?" he asked with a playful little slap to my ass, which made me arch my hips and ass off the bed.

"Not my scene, not without careful attention and a lot of lube," I said quietly. My pussy was tingling with want and I was already wet. I could feel my nipples tighten, and grow sensitive against the rough cover of the bedspread beneath me. Truthfully, the thought of

Cutter there turned me the fuck on. It turned me on even more when I felt his cock stir against my ass.

"Good to know, I'm going to leave that for another time, another day, right now I want you to turn over."

God I love how his voice held that pleasant edge, like he were talking about something as mundane as the weather, even as it held that razor's slice of command, so sharp, so stark and there it was hard not to cut yourself on it for real. I turned over and he got between my thighs. I arched ready to take him in but instead he grabbed me and dragged me to the bottom of the mattress again, almost to the point my ass was hanging off.

I put my toes against the carpet as he knelt between my knees, gazing up my body deliberately. His expression stoic, eyes liquid, dark and deep with lust and heavier things as he let my anticipation build to feverish heights.

"You like having your pussy licked?" he asked and his voice was a barely there growl. I swallowed hard.

"Oh yeah," I agreed and nodded.

"Good, I could go down on a woman for hours if she'd let me," he said and lowered his face, agonizingly slow before licking a long, deliberate wet line from my opening to my clit. I fell back against the mattress and let him do whatever he wanted. Holy mother of god that felt good.

"No argument's here, you can go as long as you'd like," I said and tangled my fingers in the cheap bedspread to either side of my hips. I moaned and writhed provocatively, I couldn't help it. Cutter's mouth was... wow.

He slid two fingers inside of me, stretching and filling me, searching out that spot and oh god, oh god, oh god, I couldn't help the cry that spilled from my throat as I rippled around his fingers and came undone. He chuckled against my clit and the vibration of it was almost too much, I jerked and his forearm braced across my hips, flattening me to the bed.

Holy hell, he provided way more than a distraction. He made me come so many times with his mouth I lost count. I was a puddle of Hope in the middle of his bed when he finally got around to ordering me up into the center of it. It took me way more tries than it should have for me to comply and the heat index went up by like a million degrees as I watched him stand there, stroking himself with sure fingers while he waited for me to fulfill his demand. I reached for him once I was settled and he came to me gladly, his smile feral and possessive and giving me an all new thrill as he covered my body with his own.

His hair curtained our faces and the world was suddenly shrouded, the diffuse light from the bedside lamp muted even further, the warmth of him against me, caged by his body... it was magical. So perfect and incredibly intimate. I wanted to stay here forever. I closed my eyes and breathed in his salty ocean smell underlying his light layering of Old Spice cologne and found bliss.

"I've got you, Sweetness," he breathed and I dragged his face to mine. I kissed him deeply, my heart crying out with relief that I had finally found a man who got me, who connected with me on that deep sublevel, who was so finely in tune with me.

He eased into me slowly, carefully, this time and it felt so incredibly good. I moaned into his mouth and he cradled me so gently in his embrace. His body met mine and filled me to the brim and I sighed out in purest satisfaction. He moved slow and deliberate, his eyes drifting shut and I don't know how long we lay in a tangle of limbs, bodies joined, moving in rhythm and synchronized beyond reason. We were drunk off each other and the communication of purest emotions through touch and glance, kiss and caress.

It was probably one of the most beautiful, sharing, joining... Hell I needed to call it what it was! It was probably one of the first times ever that I made love *with* a man, not just to him. It was exquisite and perfect and scared the bejesus out of me all at once. It left me breathless with wonder and my chest tight with wanting, for the first time I could ever remember, I allowed myself to want *for* myself. I wanted to stay like this in Cutter's arms forever and never have him let me go. I wanted to see where this went, I wanted so much to have a partner in this life instead of going it alone like I had been all this time.

"Stay with me..." I said and swallowed hard, not quite believing I had voiced the plea out loud.

"Hmm, you've got me dead to rights, Sweetheart, I'm not going anywhere," he murmured and brought the back of my hand to his lips. I had no idea how long we had been at this but I never wanted it to end. I was aware that our skins were lightly dewed with sweat; that our breathing came harsh and uneven and that Cutter's other arm, where he held himself off from crushing me, well it trembled finely with exertion.

"No, I mean after... after all of this, stay with me," I swallowed past the lump in my throat and Cutter smiled so sweetly, so serenely down at me. He pressed into me to the hilt and captured my eyes with his.

"Baby, I just told you, I'm not going anywhere. We'll figure this out, one day, one minute at a time if we have to... I'm with you. I'm staying with you." He bowed his head and kissed me into silence and tranquility.

God I was falling in love with this man. I was falling in love with him hard. It started with his confidence and carried on through his steady dedication. He was trustworthy. Incredibly so. He turned me on and turned me inside out and he just seemed to know what I was about or what I needed sometimes before even I did. I wanted to stay. I wanted to try. I had never even come close to wanting anyone else the way I wanted Cutter and as much as that scared me, as much as that terrified me because I was putting myself out there... I couldn't deny this attraction was turning into something much stronger.

I swallowed hard and came again and Cutter hummed his appreciation, he slowed in his careful love making and stilled. Holding me close and I sighed out and took the comfort and strength he offered me. We lay, panting in the circle of each other's arms for some time before he drew back and searched my face.

"I mean it, Sweetheart. You've got me." He whispered, reassuring, and kissed me one more time. We didn't even try to get up or clean up, that could be done come morning. Instead we lay close and warm and safe and slept. I woke, vaguely, sometime in the night when Cutter reached for and switched out the lamp, but he came right back to me, pulling the blankets around us both. I slept solid and I slept hard after that and it was precisely what I needed.

CHAPTER 22
Cutter

"Seriously... I hate you guys," Hope mumbled against my chest when the door flew open the next day.

"Love you too, Baby. Now get your asses up!" Pyro barked and ripped open the curtains over the window, flooding the room with bright, late morning sunlight.

"Dude, what the fuck?" I demanded.

"Ruth called, wants a sit down and is offering real fucking food as a peace offering for the hour." Marlin said, stretching in the doorway. The boys started pouring in after him and leaning against furniture and doorways, taking up seating space in the one armchair and on the sink counter.

"We having church?" I asked.

"Sort of," Beast said crossing his massive arms over his chest.

"You forget the civilian in the room?" I asked.

"Pfft! The way Hope handles herself, she ain't no civilian. She ain't no ol' lady either, we don't know what she is but whatever it is we like her," Atlas declared. I raised an eyebrow and Hope cuddled into my side more, resting her head on my shoulder.

"You're right, I'm not old, so thanks for that... or are you just saying that so I won't kick your ass? Wait..." she pushed up and glared at Atlas blearily, "What the fuck is an ol' lady to you douchecanoe's anyways?"

The guys laughed, "You're learning," Pyro said appreciatively.

"An Ol' Lady as in you're my Ol' Lady, my property, mine to keep and before you get all butt-twisted," I chuckled at her sour expression, "It's a pretty big honorific among our kind."

"It's true. Means more to a brother than a civilian wedding ring to give a woman your rag," Radar agreed.

Hope squeezed her eyes shut and clutching the sheet to her

chest, struggled to sit up. She opened her eyes and yawned.

"I'm going to need a cup of coffee and a glossary of terms to get through today aren't I?" she asked.

"No time like the present for a crash course," Marlin said with a shrug but I could see in his sky blue eyes that he was happy for me.

"Okay, so this is how it goes…" My brothers proceeded to blow Hope's mind explaining the ins and outs of a woman's place in the club.

"Wait, wait, wait… so a rag isn't actually a rag, it's one of those leather vests like you got only says that a woman is *property* of whoever she's with?"

"Pretty much but before you get pissed, you gotta understand. For us, property isn't like just a car, or a boat, or a piece of land… it's much more basic than that. Property, to us, is *something of value*. As in *something we value above all else*," I told her. I watched her wheels turn, her dark eyes searching my face before she started to nod slowly. Pyro stooped and picked up my shirt from the night before and held it out to Hope. She took it and I had to like how comfortable she was in her own skin to be sitting here naked with a room full of my brothers and not be freaking out.

That wasn't to say she was being immodest either. She had the sheet covering everything important and then some, even as she pulled my shirt over her head she was careful not to let it slip. Fucking perfect mix of tough and feminine, of being ballsy yet having grace. She was tripping all the right triggers for me and I was so incredibly struck with just how *grateful* I was that she wanted to stick around.

Hope dragged her long dark hair out of the back of the collar of my shirt and sighed, "Coffee before I kick someone's ass," she said just as Trike, our prospect, pushed through the open doorway with two of those cardboard drink holders perched on one arm, a bag of what smelled suspiciously like doughnuts hanging out of his hand.

"Thank you, Jesus! Trike, you're now officially my favorite," Hope said and reached out both hands, opening and closing her hands in the classic toddler sign for 'gimme'. The guys laughed and they fed and caffeinated her first. I smiled and took a drink of nasty tepid doughnut shop coffee that'd sat on the burner too long out of a crappy Styrofoam cup.

"I didn't think they made Styrofoam anymore," I griped.

"Me either," someone said.

We put down some coffee and munched on fried dough while Hope's crash course continued. Her mind sufficiently full and turning things over, she sat for a long minute in silence.

"Kay, get the fuck out. I'm getting up," she said finally and waved them all off. The guys laughed and stepped out into the bright sunshine, leaving the door open a sliver behind them.

"Kiss me," I demanded and she smiled, leaning across the bed. She put her arms against my chest and fell into me, and kissed me with what tasted a lot like commitment underneath the stale coffee and sugary sweetness of the half assed breakfast we'd just consumed.

"I love it when you order me around like you're all tough," her voice was pitched low and if I had to describe it, 'sex kitten' came to mind as a perfectly acceptable label to put on it. I smacked the outside of her thigh.

"Get in the shower, Hope; before I fuck you and we don't go anywhere today," she grinned and backed off of me, stopping in the bathroom doorway.

"Damn, and I was hoping you were going to join me," she said and she didn't have to invite me twice. I was up and under the spray before she got my shirt off over her head.

We showered in record time, even for us, and dressed carefully. Hope dressed to ride and pulled her hair into a tight French braid. I was putting on my boots when she bounded onto the bed behind me. She gathered my wet hair in her hands and I froze and let her tend to me. She didn't put it into a French braid like hers, but rather just combed it out and put it into a low, regular braid, tight and efficient.

"Thanks," I murmured. She put her arms around my shoulders and hugged herself to my back, nuzzling the side of my neck and giving it a quick kiss.

"Welcome," she breathed and just as quick as she'd been, she was up, shrugging into her jacket and giving a last check to her boot laces.

I pulled on my jacket and cut and pulled my keys out of my pocket. She had her helmet on and I put on my glasses as we went out into the bright light and oppressive, muggy heat that was classic Louisiana.

"About fuckin' time!" Pyro called up. Hope bounced on the balls of her feet a couple of times and gave him the finger. He grinned up at us and we came down from the second floor and went to my bike. I fired it up and Hope got on behind me. I missed Florida, and the ride we took helmet free. I missed watching her expression and the wind catching her hair. I fucking hated the impersonal black carapace looking helmet that hid her beautiful brown eyes and sharp features from me.

She snugged up close to my back, her arms around me and I took off, my boys fell in and we went back to the Voodoo Bastard's compound to one hell of a fucking barbeque going on full swing. No wonder the guys seemed excited. None of us were overtly a fan of a strict diet of fast food.

We parked and Hope wandered over to her bike to drop her helmet with it, but she wasn't fooling anybody. She wanted to make sure her pride and joy was doing okay. Satisfied she came back over and we spent the next few hours strategizing and talking about how we wanted tonight to go down.

One of Ruth's boys had been sent on some recon the night before to get the layout of Objections. Apparently it was a higher class joint. One that did jeans, but paired with some Nancy boy polo, certainly not with a jacket and cut. His man hadn't been able to get in and no one else could pass muster either. So it looked like we were flying blind.

"Well that leaves you out in the cold, Lover," Hope mused, and she didn't sound at all happy about it. Still it didn't get her down, she was already looking over the rest of The Kraken and Voodoo Bastards alike. She took a sip of her Sweet Tea out of its red Solo cup, ice cubes rattling as she contemplated her options.

"Marlin's out, too," she muttered.

"Why?" I asked casually.

"You ever see a lawyer type or judge with long hair?" she asked, "While we're at it, La Croix, is definitely out, Hex would have worked except he's got tattoos on his hands so that nixes him, Pyro stands out too much with that hair…" she sighed and twisted in her seat.

"Nothing!" she called out. My treasurer looked up darkly, "You fancy a date at a high class titty bar with me tonight?"

Laughter erupted and Hope got up, moving in Nothing's direction, he looked slightly poleaxed but she was right, he was the only white dude we had that with a little clean up could look respectable. I sure as fuck wasn't cutting my hair. Hope spoke with Nothing and he looked my way. I nodded and he gave me a nod back, listened to her some more and nodded his agreement. Hope nodded and was swiping away on her phone. She said something to Nothing and he nodded.

"Okay, we'll be back!" she called.

"Whoa, hey! Where you going?" I demanded.

"There's a Good Will thrift shop over in Metarie not far from here. Gotta look the part. We'll be back before you know it," she called.

"Nothing you going with her?" I asked.

"Yeah," he waved me off, and dare I say, might have even been blushing.

"Oooo! Can I go with you girls why you try on clothes?" Atlas teased.

"Good idea, At! Go with them!" I called out. Atlas looked over startled and I scowled.

"Son of a bitch," he muttered and set down his beer. I grinned on the inside. Hope gave me a fast kiss and was over and onto her bike.

"You watch my woman's six!" I ordered and my guys nodded. No one really seemed surprised by my declaration. Maybe they were seeing something I wasn't, who knows? I watched them go and tried not to get jittery. I knew she could, and would, take care of herself but damn.

"Fuck," I huffed a laugh.

"What?" Ruth asked.

"I think I'm straight up in love with that woman," I said.

"Shit, Brother; saw that the day you first pulled in," Ruth chuffed a laugh and pushed his girl Sherelle off his lap. She smiled and he lumbered off towards the bathrooms. I smiled and chuckled and stared off into the distance where Hope had turned off and sighed.

Some things just weren't worth fighting and with as good as it felt to be into her, I just plain didn't want to. She made life interesting. I liked that, and I usually tried to keep what I liked around. Even when it wasn't good for me. I didn't think Hope was bad for me. Not like the last girl I'd been in love with. After all, there wasn't anything worse than being in love with someone who just plain couldn't love you back.

CHAPTER 23
Hope

"Seriously Nothing, stop holding yourself so stiff, I'm supposed to be your girlfriend," I whispered harshly, smiling the whole time I did it. We were in line to get in to Objections. Line. Like this was some kind of night club except it wasn't it was a 'gentleman's club' and I was the only woman standing behind the red velvet rope, waiting along the runner of red carpet to get in.

I was dressed like a total hooker too. I'd found a skin tight LBD and with the addition of my garter and stockings, some heavy tramp makeup and some whore red lipstick I looked like the high priced escort I was pretending to be. The Metairie Good Will had been a gold mine in the men's suit department. We'd found a very nice, if a bit big, light charcoal one and a shirt and tie to match. It'd cost me more for the rush dry cleaning and alterations than it had for the suit but with Nothing standing here looking like that, we were a lock to get in this place.

Some business men came out the front door, and the bouncer looked inside before the door shut. He let the suits in front of us go and we were next at the rope. I leaned into Nothing and smiled up at him and he valiantly tried to help me, to play his part. He smiled down at me and licked his lips.

"God, my wife..." he breathed and looked tortured for a second. He was going to rabbit, he was going to bolt, *shit*. I smiled up at him and whispered.

"It's club business, she'll understand," I murmured.

"No, she won't, Hope... she's dead," he said and there was nothing I could say to that. The bouncer had lifted the rope, was checking our ID's and we were being ushered into the club. It was like the universe had hit the flush lever and we were swirling inexorably, caught in that vortex and right down the drain into the second circle of hell. For all of you non-Dante fans out there, that would be the circle of lust because holy smokes... these women were hot, the shit they had on was barely there, and they were writhing in the laps of oil tycoons and trust fund babies like their lives depended on it.

"Hope..." Nothing sounded strangled and I led him to a seat where I could see everyone, and to protect this brave and tortured man from the big bad lap dancers, I parked myself there first. Nothing's hands settled on my waist like he was afraid to touch me at first but I met his dark and twisted gaze with a pleading one of my own and that seemed to center him out. He nodded and seemed like he was back in control.

I let my eyes adjust to the lighting in here and took a more solid look. On second glance it wasn't that bad in here. The dancers were plying their trade, but the men were keeping their hands to themselves. I glanced around and spotted what was either the owner or a floor man, wandering throughout the throngs of men and dancers, checking hands with a shrewd gaze.

A girl in tasteful French lingerie, with a little round tray sashayed up to us, "Get you a drink?" she asked, and she was goooood, just a slight bite to her lower lip, a seductive and inviting sweep of her gaze over Nothing who I think had completely stopped breathing underneath me, and a subtle wink of her long lashes.

"What do you want, Baby?" I cooed for her benefit. Nothing swallowed hard, his Adams apple bobbing beneath the knot of his tie.

"Jack and Coke," he said and he at least sounded steady. I smoothed his hand from my waist down my leg to rest on my knee and gave him a winning smile that I hoped like hell was reassuring without tipping our blonde waitress off.

"What about you, Honey?" she asked me.

"Cosmopolitan please, and thank you." I winked at her and her smile grew and she flounced off in the direction of the bar.

"Oh God," Nothing muttered and blushed bright crimson when I moved his hand up my leg to rest it under the very short skirt of my dress almost at the apex of my thighs.

"Relax Nothing," I said for his ears only, "Just have to look believable. You're holding me like I'm your sister."

"Um, Hope, I'm really sorry…" he said and a second later I felt why. I dipped my head and captured his eyes with mine a second before my lips brushed his.

"Don't be, it's biological," I said against his mouth, "I know, just hang on for me okay?"

"Yeah, sure. Just," he huffed an uncomfortable laugh, "Just don't tell the Captain, I don't want to die," he said and I threw back my head and laughed. Nothing remembered then, what it was to smile, and was better able to ease into his part.

We played it up that I was the freak and it was sometime during my second lap dance that Nothing was watching me get, that I spotted the bartender give a telling chin lift to a dancer with red hair that clashed some with her royal purple lingerie. She and I both followed his gaze to a decidedly eastern European looking man who gave the dancer a hard look and a nod. He was a brutish fucker in an expensive suit, his hair barely there it was buzzed so short. His nose crooked from one too many breaks.

The dancer leaned down giving him a great view of her décolletage, but the fish she had on her hook only gave her a hard look and I think, told her to get dancing. She smiled and straightened and went to the bar, retrieving, yep… a vodka double, neat, before returning to the brute in the suit. Heh. Nothing paid my dancer, which had been instructed to dance for me but to pay attention to Nothing so I could keep playing eagle eye and he followed my line of sight.

"About fucking time," he breathed as I moved back onto his lap. I kissed him like the dance had turned me on like nobody's business and his hands were taught on my waist. He was ridged beneath me but he played a convincing game. The floor man wandered past the red head and the brute and when he was past, that's when I saw it.

Wow. Ballsy motherfuckers… but then again, the lingerie didn't leave much to the imagination. He slipped his hand up her skirt and when it reappeared it had no trace of the cylinder that'd been in it. The girl finished shaking that ass and he paid her and with a wink she sauntered a little stiffly to the bar, and with a laugh and a wink made her way to the back. I broke my kiss with Nothing and only then realized that his chest was heaving, I frowned.

"Sorry, you're really fucking good at that," he said.

"Yeah well, I'm off to follow my mark. Stay put and red really isn't your color," I said and got up. Nothing put his fingers to his mouth and wiped, coming away with my red lipstick. He swore and tried wiping it off with a cocktail napkin but I was slipping into the dressing room where Ms. Thing had just disappeared to.

I closed the door and shot the lock behind me. She wasn't anywhere I could see her just yet, but I could hear her.

"Shit!" she hissed, "Fucking asshole..."

"Too rough shoving it up there?" I asked, coming around the bank of lockers. I leaned my shoulder against the cool metal and cocked my head. The girl looked up sharply and her eyes hardened.

"I'm gonna scream, Jack will be back here before you..." I pointed the Ruger in her face.

"Can pull the trigger?"

She froze, got real quiet and held out the cylinder towards me... ewe no. Not only no but *hell* no.

"I don't want that," I snapped tersely, "I want to know where you *take it*."

Her eyes were wide and tears leaked out, I cocked the hammer on my Ruger to take advantage of the dramatic effect and purse my lips, raising my eyebrow.

"They'll kill me," she whispered.

"Bitch, you're looking down the barrel of *my* gun and you're worried about *them* killing you? Tell me what I want to know, I walk out that door and let you go on with your miserable life. You go on as if I was never here. You say nothing. You tip them off? I find you and I kill you a lot slower than a bullet to your head. You get me?" She sank down onto the bench and put up her hands nodding and cringing.

"Where. Are. They?" I demanded.

"Saint Rose!" she cried, "I make the drop at a house over in Saint Rose. 112..." she listed off an address on River Road in Saint Rose,

Louisiana. A suburb of New Orleans that I didn't think was far from here.

"Write it down," I demanded. She nodded and with shaky hands wrote it down, ripping the page off her waitressing ticket book and handing it over. She was shaking so bad it was like she had a palsy or something. I stuffed the slip of paper into my beaded clutch purse that hung crossways over my chest. It barely held the Ruger but it'd done its job and gotten it in here. I backed up towards the exit to the dressing room and left the woman shaking and bawling on the bench.

"Please don't hurt me…" she keened, "I never wanted to do this! I just owe them too much, I had a real bad coke habit… I got clean but they're making me do this to pay off my debt."

"Yeah well, drugs are bad, mmkay?" I said, shoving the Ruger into my purse and snapping it closed.

"I get that, and I'm sorry! I'm really sorry!" she cried harder.

"Yeah, you should be," I shot back mercilessly, I was only thinking about Faith, about what Joe had told me about underage victims. This bitch was part of the problem, hopefully now she was part of the solution, but right now I had to get me and mine out of here. I ducked back out into the darkened hallway, running smack into another dancer. Shit.

"Oh! I'm sorry!" I exclaimed and wobbled on my heels, hopefully convincingly, "Looking for the bathroom, silly me!"

"Oh, you passed it, Honey. It's back that way…" the girl pointed up the hall but I could tell she was suspicious. Shit.

"Oh, thank you! Must've had just one too many, I'm so sorry!" I kept babbling apologies as I backed down the hall. The dancer nodded and let herself back into the dressing room. As soon as she was out of sight I straightened and made a bee line for Nothing. He stood when he saw me. I gave him a sharp nod and we went for the exit, slipping out onto the street, walking away briskly. We made our way up Bourbon passing bars blaring blues and clubs pumping bass to the bar Ruth had told us to meet them at.

We picked up our shadows, Lightning and Hex, and they trailed us three or four groups of tourists behind. Marlin and Saint were leaning in the mouth of an alley up ahead, Nothing shot them a hand signal, and Marlin nodded and they started walking up Bourbon ahead of us by two or three tourists. We made our way through the crowds and Marlin and Saint stopped outside a bar, The Dragon's Den. Saint lit up a cigarette, which was our signal that we were good.

I slipped in ahead of Nothing and he followed me close, right on my six. We found Cutter, Atlas, Ruth, and La Croix at the back and I immediately handed the slip of paper to Ruth who was on a burner phone. He read off the address.

"Get on it and stay on it. Tell me if there's any movement," he said and hung up without so much as a goodbye. I rose an eyebrow at Cutter who was giving me a once over.

"Pyro and Radar are on it," he said. I nodded, satisfied that we had some of our own eyes on the situation.

"Doin' okay, Darlin'? You're lookin' a little pale…" Ruth commented.

"I just shoved my gun in a lap dancer's face and scared the ever living shit out of her to get that address. I'm not sure how I feel right now," I said honestly. If she'd been telling the truth, which who knew if she had been or not, then she was just another victim in all of this. I sighed inwardly. *Faith.* We were close, I could feel it, and I needed to stay focused. I could feel sympathy or whatever for the rest of the players in this damn drama later.

Cutter drew me into his side and I wrapped my arms around his shoulders, sighing, leaning into him and taking the strength that he offered.

"You ready to bounce?" Ruth asked.

"God yes, get me out of this monkey suit," Nothing griped, pulling his tie free.

"Aww, but you look so handsome," I cracked and winked at him. Nothing wouldn't meet my eyes, turning his head and fixing his gaze on the floor. I felt bad then. Ruth and La Croix led the way out of the bar, Radar and Cutter just behind them. Nothing went ahead of me and I caught his hand with mine. He met my eyes then and I smiled slightly, and mouthed the words 'thank you'. He gave me a terse nod and pulled his hand and wrist from my grip stalking out behind Cutter who glanced back at me.

I gave my man a reassuring little smile and a half shrug. He nodded, and looked over Nothing, his brow crushing at the red lipstick on his man's collar.

"Oh for the love of Christ, knock it off," I said stalking past them both, rolling my eyes. Nothing looked surprised. I patted his cheek and winked at Cutter, "I'll fill you in later," I said low enough for just him to hear, Cutter grinned broadly at me and laughing, shook his head.

I was beginning to live for these moments with these guys. The light hearted smiles and laughter no matter how dire the situation or circumstances surrounding us. I felt like I had been adopted into their tribe or something, and I was beginning to understand why this life of theirs appealed to them so strongly. It was starting to appeal to me, even though I had no fucking idea exactly how I fit into it, but hell, that had been me my whole life up to this point anyways, why change it up now?

We stepped out onto the raucous causeway that was Bourbon, glittering Mardi Gras beads, crunching broken and derelict under foot. Nothing kicked a red Solo cup out of his way as we moved up the sidewalk en masse. I trailed a bit behind the boys, off to Cutter's left when a hand shot out from a bar and pulled me by the wrist, slightly off balance.

"Give us a kiss, Princess!" a drunken frat boy exclaimed. I found my center, brought my elbow up and cracked him in his nose, blood spurted and he let go, bringing both hands to his face. I pivoted and clipped him in the balls sharply with my knee.

"I ain't a friggin' princess, Bitch. Keep your hands to yourself." Cutter looked down at the boy, gaze gone still and icy and I touched his arm.

"It's cool, I got it," I said. Cutter nodded but squatted down next to the twenty-something. He murmured something to the kid and the kid started nodding frantically. Cutter stood up and spit on the ground inches from the kid's face.

"It's worse than Ft. Royal on Spring Break," Atlas commented.

"Bet he'll think fast before touching another girl out of turn," La Croix's voice was lovely dark and deep, I would say a la Barry White if I weren't looking at a white guy standing in front of me.

"Probably," I affirmed. We'd resumed our path of travel to the van La Croix had brought us all down here in.

Cutter took my hand and squeezed, and I squeezed his back. His fingers found the spaces between mine and we made it back to the parking lot without further incident. Ruth got behind the wheel, chewing on the stub of one of his Cubans. I sat practically in Cutter's lap.

"Where to?" he asked.

"Hotel," Nothing and I coursed in unison.

"Jinx, you owe me a Coke," I told him and he cracked one of his rare smiles. Truthfully I wanted out of this dress probably worse than he wanted out of his suit. I settled back against Cutter and kicked my feet up into Marlin's lap. It was the only way to sit comfortably when you were sitting bitch. Cutter sighed and it sounded suspiciously content which made me smile. I tried to relax despite my tension.

I couldn't do anything again, I'd done my bit. I wanted a shower, some more practical clothing and to ride out and sit on the house myself. Cutter smoothed his hands up and down my bare arms. I pressed my head back into his shoulder and rolled my eyes up to look at his face. He looked down at me and smiled and I melted a little on the inside. I think he and I would be taking second watch together and you know what, I was totally okay with that.

CHAPTER 24

Cutter

I let us back into number six and shut the door behind us. I swept Hope up and down with my eyes and smiled slowly. Second watch was a few hours away and she needed a bit of a distraction, really I just wanted to get her messy before she got into the shower.

"I want you to blow me," I stated and she turned around sharply, looking me over, "Put more of that red lipstick on first."

I dropped onto the foot of the bed and she raised an eyebrow… she looked at the clock on the bedside table and her shoulders dropped. She went into the bathroom and refreshed her lipstick. Watching the creamy, smooth red of the cosmetic coat her lips had me achingly hard in my jeans… Damn. Hope was a walking fantasy. I wanted to see how far she would play along with my desires.

"Stop," I ordered when she turned around and reached the threshold of the bathroom doorway. She looked at me expectantly and I felt my lips curve into a smile.

"Crawl," I uttered and a deep fire lit in her eyes. She slowly went down onto her knees, and I smiled.

"Oh that's a good girl," I praised, "Take down your hair."

She reached up, her eyes never leaving mine, and plucked the pins holding her hair in its French twist at the back of her head. The connection we had going on was electric, thrumming back and forth between us like high tension power lines were strung up between us. Her hair uncoiled and fell around her shoulders, shiny and thick, looking soft to the touch and my breath eased out of my chest in a shuddering sigh.

God damn it Hope was gorgeous. Breathtaking, heart stopping and if I had anything to say about it completely mine. I swallowed, my mouth watering at the sight of her, this passionate wildcat, on her knees waiting for my command.

"Crawl," I whispered.

Hope dropped to all fours and her dark eyes went darker with so many things unspoken. I could see this turned her on and that turned *me* on. I sat back on the bed and watched as she stalked, slowly and deliberately across the carpet on all fours. The short, skintight skirt of her dress riding up, showing me the tops of her thigh high stockings and the gorgeous curve of her ass off to perfection.

Fuuuuuuck.

She reached me and I raised my eyebrows at her when she paused, she put her hands on my knees and smoothed her hands across the top of my thighs. I leaned back onto my hands to give her better access and she smoothed one hand over the hot bulge of my cock, the other working the tongue of my belt out of the buckle. I swear to fucking Christ she purred, humming her approval when her hand moved over my Johnson and that just made me hard to the point of pain.

She undid my belt and laid it to either side, making agonizingly slow work of my button fly. I barely breathed, and it took everything I had not to jolt when she lifted me free of my jeans. She turned those fantastic, cut obsidian eyes up to me, which were rimmed to maximum effect by her smoky eye makeup. I was a drowning man and I didn't want to be saved, those ruby red lips of hers curved into a wicked smile plaintively heated with her desire before she stretched them lovingly over the head of my cock.

Holy Christ. I thought she was a phenomenal kisser? Her kiss had nothing on how she gave head. She teased me, she tantalized me; she drove me fucking wild. Her lips were like satin her tongue like silk and I think I about fucking died. I gathered her hair in my hands and she tripped, I don't really know how to describe it. She froze for a second in her ministrations. I held her hair gently back from her face and she rolled her eyes up to meet mine. One was covered by the side sweep of her bangs and holy shit... It was one of the dirtiest, most erotic things I'd ever looked at.

Her, mouth stretched wide, red lipstick staining my cock, eyes dark and heated. I held her still by her hair and carefully tested the waters, thrusting in and out of her mouth gently; never breaking eye contact the whole time. Her eyes eventually drifted shut and she stilled, concentrating on timing her breaths, moaning around my dick. Oh shit, it was shameful how fast I was gonna go, but I couldn't help it, even though I really, really wanted to hold off.

"I'm sorry Baby, you're just too much," I grunted and she fucking gave me this devilish little smile and I came, pouring down her long and slender throat. She swallowed and I swear to Christ I felt it around the head of my cock and so I backed off. It wasn't my goal to choke her or cause her any discomfort. Her eyes were watering, her makeup blurring around the edges and for a fraction of a second she looked like this beautifully broken doll and I felt a surge of savage little boy glee that I was the one to break her.

I let her hair go, untangling my fingers from it gently, I didn't want to pull it right now. Maybe later but not right now. Hope sat back on her heels, thighs parted, and I got a real good look at the dark stain of her wetness on her satin panties. Oh yeah. I was very grateful for my fast turnaround.

"Take my boots off," I ordered and Hope looked up at me, she smirked a wicked little curve of just one side of her lips and swallowing hard, pulled first one, then the other off. I nodded and shoved my jeans down over my hips and let her take my pants. She took my socks right along with them and my girl stood up. I curved my arms around her lower back and pulled her to me, resting my chin on her stomach as I gazed up at her.

"Did I give you permission to stand up?" I asked softly.

She gave me a dark look full of lust and hands gripping my shoulders, shook her head no.

"Turn around and bend at the waist. Brace your hands against the dresser," I ordered. She turned slowly in the circle of my arms and did what I told her.

"Good girl," I breathed.

I took my time unfastening her garters, pulling off her panties, then took my time doing the garter and hose back up. She was almost at the perfect height in the heels, bent over like this, I nudged her feet shoulder width apart and she dropped just a little lower. Another nudge and she widened her stance just a little bit... perfect. I smoothed her skirt up a little so it rode a little bit higher on her back. Her beautiful flower open and glistening, throbbing with a want for attention.

I let fly and smacked her on the ass, the crack of my palm against her pale skin where she wasn't tanned, reverberating perfectly; echoing back at us from the hotel room walls. My palm stung, and I rubbed it against the perfect, red raised handprint I'd left behind and had to smile. Hope panted, breathlessly and writhed a bit and I was ready again.

"I'm going to fuck you against this dresser and you'd better not fucking come until I tell you to," I said and Hope let out this desperate groan. I had her right where I wanted her.

I pressed myself to her wet opening and slicked the head of my cock up and down her slit, making sure to tease her clit, get it wet with her cream, I'd need it that way.

"Oh my God, Cutter, please! Please just fuck me!" her voice was strained and desperate and music to my ears. I gave her a matching handprint on her other ass cheek and before she was done registering the smart from it, pushed in deep.

God, she was heaven on earth.

She all but yowled her pleasure, tightening down around me with damn near bruising force as I pumped my hips, crashing into that fine ass with a heated slap of flesh. Her hipbones cracked into the wood in front of her and she braced herself harder, rocking in her heels. I didn't back off. I didn't want to and truthfully, with how hot and slick she was, she didn't want me to either.

This was pretty much all but confirmed when she drove herself back onto my invading cock and cried out, "Harder!"

I was all for it, driving into her, the hotel television wobbling precariously on the surface of the dresser. Hope cried out, breathing ragged and sharp and picking up pace, she tightened down on me that much more and gave the first telling ripple around my head that she was on the edge, on the verge of coming and on the very edge of coming hard.

"Don't you come yet," I put just the right amount of threat

behind the words then bent over her and let my fingers do the walking. I found her clit with the middle one and put myself in her deep, teasing the pearl and stilling inside her. Hope cried out, her legs were really shaking now and the only thing keeping her up was the press of my body against hers, holding her trapped between me and the dresser.

"Don't you come, Baby, not yet," I breathed and she gave a little sob. She was right on that fucking edge and I was a cruel bastard. I was going to drive her over. I had her set up for failure and she knew it. Her breath sawed in and out of her lungs and she was trying so hard to not pitch off and over the edge of that cliff that I relented.

"Beg me," I demanded.

"Oh God! You fucking asshole!" she cried and I shoved into her just a little tighter, my cock twitched and she cried out.

"Please!?" she begged, "Oh God, Cutter, please? Please may I come? Please let me come! Oh God!"

"Say the words, Sweetheart," I intoned and with a frustrated little cry she did...

"Please may I come? Please oh, God, *I'm begging you!*"

"That's my girl! I said and gently set my teeth into her shoulder, I disengaged them and teased her clit a little more mercilessly.

"Yes, come for me Hope, I want you to come," I told her and with a wail she came apart so fucking beautifully I couldn't hold back any more if I wanted to. I let myself go and went sailing off into the ether right along with her.

CHAPTER 25

Hope

We parked alongside Pyro and Radar's bikes which were at the top of the street, set back in some tall grass. Rusty, his hand in a black cast and sporting one hell of a shiner nodded but wouldn't meet mine or Cutter's eyes.

"They're up by the house, I'm just here to watch the bikes," he mumbled.

"Thanks," Cutter said and I followed his lead, giving Rusty a short nod. Apparently once justice had been met out in the MC world, shit got dropped. The circles were too close for grudges to be held for too long.

"Go on back, Rusty, we can take it from here, Trike will watch the bikes." Rusty nodded but didn't budge from his watch. Cutter tugged me along gently and I followed him.

We crept along the side of the road and when our house was up next, slid along the outside of the tree line down the drive. A whistle that could have been a bird if it hadn't been like three am, trilled off ahead of us and to the left. We arced around and came up on Pyro and Radar crouched in the dark. Radar slapped at a mosquito on the back of his neck.

"It's quiet, there's at least a couple of dudes…" I focused on the house and let Cutter take his man's report. It was still and quiet. Most of the windows had heavy shades or drapes over them. The back ones were blacked out completely as if they'd been painted from the inside. The deep blue glow of a television set flickered around the drapes in one of the front rooms and a deep masculine cough drifted out from one of the cracked windows to the room.

"How many men?" I asked. Pyro, Radar and Cutter all looked at me and it must have been something Pyro had just said. I gave them a look that clearly communicated to stop looking at me and just answer the fucking question and Pyro shifted uneasily.

"Three that we've seen," he said and I nodded, turning my attention back to the house. Cutter's hand closed around my forearm, grasping me gently. I looked at him.

"Baby," he breathed, "We gonna have a problem with you going OFP?"

OFP, a Marine term, it meant Own Fucking Program. I considered my answer carefully and gave him the truth.

"I don't know…"

Radar snorted, "'I don't know' ain't exactly an answer that inspires confidence, Chick."

"I know, but it's an honest one… that's my *sister* in there," I pursed my lips and tried valiantly not to say anything that would make me sound like any more of an incompetent cunt.

"I get it," Pyro said, "If it were the Captain or any one of my brothers in there, I would burn the house down around their ears but you can't go it alone." Pyro did this bouncing squatting walk to get right up next to me and leaned his shoulder against mine pointing.

"See there?" he directed and swung his finger, I followed his line of sight, "And there? That's some high end fuckin' surveillance equipment for a private residence. Top notch shit." He was right, those weren't cameras you would find at your local Radio Shack. I sighed out.

"They patrol the outdoor perimeter every fifteen minutes. It's best we watch 'em the rest of tonight on through tomorrow," Radar said. I nodded and they went over a few more things. I paid attention this time and pretty soon it was just me and Cutter.

"Relax, Sweetheart, we'll figure it out. I promise," he murmured, and the best part about that was, I believed him. I nodded and took a look through the field glasses Pyro had left with us. We were on until just past dawn but before the light started coming up, we needed to move. In the dark of night this was a good vantage point but during daylight hours? We needed to find somewhere else to keep an eye out.

It showed up in the form of Hex and Nothing, just as things

started to get light enough to become sketchy. They rumbled up the road in an old 70's camper van that was wheezing and choking, which conveniently sputtered and died at precisely the right vantage just past the old house's drive where there was a gap in the trees in front of the house.

Hex and Nothing got out and made a great show of lifting the narrow hood, fanning steam out of their way and talking about what to do and this and that. Cutter and I made a break for it and made it back to the bikes just as someone started shouting at Hex in thickly accented English about moving his fucking van. Cutter and I waited in the grass, tense. He looked through the field glasses and chewed the inside of his cheek as our boys and theirs had some kind of exchange.

Finally the tension eased out of Cutter and he breathed out, "They're staying with their van. Russian went back in the house."

"They're good then," I said.

"Yeah but for how long? Swear to Christ that boy has some kind of a death wish," he muttered and I watched the two figures of Hex and Nothing get back into the van.

"Come on, let's get going," Cutter said and Trike took the binoc's and put them in his saddlebag. We pushed our bikes back down the road away from the house a good ways before firing them up and heading back to the hotel.

We grabbed some food and took it back with us. Sleep was a long time coming but we needed it. I lay in the air conditioned hush of the cheap motel room, the nude length of my body pressed against Cutter's, my head resting on his chest listening to the steady thrum of his heart and I was wide awake, my mind working in overdrive.

Finally, with a harsh exhale, Cutter was up and over me. His fingers curling around my wrists pinning my arms over my head as he settled in between my thighs, hips moving, looking for purchase. His mouth covered mine, and he swallowed my sound of initial protest and before I could buck or make another, he found what he sought, the length of him sinking inside of me. My initial second attempt at any noise protesting what was going on changed mid voicing into a moan of desire.

I was a little sore from our tryst earlier on and that just added a certain dimension to what he was doing now. His grip around my wrists loosened and he smoothed his hands over mine, palm to palm. His fingers found the spaces between mine and we locked hands which brought another moan out of me. I opened my legs, twining them around his, tangling myself with him until you couldn't tell where his body left off and mine began.

This round of sex wasn't rushed or hurried, if I had to describe it, I would say it was fierce but gentle. I loved the feeling of his skin against mine, the taut planes of his back beneath my hands, as he stroked every place that counted both inside and out.

"Mmm, kiss me?" I begged and he did. I tangled my fingers in his hair and held him to my mouth, drinking him in deep. Soon his thrusting became, hard and fast and wild, as if our kiss were the match to ignite the kerosene inside either of us.

"God I love the way you make me feel!" I gasped and was rewarded by one of the most dazzling smiles I'd ever received from him.

"Just the beginning, Baby," he murmured and God was it true. He made love to me until I was too tired to think, which I think was his whole intent in getting things started in the first place. Problem was, it was having the unexpected side effect of making me love him just that much more… this man who took care of me, took command of me, who turned me on and turned me inside out like *nobody's* business.

We slept, and woke sometime mid-day to Cutter's burner cell ringing. He picked it up off the nightstand and flipped it open.

"Yeah?"

I could hear clearly, Atlas' voice from the speaker, "Yeah Captain, lap dancer just showed up and went in, was in there maybe five minutes. She just took off."

"Shit, any movement?" Cutter asked, I'd stiffened in apprehension upon hearing the news myself, he was on my wavelength, speaking my thoughts aloud.

"No, Sir. It's business as usual, whatever the fuck that is for these assholes."

"What time is it?" Cutter asked.

"A little after thirteen-hundred." Christ, we'd had around four hours of sleep. Not enough, but better than none.

"Call us if there's any movement."

"Aye Captain," and the line went dead.

"Sounds like they're still in lockdown," I mused.

"Yeah, think it's time we crashed their party. You up for it?"

"Hell yes, when do you think would be a good time to do it?"

"Dusk sounds about right, guess we'd better sit down and make some plans."

I nodded against his chest and debated with myself, finally sighed and pushed off of him, struggling to sit up in the tangle of sheets and legs. I looked down at him.

"Thank you," I said, chickening out at the last second. He traced a thumb lightly across my cheek and smiled softly, searching my face with his gaze as if he were committing it to memory.

"Any time," he murmured.

He knew. I saw it plain as day, that he knew that by 'thank you' I meant 'I love you' and it was as clear as the bright blue sky outside that by 'any time' he meant 'I love you too' so why was it so damn hard to say the fucking words out loud?

Because to say it now was to admit out loud that the situation we were going into, that he was following me into… that only one or neither of us might come out of. Which was bullshit, but true and heartbreaking none the less. I rested my forehead against his and closed my eyes.

"Don't do that, Sweetheart," he murmured.

"Do what?" I asked.

"It's gonna be fine, we're going to get in, get her out and get gone and it's gonna be fine."

I pulled back just enough so I could nod, "Yep, so let's get planning to give us the best chance of accomplishing all of those goals in that order, shall we?"

"Sounds good, grab a shower and pack your shit. We need to go for a clean break," he said and I slipped from the bed.

I showered and dressed and while he was in showering I packed my bag. I was as dressed for the occasion as I could get. Combat boots, black of course, my black tactical pants which were none the worse for wear, but could definitely stand to be washed after this go around of wearing them. I slipped on a fitted black Under Armor brand long sleeved heat gear shirt and tucked it in. It was made of a thin, lycra or nylon type material designed to vent and keep you cool, wicking sweat and moisture from your skin and dispersing it for quick evaporation.

I liked it because it took up barely any space in my bag and it was pretty damned good at its job. We'd worn similar in Iraq and while it wasn't perfect, it did the job. Of course there was only so much you could do in that hot box when it came to keeping cool. Likewise in the oppressive heat and humidity here in New Orleans.

Cutter put on something pretty similar, although where I looked like I was trying to participate in the summer gothic weight loss program, (wear all black all summer long guaranteed lose fifteen pounds,) the coloring he donned was much more… I don't know… hunter chic.

He wore some desert issue combat boots and a pair of cargo pants in the classic civilian deer hunter camo. He pulled a long sleeved olive green tee over his head and tucked it in. Over that, he shrugged into a brown leather holster. While I tucked my Ruger into my inner pants holster at the small of my back, he tucked a big bad .45 something or other under his arm.

We silently went about strapping on weaponry, which for me was just a knife along the outside of my thigh, but for him was a whole lot of knives. I blinked and watched as he tucked them in just about every pocket and added holsters to the outside of his calf and one to each wrist and one to the opposite thigh from the one he'd strapped to his lower leg.

"I take it this is where you actually got the name Cutter?" I asked.

He grinned at me, "Where'd you think I got it?"

"Truthfully with all the maritime stuff I thought you took it from the type of boat, you know like a Coast Guard Cutter."

The corners of his mouth turned down like he was impressed at my line of thinking, then he spoke, "Naw, got it because a motherfucker pissed me off, so I cut him up."

"Adorable," I commented dryly.

"Was still dealing with a lot of the shit from over there, wasn't exactly in my right head back then," he fixed me with a look like he was waiting to see what I would do or say so I left my sarcasm at the door.

"Who the fuck am I to judge? I'm the one about to march the lot of you into a house full of Russian mobsters with every intention of killing them all so I can extract my drugged up and probably fucked up sister."

"Yeah, and we're the crazy bastards who are excited to do it with you," he said.

"You know I once saw this quote on the internet, I think it was by I wanna say Nanea Hoffman, I remember the blog had a funny name... Anyways, it said 'When you find people who not only tolerate your quirks but celebrate them with glad cries of "Me too!" be sure to cherish them. Because those weirdos are your tribe.'" Cutter barked a laugh and I couldn't help but chuckle with him.

"Okay, I take it you feel like me an' my rag tag crew are that for you?" he said and I smiled broadly.

"You know it," I told him.

"I'm glad, Baby," he said and pulled me against him. We hugged for a long minute and with a sigh broke apart before getting back to rounding up and packing up the rest of our shit.

"You ready for what we might find?" he asked.

"Nope. Not in the slightest," I said honestly, "There's no way anybody can be prepared for something like this. You can talk yourself up, convince yourself that the worst shit you could possibly think of is behind those doors, but once you see it, you know that whatever you convinced yourself of is nothing but a pack of lies. Like what processed cheese is to real cheese. This is going to be ugly, and what we're about to do is going to be ugly. That's just the way it is."

"Jaded ain't you, Sweetheart?"

"Isn't that part of why you love me?" I asked, holding my breath. I knew I was fishing here but I couldn't help myself, I wanted the admission so badly.

"Yeah," he said, looking me over, "Yeah it is. You're real, Sweetheart. That's exactly why I love you."

I let out my breath and nodded, "Let's go get my sister," I said.

"Sounds good to me," he smiled and held the door open for me and I hefted my jacket and helmet with one arm and shouldered my pack with the other, slipping out into the slightly overcast day.

Seemed like the Louisiana sky decided it wanted to match my mood and the circumstances we all found ourselves in and I was totally okay with that.

CHAPTER 26

Cutter

We stood around one of the gaming tables at the Voodoo Bastard's clubhouse and looked over the sheets of butcher paper. Atlas had roughed out the property on the surface of one sheet and we were deciding how best to proceed.

The cameras were a problem. We didn't know if they were closed circuit or not and we were waiting on some communications from one of the Voodoo Bastards who was a security systems guy by day. He'd been texted some pictures of the cameras and it was going to be one of the deciding factors on how we played this. Cameras or no cameras we wouldn't be going in flying colors. The whole point to this was to get in, get the girl; get out and to go the fuck home.

Ruth's phone rang and he wandered off from the table and returned a moment later, "Not closed circuit, the feed goes somewhere off site. My guy says it'll be easy to jam the signal, he can be here in a few hours with a device."

I shot Ruth a thumbs up and we made plans on how to breach the place. It was a white, one story house, pretty sizeable. Maybe a two bedroom one bath. There wasn't really any telling the inside layout from the outside. What we did know was there were two doors, one in front and one in back. A long drive to the left of the house as you faced it, led right past it and into the back yard where there was some kind of outbuilding, from what we'd been able to see, which wasn't much, it looked like it could be a two car garage.

The front door had a broad front stoop painted red, with some brick accent columns about knee height at the bottom and two more waist height at the top of the step. It was a bottle neck at the bottom before widening some at the top. Still there was only room for about two men on the front step and the back wasn't much better.

The back of the house had a thin decorative iron rail around the back stoop. The advantage was the back windows, even though there were a lot of 'em, were painted over from the inside. So we may not be able to see in, but they couldn't really see out either. Some of the local boys had some guesses to the layout of the house based on their experience living in some of similar make around these parts all their life.

Hex and La Croix both agreed that the back probably went right into the kitchen, the bank of windows on three sides to the right of the kitchen door was probably what passed as a dining area. No telling if there was a wall or just an archway leading into the living room from there but they cautioned us to look sharp and try not to shoot our own boys if we breached front and back simultaneously which was the plan.

I looked across the expanse of table at Hope who was a study in concentration and tension. She wanted to go and she wanted to go *now* but she was hanging in there. She met my gaze and gave me a cool nod and I gave it to her back.

Before we rode out, we split into teams, I would go in the front with Pyro and Marlin. Hope was taking the back with Radar, Atlas, and Beast while Ruth and his boys secured the outbuilding.

Trike would keep the crash truck running and watch the bikes along with one of the Voodoo Bastard's prospects and we would try and keep this neat and clean. Like I said, we wanted to get in, get out and get on with it. Nothing was our rear guard, and was on watch to alert us to any incoming trouble from the road, cops included. All of me and mine were retrofitted in body armor from the crash truck. Hope was making due with a vest a size too big but it couldn't be helped, at least it was black and matched the rest of her.

I adjusted one of the Velcro straps on my tan vest and tightened it up. We were riding out in three vans with the crash truck bringing up the rear and each of us were as strapped as you could make us. There was no riding through town with as armed and ready as we were and not drawing attention so cargo vans rented under assumed names was the way to go on this one.

We loaded up and rode out, Hope and I agreeing that it was in our best interest to divide and conquer in this instance. I wanted so badly to be able to watch her back but I trusted and believed in my guys. They would watch her six as if it were my own and if they didn't, well then they knew the consequences of that. I wasn't going to have it any other way...

CHAPTER 27
Hope

Adrenaline started to surge through me as soon as the door on the van shut. I used every bit of my training to quash it down. Deep, steady breathing, it helped until we turned onto River Road in Saint Rose, then my heart picked up again.

"Okay, their signal is gonna be jammed as soon as you throw back the doors," Ruth's security guy, Spec turned around in the passenger seat and smiled, waving a device with a switch on it no bigger than an RC car controller and looking suspiciously like one. I nodded and pulled my Ruger. We rolled to a stop and Spec threw the switch, I looked forward, Radar nodded, I nodded back and he threw open the van door. I was out into the deepening twilight with Atlas and Beast riding my six. I hit the ground and moved swiftly. A man came around the side of the house as we strode down the driveway and I rose, aimed and fired in one fluid movement. The shot hit center mass and he flew back. As I passed him I put one in his forehead just to be sure.

Shouting in the house, Beast passed me and we heard Cutter's cue. Fast and faster, that was how this needed to be done. Beast let fly with a massive booted foot and the door flew open on its hinges. I followed his breech and put one in each man sitting at the table to my right before they even got up and that's when shit got real. A bat or stick or something crashed into my arm from above, my nerveless fingers dropped the Ruger and I let muscle memory take over.

I ducked and came at him up and under, my shoulder connecting with his solar plexus, but this was bad. Real bad, I needed to back off. Disengage before he got me. Shouting, screaming, guns going off in the front of the house but I was engaged and in it to win it. His elbow crashed down between my shoulder blades and *fuck* that hurt! I went down and Atlas or Radar, one of them popped him. He jolted back, once, twice a third time before falling to his knees in front of me.

I rose, knife drawn and ran it across his throat for good measure. I moved past him deeper into the house, I kicked the door directly in front of me open and plastered myself to the wall to the side, Radar had his gun raised and at the ready but lowered it. I ducked around the corner and looked into a bathroom done in god awful turquoise. A girl, maybe mid- twenties was crouched in the bathtub hands raised shaking and crying. Not my sister.

"Stay down," I told her.

Radar passed me up and lined up to breach the next door, I could see Cutter just past him waiting for Marlin to breach the last door up the hall. I nodded and Radar and Marlin let fly simultaneously.

These doors were padlocked from the outside. I went in low since I didn't have a gun, Atlas right on my ass, aiming for corners, he fired at the dude in the center of the room and I felt wet rain down on me as my knife buried deep in his groin. Blood, hot, slick and wet ran down over my hands and he fell back, crashing like a felled tree. There were two girls to either side on dirty twin mattresses. The dude in here with them was obviously sampling the merchandise which made my gorge rise and stab him a few times out of pure fury and hatred.

The two girls in this room were crying the one on the right trying to cover her naked lower half with her hands. I looked at their faces, really looked and finally the one on the left looked back. We froze for an instant...

Faith...

My sister's aquamarine eyes stared out at me from the days old cruddy makeup smeared around her eyes. I sheathed my knife and held out my hands to her and realizing they were bloody, did my best to wipe them on my pants.

"Faith..." I tried and she stared at me with confusion. Her pupils dilated to where there was barely any color.

"Faith?" I tried again and went to her and she started to cry again.

Big wracking sobs that hitched her too thin shoulders in her dirty skin tight dress.

"Hope, is it really you?" she asked and I nodded emphatically.

"It's okay Bubbles, I got you. I got you now, I always got you, Sis," she collapsed into my arms and I dragged the dirty, dark wig off her hair. Her blonde tresses fell free, equally dirty and brittle like straw and I felt tears burn the backs of my own eyes.

I stood up and dragged my sister with me, her arm over my shoulders. She was so *light*, painfully thin and malnourished and I wanted to kill some more motherfuckers. I wanted to scream and to shout my rage into the sky but *Faith*... I had my sister in my arms again.

"It's okay, I got you, Bubbles; these men are here to help, easy..." I helped her out into the darkened living room, the only light source the busted in front door.

"Awe fuck," I heard and looked up into Cutter's face, which was equally devastated by the horrors we were taking in.

"*Marlin!*" he boomed and Faith jolted in my grasp and started to cry harder.

"Easy, it's okay!" I soothed.

Marlin came around the corner from the kitchen, "Yeah, Captain?"

"Tend to the girl, you're the only one with the experience for this," he said and I followed my man's gaze to the inside of my sisters arm, to the black and blue scabbed over track marks and the infection taking hold there.

My vision flashed on and off and the blood roared in my ears, "Awe shit," I heard Marlin exclaim and the slight weight that was my sister, her easy burden disappeared from my shoulders. Marlin had scooped her up, arm under her knees and around her back and had lifted her easily as if she were light as air, he strode for the front door, Pyro right behind him and Cutter caught me as I went to go after them. I blinked, overcome, bent at the waist over Cutter's arm and vomited.

"It's okay. Come on Babe, let's get your shit together. We ain't done yet," he said and he was right. We weren't.

"How many?" I inquired and wiped the back of my hand over my lips. Beast was there and handed me a bandana I wiped my mouth and looked up at Cutter.

"How many?" I repeated.

"Seven girls, five guards. You took out all five almost all by yourself," he sounded proud and I barked a bitter broken laugh.

"Died too quick," I said and straightened.

"Don't disagree, Sweetheart,"

A feminine bleat of fear and a shot rang out, we all jumped. Ruth came out of one of the rooms behind us I stared at him, he looked regretful and heaved a sigh so big there just were none bigger.

"Too far gone, I know the look. Never would have made it through detox. Sometimes death is the kinder mercy, Darlin'," I blinked, long and slow.

"What about the other girls?" I asked.

"We'll get 'em cleaned up," La Croix shouldered past us with another in his arms and soon it was a steady stream of victims being carried out to the vans outside.

Shaking, I stood there and blinked when Pyro ducked back in, "You find the junk?" he asked.

"What?" I asked.

"The drugs, did anybody find the drugs?" he asked.

"Yeah," Hex held up a plastic sandwich bag, smaller little glassine bags filled with off-white powder coming a third of the way up.

"Gonna need some of that, Man," Pyro said.

"What? What for?" I asked, numb.

"Tell you later," Cutter said and gave Ruth a raised eyebrow.

"They gonna need it to wean your Sis off it," Ruth said and told Hex, "Hand it over Man, there's plenty more green to be had other ways. Let's get this mess cleaned up." Hex tossed the bag to Pyro who passed it off to Atlas who ran it out the front door.

"Cleanup is my area," Pyro said and he pushed back further into the house.

"Come on, Sweetheart."

I let Cutter lead me outside, my arm beginning to throb and

fucking ache fiercely now that the adrenaline was wearing off. I sucked it up and moved out. Halfway up the drive there was a shout, we all froze and turned. A neighbor, a fucking neighbor the next house over, a pond separating the properties.

"Go, on... we got this," Ruth declared and Cutter hauled me back to the vans. We got in, the door rolled shut and the van lumbered into an awkward three point turn, the road too narrow to pull a full U-turn.

I sat on the metal floor of the van in the circle of Cutter's arms, bracketed by his strong thighs and shook like a new born calf, my gaze fixed on my sister who was trying to push out of Marlin's hold.

"Bubbles, it's okay! It's okay! He's trying to help!" She started screaming and crying until Marlin finally let her go where she wedged herself into the back corner of the van, legs curled to her chest, shivering despite the heat. My gaze fixed on her ankle, to the raw skin there, flat and shiny and pink with scar tissue. Those fuckers... those fuckers had kept her chained, like a goddamn animal. I shook harder, this time with anger as I wanted to kill them all over again.

Someone was making soothing noises and a woman was crying, it took me a minute to realize that Faith was out of it and mumbling to herself and the woman crying was me. Those soothing sounds were meant for me too, uttered repeatedly by the man who held me fast. God wasn't this some seriously fucked up shit?

CHAPTER 28
Cutter

I waved my boys off the highway. I don't think she realized she was doing it but Hope wasn't even using both hands on her handlebars anymore. Her right she kept coiled against her chest. Had she been hurt and I hadn't realized it? I swore six ways to Sunday and led us off the interstate. We'd left Louisiana behind an hour or more ago but that didn't even put us close to home.

I pulled into the lot at a run of the mill roadside motel and shut off my bike, swinging a leg over. Hope was working the catch on her helmet with her non-dominant hand and wasn't doing awesome at it. I helped her get it off and double cursed my own ass. Her face was pale, a sheen of sweat coating her skin and her expression was drawn tight with pain.

"What hurts, Sweetheart?" I asked and she shook her head, shrouded in determination.

"What's up, Captain?" Marlin called from the crash truck, Hope's sister was curled up on the passenger side floorboard, Marlin's jacket and cut wrapped around her. Trike was riding Marlin's bike so Marlin could stay with the girl and monitor.

"Hope's hurt!" I called back and my VP swore.

Nothing pushed through the guys and bikes around us, he'd been a medic by trade once upon a time, before tossing in the towel after his wife and kid died. Now he just painted houses for a living. Waste of talent you ask me, but he didn't so I kept my mouth shut. He took Hope's hand gently and tried to extend her arm towards him. She grimaced and a tear snuck free but she didn't make a sound.

"Fuck this," I snarled and called out, "Pyro! Get us some rooms, I want Nothing to check this out."

"Can you remember what happened?" Nothing asked.

Hope licked her lips, "Must have happened at the raid," she said and shook her head defeated, "I don't remember when or what," she said and frowned, squeezing her eyes shut.

"A lot of heinous shit in that house, girl. Doesn't surprise me none," Beast said. Hope sniffed and nodded, wiping sweat off her upper lip with her good hand.

"Gotta wait until Pyro gets us a room so I can have a real good look at this, get her coat off, but I can already say this is going to need an x-ray, Captain." Nothing looked worried and if Nothing looked worried then it was definitely something to worry about. We stood around with our thumbs up our asses while we waited on Pyro, who finally came jogging back across the lot.

"They got enough rooms?" I asked.

"Yeah, some of us are doubling up," he handed me a key card and for once it was good to be King, or Captain as it was in this case, then Hope opened her mouth and blew any notion I had of some privacy with her out of the water.

"Better put us in a room with two beds," Hope said, voice strained and breathless with pain, "I just got her back, I'm not staying separate from my sister."

"Don't you worry 'bout that none for now, let's get you checked out."

We trouped into the roadside motel and went into the first room we had a key for. Nothing led Hope over to the little two seater table and pulled out one of the chairs for her. She obediently sat down and let him ease her out of her jacket while Marlin helped ease her sister into one of the beds in the room.

She was in real rough shape, the sister, shaking and jerking and just as fucking miserable as they got. Marlin had his hands full, but the determination on his face sealed the deal. He had every intention of doing right by the girl, I just couldn't help but worry that he might lose his shit a little in the process seein' as what he'd been through before. I worried about my brother but my girl's sister was in the right hands for her particular needs. I sighed and turned back to Hope who gasped in pain.

"I know, I'm sorry," Nothing said through gritted teeth. He was easing her black fitted top over her head, peeling the long sleeve down her injured arm so he could see it carefully, but there was only so much he could do with her arm lookin' the way it did. It was bruised so deep the result was black edged in a deep grape purple midway between her wrist and elbow. What's more, it was grotesquely swollen. Shit. It was broken just looking at it, didn't need no x-ray to tell us that.

"Pyro…" I started but he beat me to it.

"Already looking for the closest ER, Captain," and he was, nose buried in his phone, scrolling through some damn internet page or other.

"Okay, let's get a shirt on you," I said and was about to pull off my jacket and cut to give her mine to put something on her other than having her just sit there in her bra when Radar held out his plain white tee. I blinked and turned to look at him. He shrugged and I took the proffered shirt and let Nothing help ease it over her arm.

"Did you seriously just give me the shirt off your back?" Hope asked him.

"Yeah," he grinned and Hope smiled back, though it was pinched.

"Aww I've been adopted," she said and a chuckle swept through the guys. Faith let out a whimper and Marlin sighed loudly.

"Extra people, out! Get out, you're making this harder than it needs to be," he said curtly and the boys filtered out the open door and to their own rooms and shit.

"I'll ride with you guys, she can't ride on her own but she should be okay as a passenger. Best we can do." Nothing didn't look happy about it but he was right, short of taking the crash truck.

"I'll be fine," Hope said and shot a worried look over to her sister. Marlin was at the door speaking low and insistent to Trike sending him on some kind of errand run.

"Let's go," I ordered.

We rode to the hospital, Nothing and Pyro with us. Pyro stayed out with the bikes while Nothing and I took Hope inside. It was a chilly reception by the hospital staff, a couple of bikers escorting a wounded bird, but Hope set 'em straight.

"How did this happen?" she was asked by the nurse.

"I'm a defense contractor, my boyfriend and a couple of his guys rode with me to New Orleans where I was giving a training and demonstration, it's what I do for a living. Anyways, I was doing a live action demonstration and got hit with a Kendo stick, brought it down right on my arm, it was an accident. You can call Detective Joe Thibault, he was there," she said. She even started going through her phone to give them the number.

"That won't be necessary," the nurse said frowning, "You're an awfully long ways from New Orleans though; didn't this hurt?"

"Hope's Army," I explained and gave the nurse my best winning smile, "She'll always try to walk it off, I noticed her favoring it to the point she wasn't using both hands, made the call to bring her in."

"Well, at least she listens to sense," the nurse smiled and Hope gave her a tight one in return. They weren't busy which was good for us, Hope was taken right back into a room and was wheeled off to x-ray; much to her protestations that her arm might be busted but her legs were just fine.

She lay on her side, her injured arm tucked into her side on top of her body when the doctor came to see her.

"Well Ms. Andrews, all things considered it's not a really *bad* break, but it *is* fractured," he said by way of greeting and snapped the x-ray up onto the little room's computer monitor. I guess they didn't do film anymore.

"Great, what does that mean?" she asked.

"Only one thing for it, going to have to put you in a cast."

Hope groaned and the doctor chuckled, "Six weeks, preference on color?"

Hope glared at him, "Black, like your soul for telling me I have to wear a cast in the first place."

The doctor laughed outright, "Well, now, don't shoot the messenger…"

I half watched Hope and the doctor banter and half watched Nothing who was studying the x-ray with some intent, nodding to himself. He glanced at Hope when she made a childlike noise of protestation and a real unhappy face.

"What?" I asked.

"Ms. Andrews, I really recommend you take the pain medication, I wouldn't wish setting a bone without it on anyone," the doctor was frowning in clear disapproval.

"Fine," she grated out, sullen.

I think she was grateful she took it when he did what needed to be done. He put her in a cast which wrapped around her hand and thumb and went to her elbow and wrote a prescription for pain which I would have one of the boys fill for her. It was dicey getting her back to the motel, the drugs the hospital gave her making her both loopy and tired, adding to her already mounting exhaustion.

When we got back to our room it was to a whole lot of whimpering and whining coming from the closed bathroom door. Hope threw it open, her sister curled in a ball in the back of the bathtub, the water running but she was in here alone. Hope knelt by the tub and Marlin came through the motel room front door.

"Shit, was hoping to have this taken care of before y'all got back but it's been an ever loving bitch talking her into things," Hope glared up at Marlin and he put up his hands, a box of something in one and some kind of comb in the other.

"Not saying I blame her, just taking longer than I'd like. She's got head lice, I'm just trying to get her cleaned up is all. You up to helping?" he asked Hope.

Hope held up her casted arm, "Duct tape and grocery bag. Go! Go!" she said and it was cute as hell. She was loopy as all fuckin' get out but I wasn't about to deny her, not on this. She was the only other woman aside from Faith on our crew at the moment, so I took one of the latex gloves Marlin had bought as part of the head lice rid kit and pulled it over Hope's casted hand. I duct taped a grocery bag to that and covered the rest of the cast, duct taping the bag in a good seal to the skin of her upper arm.

"Thanks," she said, swaying on her feet.

"You up for this?" I asked.

"No one is ever up for this," she said somberly and I nodded.

"Out here if you need me," I murmured.

"Yeah," she said, "Not even gonna lie, I'm gonna need you after this," and then she took top spot for bravest woman I'd ever met, she marched unflinching into that bathroom with my VP and spent the next hour bathing her sister, dosing her long blonde hair liberally with pesticide shampoo while my VP did his best to help keep the fidgety junky victim still. Christ, what a mess.

At one point she booted Marlin clean out of the room, when Faith started getting a little too loud and a little too panicky. Didn't need someone in a neighboring room not knowing what was what to call the cops.

Marlin dropped heavily into the seat across from me, where I'd been fucking around with some damned game on my phone. I tossed the phone onto the table and gave my First Mate, my second in command, a hard once over.

"You good, Brother?" I asked.

Marlin scrubbed his face with his hands and pressed his fingertips into his eye sockets, "Hell no, it's like Danny all over again, except he wasn't half as pretty. You get a load of those eyes?"

"Naw, not really," I searched my brother's face, "I gotta be concerned that this is gonna be too much for you?" I asked.

"Yes… No… Hell, I don't know, Cap'n. Your girl know what comes next?"

"Don't think so, we'll have to worry about that when we get to it."

"I gave her some, but there was no telling how much they had her on. I don't want to overdo it, we don't need her ODing on us, but fuck… This is gonna get a hell of a lot nastier before it gets any better."

"How long you think?"

"Week, maybe two of the real nasty withdrawal symptoms, a full month or more for the rest of 'em. This ain't no quick fix brother."

"Yeah, I figured that."

"Had Trike hit the local Wally World and grab her some clean sweats, and some shit, hopefully at least clean she'll feel a little better."

"I can't even begin to know what this shit is like, you want I should call in a favor with the guys up North? Reave and his buddy Trig have some firsthand experience with this shit, that doctor of theirs might be of some help too…" but Marlin was already shaking his head no.

"No man, last thing that girl needs is more strange men around her, it's gonna be an uphill battle just for me to get up and over them walls," he let out a gusty sigh and I nodded.

"Round two?" I asked when he heaved himself onto his feet.

"Yeah, after I have a smoke."

Marlin let himself out of the room and I sighed. He was right, there was no quick fix for this shit. I closed my eyes and listened to the wretched sobbing coming from the cracked bathroom door, and the soothing sounds my girl made as she tried to fix up her busted sister. It wasn't pretty in any way, shape or form.

CHAPTER 29
Hope

I lay staring across Cutter's gently rising and falling chest at my sister perched on the edge of the bed next to ours. She was sleeping the sleep of the exhausted, her brow drawn down, creased with some nightmare as she lay curled on her side, facing us. She was in an oversized tee shirt and some black stretchy yoga pants that were still a size too big for her but were better than the filthy stained dress we'd found her in.

Marlin and I had gotten her cleaned up as best we could but he'd had to put more of that poison in her veins to calm her the fuck down. I didn't blame her, but it broke my heart and killed a piece inside of me to see what kind of a state she was in. Marlin and I talked about it. He seemed to know his shit and he'd finally shared exactly why he did and my heart broke all over again, for him this time.

When Faith had gone all dreamy eyed and out of it and we were sure he hadn't given her too much, we'd been able to take stock of what was what with my sister. She was a mess. Bruises on her arms where she'd been held were bad, but the bruises on her thighs, that'd made me murderous all over again.

She was malnourished, lice ridden, track marked and some of *those* were infected. There was no telling if she had any STD's but probably. I prayed that whatever she did have, when we got her checked out in Florida, that it was all shit that was treatable. I was terrified she had HIV or Hepatitis, both from the rapes and from the needles they'd been shoving into her flesh.

"Hey… shh," Cutter's voice was low and soothing as I choked back a sob, stuffing the back of my hand into my mouth to try and quell it. It made Marlin look over from where he sat behind my sister, back against the headboard, arms crossed over his chest, legs straight and crossed at the ankle in front of him. He looked like some kind avenging guardian sitting behind my sister like that and I was grateful for it. That her situation tripped all his protective instincts because just after trying to bathe her and get her fixed up I knew beyond a shadow of a doubt that I just wasn't equipped for this. I didn't have the first clue on how to fix this. I was fucking lost without these guys.

Cutter's hand smoothed up and down my back, and he made soothing sounds like I was some messed up child and for once, I let myself be just that. I let him hold me, and comfort me and believed the lie, "It's gonna be okay…"

I needed to believe it, not just for me but for Faith and even Charity. Oh God. Char. I hadn't called her, hadn't told her we'd gotten Faith back but looking across at Faith, shit. I couldn't call Blossom just yet. Not when I was staring at this tweaked out broken junkie girl wearing my sister's face. I couldn't. I just couldn't. I mean, I knew I had to but I didn't have to *right now*, did I?

"Hey," Cutter nudged me.

"What?" I asked looking up at him.

"Whatever you're thinkin', just stop. This whole mess is gonna be here when you open your eyes, Baby. We just gotta take it one day at a time. You get me?"

He jostled me a little, gently, when I didn't answer right away, I startled and agreed and his words somehow made it bearable again. He was right, there wasn't anything I could do about any of it right this second. I closed my eyes but sleep was still a long time coming.

When I woke, I felt like shit. My sister looked like shit, Marlin looked like shit and Cutter… well he looked rough around the edges too. We all moved around the room slower than usual and I stood with some serious misgivings while I watched them load my baby into the back of the crash truck. They had some apparatus on there to keep her upright and they ratchet strapped her in place, still, I was pissed I couldn't ride.

Instead, Cutter helped me into my helmet and I got on the back of his bike. I wasn't good to drive but I would be damned if I couldn't ride. Besides, I didn't want to crowd Faith and driving the crash truck didn't appeal to me in the slightest. Selfish moment? Yeah. Yeah it was.

Marlin gave me a nod, my sister was in the seat this time which was an improvement over yesterday's floorboard adventure. She stared at me through the passenger side window and put her hand to the glass. Cutter pulled us up even so I could put my hand over hers. I held up three fingers, the classic sign for 'I love you' and she did it back. She looked so haggard, so worn and tired and like everything sparkly and vivacious about her had been strip mined out of her and I felt helpless.

The ride back to Florida was a fucking long one after that. We had the better part of a day ahead of us, we'd only been about an hour out of Louisiana when we'd been forced to pull off for my lame ass the day before… or was it earlier today? Man everything was such a mess. A jumble of time, too much happening in too short a span of time and the days just blurred together. I had no idea what time it was let alone what day it was. I knew the sun was out, but that was about it.

I hugged myself to Cutter's strong, lean back and let the vibration of the bike, the rushing wind and the blur of pavement beneath the wheels lull me, almost hypnotize me. It didn't help as much as I would have liked.

I knew when we crossed the Florida state line, not by any signage but by the guys popping off their helmets with joyous whoops. I even brought mine off and the fresh blast of wind in my face, man was it nice. I let my hair whip back in the wind and it was like it blew out the cobwebs some. Reviving, that was the best way to call it.

"I want to check on my sister!" I shouted and Cutter nodded. He held up his hand and shot a series of hand signals and we started dropping back in the pack. I hugged my casted arm around his waist, my wrist through the chinstrap on my helmet. We rode alongside the crash truck's passenger side and I reached up my left hand. The window rolled down and my sister reached down and we clasped hands for as long as we could.

"I love you, Bubbles!" I shouted over the wind and a ghost of a smile teased my sister's lips. She laid her head down on her arm and Cutter gunned it just a little bit and the link of our hands was broken. I held onto my lover and he took us back up front to lead his crew. It was still an hour and more to Ft. Royal.

When we hit town, hand signals were thrown and some of the guys started peeling off to go to their respective homes until finally it was just me and Cutter, Trike on Marlin's Harley, and Marlin and my sister in the truck. We rolled up to the house we'd all left from and the ride from hell was over.

I stood and stretched and Cutter did a few last minute things before shutting off his Indian and getting off of it himself. I was already helping my little sister down from the truck.

"It hurts," she whimpered and I frowned.

"What hurts?"

"Everything," she moaned.

"She's Jonsing for a fix *hard* right now," Marlin said coming around.

"I want it but I hate it and I don't know what to *do*, Buttercup," Faith was whining and it broke my fucking heart.

"Come on Sis, let's get you inside and figure out what to do from there," I looked at Marlin over my sister's head and he nodded, the sigh he heaved unmistakable.

"Take her on up to the master bedroom," Marlin called after us.

I helped my sister and the guys let me do it and as soon as we were in the house my sister hissed at me, "Hope, who are these guys?"

"Easy there, tiger. They've gone above and beyond helping me get you out of there. I've got questions too, like what the fuck happened?"

My sister whimpered and we took the stairs slowly, one at a time as she moved like an old woman. Like her entire body was arthritic and pained her.

"That bitch, she sold me, Hope... Tonya *sold me...*" and then she started to cry and I really didn't feel so fucking bad that the bitch had met her end, in fact, I found myself sort of hoping that it'd been real slow and painful, terrifying even. What kind of bitch did that make me? A vengeful one. That's what.

I got Faith into the big king sized four poster bed and got up in it with her. I held her hand with my good one and we lay facing each other. She wept, big wracking heaving sobs and I held her, smoothing her tangled, brittle blonde hair back from her face. The fucking drugs they kept pushing on her had ravaged her, I was terrified beyond repair. I fingered the black leather cuff bracelet that her two thin wrist practically swam in and wondered what it meant. I'd never seen it before. It was a wide brace of leather, with an old fashioned key-hole plate riveted to it.

It had been on the closed lid of the toilet when she'd been in the bath and she'd had an epic freak out, panicking and screaming, thrashing when I'd swept it into the plastic grocery sack we were using as a trash bag. Marlin had immediately gone for it with a baleful look in my direction, and had spent the next five minutes convincing Faith that it was okay, that it was there and that no one was going to throw it away. We had to keep it in her sight or she would have a whole new meltdown over it and as soon as we'd gotten her out of the dirty bathwater with drowning head bugs in it, she'd snatched it to her and had held onto it for dear life.

I tried asking her again now what it was, why it meant something but all that did was set her into a fit of crying harder. So I lay still with my sister until she'd cried herself to sleep and sighed. I didn't know what to do. How to help her. Fuck.

"C'mere, Sweetheart. Marlin and I need to talk to you," Cutter murmured from the doorway. I slipped out of bed and left Faith sleeping and went down to the kitchen with them.

"I don't know what to fucking do," I confessed and rubbed my eyes.

"That's what we wanted to talk to you about," Marlin said.

"I'm all ears, shit… start talkin'," I told him.

"Marlin here is confident he can get her physically better, I pulled another favor with the SHMC up North, got one of their members, a bona fide doctor coming down to check her out. Bloodwork, and the more unpleasant things that go along with this kind of thing."

I nodded wearily and Marlin and Cutter exchanged a look, a look I didn't like, "What was that look for?" I asked, immediately on the defensive.

"Now, just hear us out," Cutter said softly. I gritted my teeth and nodded slowly. I mean fuck, hadn't these guys earned at least that much?

"I want to help your sister, I have some experience with this kind of thing, I can get her clean. Now I gotta ask, have you ever been with a junky kicking dope before?" Marlin was giving me a rather intense once over. I shook my head.

"First week is going to be hell on earth, for her but also for me as she goes through the physical symptoms of withdrawal. I'm talking vomiting, diarrhea, excruciating pain, begging, pleading… it's not pretty Hope."

I swallowed and nodded, but I couldn't look at either of them, "What do you need me to do?" I asked.

"That's just it, I need you to do nothing," he said and he fixed me with an intense look.

"Wait, what?" I frowned.

"I need you to go upstairs, kiss your sister and go with Cutter and stay the fuck out of this house for a week, you get me?"

"Oh no, I can't do that." I was shaking my head emphatically and Marlin crossed his arms.

"I mean it, I need you to trust me on this, the first week or two is the worst, the physical withdrawal is… well it's something you don't need to see. Your sister is going to be a complete basket case. She's going to be going through shit you can't possibly imagine and you don't need to be here for it. She isn't going to want you to be here for it. Trust me."

I was shaking my head softly back and forth. I wanted to reject everything he was saying. I wanted to be here for my little sister like I always had been. I swallowed hard, eyes welling.

I would fight him on this. I would, but then Cutter's voice cut through my unreasonableness, "Why haven't you called your littlest one?" he asked, and I jolted.

"Because she doesn't need to be here for this part," I said and

Cutter came to stand right in front of me, he put his hands on my shoulders and I looked up into his sorrowful face.

"Neither do you, Sweetheart. We've helped you this far, Baby. I know you're tired and I'm telling you, your sister may hate you for a minute for you not being right physically there but I promise, she's gonna be glad you weren't when it's all over.

"Shouldn't this be up to her?" I asked softly. I was seriously torn by now and Marlin sighed.

"Right now she is craving that shit with every fiber of her being. She wants it so bad, just to make the pain stop that she'd do anything for it. Pretty soon she'll come to the realization that she ain't got no way to get it, then the real begging is gonna start. The kind where she starts begging you to kill her. Trust me, Hope. We've all seen the lengths you're willing to go to for your family. It's part of why we like you so much. We're glad you're with the Captain here, but *you're with the Captain now*. Which means you're one of us and you're our family now, too. You ain't gotta carry this alone. Let us help you."

It was a moving speech, it really was but... "Faith is my sister, she's not a burden, she never has been, but she is my responsibility – " Cutter cut me off.

"Babe, you aren't listening to Marlin here, she's *our* responsibility. You only thought you were joking when you cracked that you'd been adopted," he shook his head, "You have, you really have, you're mine, Hope; and I'm tellin' you, you ain't gotta do it all by yourself."

"Is it really going to be that bad?" We whirled and there was Faith, leaning hard against the wall where the kitchen started.

"Not gonna lie to you, Baby Girl, it's gonna be that bad and worse..." Marlin said and his tone more than anything put me at ease. It was low and soothing but more than that, when he spoke to my little sister it was deferential.

Faith got teary, dashing at the moisture on her lashline with her fingers like she used to when she was little and had scraped her knee and my fucking heart broke all over again.

"It's up to you, Peanut," I said and sniffed myself, "I went through Hell in gasoline boots to find you, I never gave up and I'm not giving up now. It really is up to you. I'll do whatever you want."

My sister pursed her lips and looked like she was having a hell of a time deciding, she was lucid for the time being but who knew how long that would last?

"Does Char know you found me yet?" she asked finally.

"Not yet, Babe, I gotta call her."

"Don't. I don't want her to see me like this, I don't want *you* to see me like this... Let me get better first, please?"

I cracked, little pieces of me tinkling to the floor and the tears ran free. I nodded and it killed me, letting her go. Letting her be all grown up.

"I'm not going anywhere, this is a small town, Faith. You change your mind, you need me, you tell Marlin and I'll be here. You understand me?" She nodded a bit too rapidly and came to me then, we hugged each other fiercely and cried.

"About two weeks," Marlin said, "For the absolute worst of it, one but two if you want to be out of feeling physically crappy... the emotional part takes a lot longer. A month, month and a half... although you got a lot more going on than just addiction issues on that front." Marlin didn't sound happy at all to be delivering the tough news but I appreciated him for it. So did Faith, I think. She pulled back and nodded.

"Okay, when does this start?" she asked bravely.

"Now," Marlin swallowed hard and looked a little green around the gills, I could tell this was going to hurt him too. Fuck, what a goddamn mess. The whole thing.

"We'll stay on the Mysteria Avenge," Cutter said, naming his boat.

"Can you go by the Scarlett Anne for me, Bro? Pick me up some clothes and shit?" Marlin asked.

"Yeah, let me get Hope settled and will do. You hang in there, Firefly," he said to my sister and she nodded. We hugged one last time and I swore I would be doing a preemptive lice treatment, we'd be swinging by a pharmacy on the way to his boat. I loved my sister, lived for them both, but the head bugs and the thought of getting them made my skin crawl. I couldn't help it.

"I love you, Peanut," I whispered and Faith shook, so frail, and whispered it back...

"I love you too,"

Leaving my little sister in the care of someone else at a time like this killed me. Destroyed a part of my soul I wasn't ever going to get back. I followed Cutter out to his bike and he asked me...

"Need anything?"

"Yeah, swing by the local pharmacy, then take me home. Do whatever it is Marlin needs you to do and then get your ass back to the boat because I can't be strong forever and I'm under some extreme load here."

"I hear you, Sweetheart. Come on, let's go."

He took me to the pharmacy, he took me to his boat; he kissed me hard before he went to run the other errands that needed to be done... It was the most agonizing alone time I'd ever spent... waiting for him to get back to me which was rough for the girl who was always alone, who was used to carrying it all and all by herself. It was real damn rough.

CHAPTER 30
Cutter

I made record time, leaping across docks and boats to the other end of the harbor to Marlin's sport fishing vessel he lived aboard. He was right across the harbor something like ten slips away and yet most of the time he and I were on opposite ends of the planet, which truthfully had never bothered me until now.

I knew Marlin was a standup guy, knew the tragedy he'd come from and how much it affected him, still, my girl had a lot riding on this. On him succeeding this time. I threw a bunch of his shit in a duffel I found randomly in one of his cupboards and slinging it over my shoulder, locked up and dashed back across everything.

I rode back to my house and found Marlin and Faith sitting across from each other in the living room, talking quietly. Faith looked scared, and I didn't blame her. This was bullshit. Hardcore bullshit that she had to go through this on top of everything else. She looked blasted apart, freaked out but her aquamarine eyes held that glint of stubborn, a subtle flicker of that fire her sister Hope held inside.

"You cool, Firefly?" I asked her and she nodded, not quite looking at me. That was cool.

"Thanks, Man." Marlin nodded.

"Doc an' them should be here in the next day or so, I don't know if he's flyin' solo or not."

"Aye, aye, Captain," he said but he was distracted, his full attention on Faith.

"You call you need to tag out for a minute. Nothing's got medical training, said you could call him."

"I got this," he said and I gripped his elbow he looked at me then.

"I mean it, you tap out if you need to; you feel me?"

"Copy that, Sir."

I let him go.

"You hang in there, Firefly; see you soon."

She nodded, and I left, I didn't want to leave Hope for too long. I rode home and put my bike up in the garage. When I went below deck I found Hope exactly as I'd left her, slumped on the arm of my couch, staring off into space.

"C'mere, Baby," I murmured and pulled her by her good hand up and into my arms where she crashed and shattered into a million pieces. I held her tight, held her close while the storm raged and like any rainstorm, I waited out her tears patiently because what else could you do?

"Some tough bitch I am," she muttered brokenly after she'd been calm a while.

"What do you want to do?" I asked her softly.

"You're gonna love it," she dumped her bag from the drugstore out on the couch, boxes of pesticide shampoo falling out and bouncing to the floor.

"Preemptive measures?" I asked.

"Full tactical assault," she affirmed.

"Hell you know I'm all about those…" and so that's how we spent our first night as a fuckin' couple with her moved into my place. Drinking beer and shampooing and combing the hell out of each other's hair looking for any stray head lice accrued from her sister.

Ain't love fuckin' grand?

CHAPTER 31
Hope

I closed my eyes. It had been years and years since anyone had combed my hair for anything other than a precision trim. I'd forgotten how relaxing, how meditative it could be. Cutter's fingers were sure but very gentle as he combed my hair carefully. Since it was less likely that he had anything I'd done his first. Not so much as a nit.

"Anything yet?" I asked and my voice sounded dreamy and relaxed. Between the hair combing and the buzz I had going on from my beer, I wasn't in a bad place right now, but leave it to Cutter to make it better. He pressed a kiss to the back of my shoulder, I sat on his floor wrapped in a towel, peeling the label off my beer, holding it awkwardly in my casted hand.

"A few," he murmured, "No eggs that I can tell, I think you're safe."

"Hmm," I huffed a laugh, "My hero," I said softly. He drew the comb through the long strands of my hair, and I sighed.

"Hell of a way to get you moved in," he commented dryly.

"I don't recall agreeing to live with you," I said and took a deep swallow of my beer. I wanted to. I wanted to put down roots so bad but I was afraid. I wanted to maintain my independence too. I felt like I was relying on Cutter entirely too much by this point. I wasn't, nor would I ever be, a woman who couldn't handle her own shit.

"Let's get something straight, Sweetheart. I said you were mine back there and you didn't disagree so that makes you mine."

"Oh, does it?" I asked amused but my temper was also getting a good start, fueled by alcohol and the sense that I was somehow being cornered. Except how could I be cornered into something that I *wanted*?

"Yep," he cradled me back against him and pressed his lips a little more insistently against my skin, and of course he had to say the one thing that would unravel me completely...

"I love you," and just like that I came completely undone all over again.

I took a deep breath and fought down the welling tears but he'd more than earned it, more than deserved me saying it back and so I said, "I love you too," my voice cracking.

"Oh, Sweetheart," he tugged on me and I stood up, turning around. He pulled on my towel and it fell to the floor and with a final guiding tug he pulled me down across his lap, I straddled him, and his towel was very much in the way.

His arms snaked around me and our lips met, carefully at first, then more insistent, hungry then ravenous, we devoured each other. I loved his wandering hands on my body, how they teased me how they gripped my ass and the appreciative and very enthusiastic noise that occurred *when* they gripped my ass. He pulled me tight up against him, one arm pinning me against his body the other teasing my pussy, fingers rubbing, looking for a way in though he couldn't see what he was doing the way he had a hold of me.

I held my casted arm against me, my other hand tangled, fisted, in his long, damp hair as our mouths attacked each other. The fact his towel separated us quickly became infuriating. Cutter reached between us and gyrating his hips shoved the terrycloth out of the way and in a perfect moment of synchronicity pushed himself so I could glide down over the top of him.

I moaned into his mouth as he filled me and sighed in satisfaction as he became fully seated inside of me. He broke the kiss just long enough to look up at me. He leaned back and with a soft sigh said, "Take your pleasure Baby, I wanna watch you move."

So. Hot.

I rode him, slow and deliberate, never breaking eye contact, and the depth of the emotion in his eyes left me breathless. He talked me up, his voice low and intense telling me things every woman wants to hear but never really believes. He told me that I was beautiful, that I was tight; that I felt so fucking good. That he loved my body, that I was everything good, and perfect for him and when he spoke, I listened and I couldn't stop myself from *believing* him if I wanted to.

It heightened the experience like nobody's business, a warm glow suffusing me from the inside out until I felt positively radiant. When his hands smoothed over my skin I tightened around him and it brought me that much higher. When his thumb found my clit, gently stroking, teasing me there, the world stopped spinning, the universe held its collective breath, my pussy gave a deep, satisfying throb and all that time that stood still, caught up all at once and I was spinning, hurdling back to earth, beautifully free falling through space and time and sensation, until I came back to myself, safe in Cutter's arms.

God damn, orgasms with him were the most intense thing I had ever felt in my life. I shuddered with little aftershocks as he held me, blinking stars out of my vision, yeah, stars, as in blotches and fire bursts of color swimming across my vision, obscuring the room. My head lay on Cutter's shoulder as I panted and his arms held me to his body. I was up on my knees and he took full advantage of that, thrusting lazily but evenly up inside me, drawing out the crashing waves of my orgasm until they gently lapped at my edges, the tide of intensity receding gradually.

"Holy God!" I half gasped half groaned and Cutter chuckled.

"Can you hold onto me? I want to finish this in my bed," he murmured into the side of my neck, kissing me there, lips, tongue and teeth worrying at the erogenous zone, sending a wash of tingling bliss skittering along my edges, washing over my skin.

It took me several moments to get my shit together enough to wrap my arms around his strong shoulders in any kind of grip that left him secure enough to lean forward and propel us up with his strong legs. The cast on my arm made it awkward at first and I thought for sure I was going to slide off him and crash through the coffee table at one point, before he got his hands under my thighs and hitched me up so I could wrap my legs around him.

He slipped out of my pussy and I mourned the loss for only a moment but then we were moving, Cutter striding with some serious purpose and intent up the narrow hall, the cool wood paneling brushing my knees to either side of him as he propelled us towards his bed cupboard where I was pretty sure he had every intention of fucking the last bit of sense I had right out of me for the night.

I was on board, in fact, as soon as he set my ass on the edge of the mattress I made to pull myself back, into the bed. Wrong answer. Cutter wrapped his strong arms around my thighs and pulled me back towards him and the edge.

"Where the fuck you think you're going?" he asked, an edge of humor to his tone.

"Not going to finish what you started?" I asked.

"Oh, I always finish what I start, Sweetheart. I'm just finishing it my way."

He pressed into me from his standing position and I let my arms fall above my head in supplication, back arching. God he felt so damn good. Filling me, stroking all the right places, rough, slow, it didn't matter this man was every kind of hot and then some and was a god with the way he used his dick. Cutter laughed, a bright rich sound that coated my soul in warmth. Such a sexy sound. I sighed, arching.

"A god, eh?" he asked and I giggled. Had I said that out loud?

He bent over me and kissed my mouth, slipping in and out of me at a sedate pace that just stoked my fires higher.

"Harder, please harder," I begged, breathless with need. Cutter laughed again, a low, deep, dark chuckle and it was just such a turn on. I mean, his laugh turned me on like nobody's business and I'd never encountered that before. His hands found purchase at my waist, above my hips, where he held me tightly so that he could drive himself into me and *oh* like that! Yes, just like that!

I was boneless, voice lilting as I cried out with every deep thrust. It felt so incredible, and every time his body met mine, his cock went just deep enough to bottom out, to bump my cervix and that slight edge of pain was just perfect, giving such a sweet, intense sharp edge to the pleasure building between my thighs, pooling in my lower body. That heavy glow of impending explosive orgasm.

"Oh yeah, you're close aren't you, Sweetheart?" his voice was low and intense, I opened my eyes and met his which were positively molten, his expression set in lines of concentration.

"Yeah," my voice came in a breathy, girly gasp and I didn't even care. I could be something soft, something feminine and sweet, I could be a woman with Cutter and he wouldn't hold it against me later when the clothes were back on and I had shit to take care of. He wasn't like that with me, he was the only one who wasn't. I liked letting go for him, he made me feel secure enough to do it and that was pure magic on his part.

"Good, I want you to come, I want you to come all over my dick and then I'm gonna make you come again. You like that idea?" he asked, but he wasn't asking, he was telling me exactly what he was going to do and he already knew *exactly* how his words would affect me.

The sensations coiled tightly in my body sprang free with his words and I cried out, body tightening, shuddering, spine bowing backwards until just my ass and the crown of my head met the sheets. Cutter let out a triumphant whoop and drove up into me with a renewed vigor as my body fluttered and pulsed on the inside.

"God I love the feel of you when you do that!" he cried and he wasn't about to let it stop. He found my clit with the pad of his thumb, just when I thought I could begin my descent from the clouds, and with some gentle strokes, he brought me again, the pleasure and intensity of it bringing a shout from me. I came again and he made me come at least one more time after that and I had no idea how, but he just kept the orgasms *rolling*, until I was completely steamrolled flat in his bed and didn't care what he did. I think that had been his entire plan in the first place.

He pulled from me, and I knew he was soaked, I felt slick, drenched and it was all because he wrung me out so beautifully. He urged me to crawl up into bed and got up into it with me.

"Not done yet, Sweetheart. On your knees for me, Baby." I complied and he knelt behind me. He shoved into my soaking cunt and I guess I wasn't completely out of it because I shoved my ass back at him, meeting his body with mine. I arched low and moaned loud and almost missed it when he opened the cupboard beside him. A plastic clack, the lube was cold between my ass cheeks, against my asshole but I was close to coming *yet again* so I really didn't care.

"Tell me if any of this is too much," he murmured and his voice had gone from demanding, to velvet wrapped steel. Warm and alive, his tone genuinely concerned and loving, I don't know how... but it somehow added sensation to what was already going on with my body. I squeezed down on him, close, so close and I couldn't believe it but I wanted to come again so badly.

He teased the pad of his thumb against my asshole and *oh wow*, close and closer still... and then he pressed in carefully and breached my opening and I came all over again. Hard and fierce I shivered violently, collapsing onto my chest gasping. His thrusting slowed and eased and he rode me out, withdrawing from my body slowly as I shook and quivered a beautiful nerveless mess.

"Ready to try this?" he asked and I could only nod dumbly. He murmured sweet things, encouragement, yes, but also gave me an out, as he continued to play with my body, working me up to the girth of his cock. He really wanted this, the idea really turned him on and admittedly, I had never had a good experience with anal but holy god... this was different. I'd never felt anything quite like this before and it was *good*. A tingling wash swept down my entire body from the back of my neck to the soles of my feet, wrapping around and teasing me from the inside out, sparks of pleasure flitting along my nerve endings like will-o-the-wisps.

He pressed his cock against me and slipped in, stretching, there was a bit of discomfort, my body spasming a time or two around him, trying to adjust. He murmured a suggestion and I obeyed, pushing out against him and he eased his way in, slow, deep and the sound of pleasure that rumbled from his chest had me sighing and relaxing further. He took his time, moved slowly, took such tender care not to hurt me, but it didn't hurt. It did just the opposite.

"Oh my *god*..." I heard myself say but I couldn't be sure it was my voice. I was in a euphoric haze, like I was riding out the longest, softest, purest orgasm of my life. My whole body floated and it was a little bitter sweet as I recognized that this was one of those moments that sure, subsequent times would be really fucking good, but there was nothing as awesome as your *first* time. I recognized that in this, and oh my god, I was determined to enjoy it, to ride this out as long as I could because it felt incredible.

Cutter was amazing. He moved slowly, his stamina beyond fucking compare. He took his pleasure now, at his own pace. From the feel of his long, leisurely, strokes he was in no hurry to come. He would ask how I was doing every once in a while, and I would try to pull it together long enough to moan but I was in that place between worlds now, loving every minute of it.

"Don't stop, God please don't stop," I whispered and he made a satisfied hum, his hands stroking leisurely over my ass, my hips, up my back in a sweeping arch to my shoulders and back to my hips.

"Oh, Baby, oh Hope, I can't help it, I'm gonna come," he said, voice breathy and almost as euphoric as my own when I found it. His hips jerked and he came inside me and it felt so, deliciously *dirty*. I loved it, he slowly and carefully pulled out and smoothed his hands over my body one more time as I giggled and just sort of keeled over onto my side, panting. My legs were numb from kneeling so long.

Cutter lay facing me and gathered me to his chest, kissing my forehead, which made my eyes drift shut. Reverent, cared for, *loved*, that was what his kiss made me feel in that moment and it was all I had ever secretly longed for… It was a powerful spell he wove over me.

"Jesus Christ that was good," he uttered when he had mostly caught his breath.

"Hmmm…" I hummed gently, words were not in my forecast just yet.

"C'mon Baby, let's get you cleaned up, I'll change the sheets while you're in there and tuck you in, wash up myself and be back before you know it." I nodded reluctantly. It needed to happen, it really did.

"Be right back, let me get the shower heated up for you…"

He left me and I dozed lightly, I wondered if I were going to be sore tomorrow… then I lazily drifted from that thought to wondering if I would care. He came back, made me drink some water and helped me into the shower. It was a pain in the ass holding my cast out of the spray but I managed a good wash and rinse of my body and only mildly got my hair wet.

Cutter was a man of his word. He had the sheets changed and the bed ready when I got out. He dried me off, tucked me in and kissed me with that same reverence of before and I melted. I couldn't ever remember a time when anyone took such care of me...

He kissed me, and smoothed my hair back from my face, "Back before you know it... I wish my damn shower were big enough for two. You good?" he asked.

I smiled, "I'm good," I whispered drowsily.

"Okay, back in a minute," he promised again and I was alone.

I lay in the soothing dark, lulled by the sound of his small shower and the water lapping against the hull of his boat, the gentle bob and sway of the vessel in the harbor. This was peace. I opened my eyes, I didn't want to fall asleep before he came back, despite how it sucked at my edges. Light from one of the portholes fell across the image of the sad girl I'd examined the first time I'd ever been in his bunk. I closed my eyes then. I didn't want to think about him with anyone else. Not after what we'd just shared.

I was barely, vaguely aware of him coming back to bed, he slipped in behind me and pulled me back into the curve of his chest, kissing the back of my shoulder with that same reverence, making me sigh and drift off more soundly, more completely into the deepest, securest, dreamless and probably most restorative sleep I had ever had.

CHAPTER 32

Cutter

She slept soundly, and I drifted off right along with her. The sun was streaming bright through the portholes the next morning when the sound of people boarding the Mysteria Avenge jolted me awake.

I carefully slid my arm out from under the curve of Hope's neck and slipped to the end of the bed. I pulled a pair of blue and white board shorts out of my cupboard without really caring and pulled them on. If it was some of the guys, which was likely, they didn't want a view of my junk. Not that I cared. I stood up and stretched, yawning and plucked a hair tie off the hook from under my cut, replacing it. I whipped my long hair into a low pony as I trudged the length of my boat just for the first knock to fall on the hatch leading above deck.

"All right!" I called out and flung it open.

A keen girly excited shout and I was stumbling back into my living room confused, the glaring light of the outside which had stolen my vision resolved into the smiling pixie face of Li'l Bit who was legs around my hips and arms around my shoulders.

"Hi!" she crowed and laid one on me, her lips as soft as I remembered, lush and warm. Her enthusiasm caught me off guard and I froze of a second, eyes wide, hands on her hips and the world lost focus for a second.

Damn. I was completely caught off guard. I'd wanted the woman in my arms for fucking ages, had been bitter as hell to let her go back to her man, to her life and now she was here, warm and enthusiastic and all I could think about was putting her down, putting some distance between us before…

"Eh he he hem…"

Fuck.

CHAPTER 33
Hope

Fierce, hot, intense and immediate. Jealousy ripped through me like a rocket propelled grenade. I finished buttoning the front of my black shirt dress and watched the man I loved, who supposedly loved me back, kiss another woman in front of me and I didn't have a damn thing I could really say. I reached down and pulled my flip flops out of the pocket on the side of my pack that just happened to fit the two pairs I had perfectly and dropped the black ones to the carpet by the bunk step.

I shrugged my feet into them while Cutter stared at the woman in disbelief and then it registered, not what I was looking at but *who*. Fuck. It was the sad green eyed girl. The one whose picture was taped, wrinkled and forlorn to the inside of Cutter's bunk. Where he could wake up to her image every morning and fall asleep looking at it every night... like I had last night.

Holy Christ. It hurt. Deep in the center of my chest, it fucking hurt and I just didn't have any room to process, to deal with it, so I did what I do best. I put on my resting bitch face and ghosted up the hall. I leaned my shoulder nonchalantly against the beautifully restored, wood paneled wall and cleared my throat.

"Eh he he hem..."

Cutter's eyes drifted shut and his shoulders dropped and I could see it written all over his face... *Fuck*. The woman turned her head and looked taken aback and blushed furiously.

"Oh..." she said and unwound herself from Cutter's body, sliding down him to the floor. I kept my face impassive. I wasn't going to fucking cry. It wasn't happening.

My phone started ringing, shrill, filling the weighted silence as the thump of another man boarding the boat, made the woman and Cutter both redirect their attention to the open hatch. My phone rang and rang and I went for it, pushing off the wall and reaching for it with my casted arm, which I really, *really* wanted to use to beat the fuck out of the man I'd let fuck me last night.

I picked it up off the table as Cutter drew breath to speak. I put my hand up and arched a brow coldly. I didn't want to hear it. Not right now. Not yet. I wanted him to save it.

"Hello?"

"It's Marlin, the doc from up north is in town, I'm taking your sister to the clinic to have him check her out and she wanted me to call you, wants you to be there for the exam."

"Location."

There was a pause on the other end of the line, "Everything okay, Hope?"

"Location, Marlin." I said and I knew I didn't sound okay which just made me want to leave more. Cutter and I were staring hard at each other across the short space between us. The atmosphere tense. The woman's head bobbing back and forth between us as if she were watching a demented tennis match.

"Pear Street, other side of the Boulevard, down two blocks on Vine."

"Copy that, en route." I hung up.

"Hope..." Cutter tried.

"Fucking save it," I snarled bitterly.

"Oh hey, it's not what you..." I glared the woman into silence and she rocked back, a dubious expression on her pixie-like face.

"Hope!" Cutter tried again but I'd snatched up my jacket which had my wallet and sunglasses in it and dug them out. I left the too hot garment to flop onto the recliner it'd come from and marched for the steep steps out the hatch.

I didn't have time to deal with my fucking feelings on this. Faith needed me and I could deal with it later. I shoved it down, and when that didn't work I shoved it aside and burst into the bright Florida mid-morning sunshine.

"Whoa, hey!" A dude with a light brown, almost faux hawk, with sparkling blue eyes and a row of switchblade patches on his vest put up his hands. He had a smart phone in one of them and looked like he'd just finished a call of his own. I blew past him.

"Hope!" Cutter called from the hatch, the woman was on deck behind me hugging herself looking like she was about to cry.

"Go fuck yourself, Cutter! Faith needs me," I leapt to the dock, chest heaving with uneven breaths borne of too much emotion. I didn't break stride all the way to the clinic.

I got there just in time for Nothing to pull up with Faith and Marlin in the back of what I presumed was his Subaru Outback, an older one, probably early two-thousands, that had seen better days. Behind them was a man on a Harley. He was older, wearing a vest like the guy back on Cutter's boat. A Sacred Hearts vest, I realized as he rolled to a stop. Shit, this was the doctor?

My sister was curled up in a ball on the back seat, staring sightless out the passenger side window of the Subaru. She didn't look good. Pale and sweating, brow creased with pain. Nothing got out of the driver's seat and was frowning at me.

"What's wrong?" he asked by way of greeting.

"Nothing," I said and he raised his eyebrows at me. I scoffed, "You know what I fucking mean," I said and scowled. I knew my tone was acerbic and I also knew that Nothing didn't deserve my pissed off but I didn't have time to apologize, but rather, just enough to change my attitude for when Marlin came around to help my sister out of the car. The older man came up while Nothing used a set of keys to let us into the clinic's side door.

"You the doctor?" I asked.

"You must be the sister?" he asked and I dismissed the skepticism. I was the tall, dark and fucked up one in our family. Didn't look anything like my sisters, my mom, and while he'd been around, my stepdad either.

"Yeah, I'm Hope."

"Doc," he said and he was smiling but it held the ghost of something in it, like the smile had once been something much more than what I saw now.

"Thanks for coming," I said.

"No problem, these boys did us a big boon not too long back, we owe 'em a whole lot more 'n a house call," he was looking me over, and nodded to himself, "You wanna talk about whatever it is, I *am* a doctor, may not be a headshrinker by schooling or degree, but I am fair good at listening."

I startled a bit and hoped it didn't show, "No I'm good, just look after my sister please."

He nodded, and turned to follow Marlin and Faith inside, he had to help her. She was moving like an old woman and I was betting the withdrawals were setting in hard core.

I followed the doctor, Nothing stayed outside to look out and warn us of trouble but the clinic was deserted. I wondered about that, but Marlin was talking.

"We have to hurry up some, the place is only closed down for two hours for lunch." He helped my sister onto the edge of the exam table and the room was already prepped for the doctor to do his thing. He slid his big black bag he had slung across his chest off, and set it down.

"Won't be needing that, you guys are good and stocked here, let me have a look at you if that's all right, Sweetheart," he said to my sister and the term of endearment made me close my eyes and count to ten. I needed to be strong, to be here for Faith. I stood at her side, and she held my hand and I held hers as the doctor looked her over.

He left me with her to help her into an exam gown for the pelvic and Faith started to cry. She hadn't said anything yet, and that was okay. I just helped her get into the gown and laying down. I cracked the door to give them the signal she was ready and went and leaned a hip against the table by hers. I faced my sister and gathered her hand up between mine while the doctor did his thing behind me.

"Remember the first time we did this ever?" I asked and she laughed brokenly, her aquamarine eyes swimming with tears, the clear liquid magnifying her eyes and making them luminous. My sisters both managed to remain pretty when they cried. Not me.

"Yeah," she said brokenly and jumped.

"Easy, Faith. Ready? Going to use the speculum now," the doctor was kind, treated my sister gently and with respect. He was good. I had to appreciate that.

My sister and I murmured back and forth, talking about that long ago first pelvic exam and even managed to laugh a time or two. She was so afraid, so broken and in so much pain that I couldn't stop the tears from leaking out if I wanted to. We cried together, the doctor paused.

"Faith, I have to ask you something..."

"Yeah?" her voice warbled pitifully.

"Honey, you ever been pregnant?" he asked.

My sister dissolved into tears and I saw Marlin just outside the door, stiffen through the crack in it. I held my breath...

"Yeah, they had some doctor come... they killed my baby."

I hadn't made them suffer enough...

Faith sobbed and shook and I bent over her and over the table and held her from the waist up while the doctor made soothing noises and finished what he needed to do. I let the tears drip hot and salty slick down my own face and didn't even try to wipe them or slow them. The doctor's tone had said everything I'd needed it to and Faith didn't need it up front and center any worse than it already was.

"Okay, Honey, we're all done." Doc murmured and he got up and went for the door, we exchanged a meaningful look and he gave me a nod and I helped my sister back into her cheap bargain store sweats someone had found her.

"Thank you for coming," she said and it was as if she were completely drained, hollow, a husk... nothing more.

"Faith, I will always come for you, you're my girl," I said and we hugged. I kissed her forehead and Marlin stuck his head in.

"We gotta go," he murmured. I nodded.

"Okay, I'll come with you," I said.

"No," Faith shook her head, "I really needed you for this part but Marlin told me what's coming, Sis; you don't... I don't want you there for that. I promise. I'll call when it's over." I'd never seen such a look of sheer iron will and determination on Faith before. She had always been my little party girl. Had never taken life, school, her grades, any of it seriously until she'd graduated... and had nothing to do and nowhere to go and no scholarship like Char to get her to the next level.

She'd had to waitress, take community college courses, take out student loans and claw her way into college and I had done what I could to help her... not as much as I could have or should have, which was why she had sought cheaper off campus living... which is why she'd met Tonya, which was why this was my fault.

I always had to be such a fucking hard ass and look at us now.

"Okay," I said finally and let Marlin take her from me. She seemed to have some kind of understanding with him. Which, that was fast, but who was I to bitch? I hadn't exactly been there for her before, we'd had some knock down drag out screaming matches. Fuck. Fuck me.

"Faith, can I talk to your sister about your results and what needs to happen?" the doctor asked her.

She nodded, "Yeah sure. I just want to go lay down, get this started, get this over with." My sister closed her eyes and swallowed and Marlin took her away from me, and I let her go. Against every single urge and raging desire I had to snatch her to me and never let her go again.

The doctor picked up his bag, and slung it across his chest and I followed him out. Nothing gave me a lingering look of concern as he closed Marlin and Faith into the back seat of his car but my last lingering look of longing and ache was all for my sister.

"Give you a ride somewhere?" Nothing asked.

"Nope. I'm good," I said and closed it down.

"Hope..."

"Take them back to the house please, Nothing. Make sure my sister gets there safe and make sure Marlin knows I *need* him to take care of her. Please? I need Faith to be okay before I'm good to handle my own shit."

Nothing nodded readily, "Yeah, no, you can count on us, Hope; you can count on all of us. Just take care of you, too."

"Not worried about me, worried about my baby girl," I sniffed and Nothing nodded.

"I'll call you and the Captain later, report," Marlin called from the back seat.

"Call me," I said and he nodded, Nothing got behind the wheel and the doctor stood beside me as I watched them go.

"Why did you ask about pregnancy?" I asked when they were gone.

He sighed, "There's scarring. Even if she got pregnant again she'd never be able to carry a baby to term... Those bastards really hurt your sister, I'm sorry."

I just wished I'd killed more of them. I didn't say that though. I wasn't about to admit to murder out loud, even if he was cool with back alley dealings like this.

"What happens now?" I asked.

"I wait here for the clinic people to come back from lunch and they let me run your sister's labs, Cutter has some kind of deal with them. We just wanted her to have as much privacy as possible. Far as anyone knows she's Faith Andrews."

"That's right," I agreed. My stepfucker's name had never suited either of my sisters. Of course he'd never treated either of them like he'd treated me, and my mom and the girls never knew about that. I scrubbed my face with my hands.

"It'll be a day or two for some of the tests, Cutter's fronting a lot of money to get her tests to the front of the line. Should know everything by the end of next week. I'll be here a day or two with Hayden and Reave. Cutter's putting us up at a local B&B, away from your sister, but I'll be on hand in case she needs another IV or methadone becomes imperative..." I kind of lost him after that. Tuned him out, while my brain wrapped around and around that name...

Hayden.

So that's who she was. I faked my way through the rest of the conversation and totally whooped my own ass on the inside for having to make him repeat himself on some things. I mean fuck I was supposed to be here for my sister, *focused* on my sister... But I couldn't help it. I had never in my life wanted anything more for myself than I wanted to try and forge something with Cutter.

I was so incredibly angry with myself. For allowing myself to be fooled into thinking that he could love me so easily, or that he would want only me... Gah... past insecurities, current events...

they swamped me, rolled me under and drowned me. I was suffocating, I was sick of it and so when I parted ways with the doctor at the clinic I did probably one of the worst things I could do, but fuck. I'd earned it. I went straight for the boulevard and for one of the nearest open bars.

Time to fight fire with fire. My sorrows wanted to drown me, well I was going to drown them right back.

CHAPTER 34
Cutter

"I'm so sorry, I didn't know..." Li'l Bit turned and looked at me and looked totally freaked out. It was about the thousandth time she'd said it and it wasn't freaking helping the situation.

"Not your fault, Li'l Bit... this whole thing has been a lot of flying by the seat of our pants since she hit town and we haven't exactly had enough downtime to set the rules," I said in a bid to make her feel better.

Hope had been and gone from the clinic and she wouldn't answer her phone for me. At first it'd rung and then gone to voice mail, so she was hitting the 'ignore' function on me. I tried to have one of the boys call her which ended in Atlas calling me back calling me all kinds of names for him getting told to fuck off.

It'd be funny if it didn't feel like I was dying on the inside. Despite the calm exterior I was going out of my mind. Thoughts racing, one careening through my head right after the other before getting caught in the track and looping around and around and around and fuck this... Just breathe. My PTSD was having a fucking field day, anxiety riding at an all-time high letting its freak flag fly and all those thoughts in my head funneled right on down to the unthinkable...

I'd lost Hope.

Reaver held Li'l Bit in his lap and turned her face in his direction, eyes sparkling, he whispered something to her and kissed her and she smiled and nodded. Worlds away from the broken and sorrowful angel she'd left as months ago. Finding out your dead husband was alive after six months of grieving him being gone, spiraling down further every day... well, it wasn't exactly something you bounced back from overnight.

Li'l Bit had left here with her man, my friend, and it looks like she was worlds better in a matter of just a few months. She pretty much oozed vitality. Put on weight and got her color back. Her sparkle and her fire... and while I was glad, I didn't really feel a damn thing for her. There was no more jealousy, there was no more envy... I looked at them now and I was genuinely *happy* for my friends and terrified at the same time that my shot at what they had, had just been blown clean out of the sparkling coastal waters in which we sat.

"You know how I know you're in love? Like finally met the real deal?" Reaver asked me.

"How?" I muttered, not really giving a shit what was going to come out of his mouth.

"You got the same look on your ugly mug I did when I thought I'd lost my Doll forever. Fuck man, this your first fight?"

"No," I said thinking back to our brawl in the sand.

"I think it is," Li'l Bit was smiling and she winked at me.

"Jesus Christ, you think you two are in love and you got it all figured the fuck out for the rest of us?" I asked.

Reaver and Li'l Bit exchanged a look.

"What?" I demanded.

It was Hayden who answered, "She's your air to breathe, your water to drink, your nourishment," she said and fixed those bright green eyes on me. I leaned back.

"Yeah, yeah I guess she is. It's like I'm missing an arm over here or something, not knowing where she is, knowing she's hurting..."

Li'l Bit smiled beatifically, "That was how Ashton explained it to me, about her and Trig. I didn't really know what she meant until Reaver," she looked her man in the eyes and just that act alone put a smile on her face, made her fucking glow from the inside out. He leaned forward and kissed her, holding her face to his, deepening the kiss by slipping his tongue past her lips and the thought that I might never do the same with Hope... fuck man. It left me gutted.

I knew, deep down, she wasn't going nowhere. I'd called Marlin and he had a hold of her sister still. From what he and Nothing told me she'd shown up at the town clinic and looked upset, and when they'd left, her agitation had been off the charts. I didn't know how my girl typically dealt with stress but if I had to hazard a guess I would bet it was punching something, which was out on a kind of her cast.

I had every man not workin' out looking for her right now and was just waiting on a call. Reaver and Li'l Bit stopped sucking face long enough to remember I was here and to rejoin the conversation.

"I'm sure she's fine, man. You said she could take care of herself."

"That's not the point bro – " my phone rang and I snatched it up.

"Report," I said by way of greeting.

"Yeah Captain, she's at Jacks at the bar and nursing some bitch drink," Lightning said.

"She okay?" I asked standing.

"Looks like she's been cryin', keeps glaring guys off. Doubt she's sober enough to effectively fend one off should they make any kind of real play but she's holding her own. Want I should bring her in?"

"No, don't try. Just sit on her and watch her back, I'll be there in a minute." I looked up, Reaver slid Hayden off his lap, stood and stretched.

"Aye, Captain." Lightning hung up and so did I.

"I think you should sit this one out, let me go down there, bet you I'd have a better chance of it than you would," he said.

"Oh yeah, how's that?"

"I'm not you, and I'm not Hayden. Hell, I'm not even Kraken. Neutral party… Come on. Let me give it a try."

I wasn't biting, but what he said next had me leaning back in my seat, he had me hook line and sinker with it. He said, "Come on man, you gave my woman back to me, delivered her safe and sound and took care of her… Let me return the favor; even though this won't even come close to what you did for us."

I rubbed my hand over my mouth and beard thoughtful, and finally nodded, "Alright man. Try not to take too long."

"You get some dinner going on the grill of yours, I'll bring her back here. The four of us will have a nice dinner and act like civilian grownups for a minute," he grinned at me and winked and I huffed a laugh.

"I'll help you cook," Hayden murmured.

"Okay, Li'l Bit can stay here, I'll run to the store and she and I will grill up some food. Surf or turf?" I asked.

"Surf," he and Li'l Bit said in unison and laughed.

"We get plenty of turf at home," he said and leapt down onto the dock. His running shoes making a soft thud.

"Yeah, kind of figured," I said.

"I'll bring her back, give me an hour. Maybe two if she's stubborn."

"She's definitely that," I agreed.

"If she doesn't try to kill me, I am so telling on you," Li'l Bit giggled.

"You don't need to give me an excuse to spank that ass, Doll. If you wanna insist you know I'll take you up on it though." Reaver pointed both index fingers at her about chest height as he walked backwards down the dock. He winked at her and dropped both thumbs down. She laughed high and bright and blew him a kiss which he caught and tucked inside his cut before turning and strolling away, up towards the boulevard.

"He won't let you down, you know. He'll talk her into coming around."

"It hurt her, Li'l Bit. It hurt her a lot."

"I know, Sweetie, I really am sorry, but if she didn't love you it wouldn't bother her and if she loves you she'll come back here and work it out. She'll listen to reason."

"I hope you're right."

She rolled her eyes and scraped her short bangs off to the side, "Of course I'm right. I'm *always* right about these things."

"Now who is gonna tattle on who?" I asked. She blushed and bit her lower lip, and I could tell the prospect excited her. Yep. She and Reave were doing just fine. A weight, a worry I hadn't known I was carrying lifted at that. She was okay. Reave was okay.

Good. I was glad for that. I really was. Now I just needed Hope to be alright and if that went down like it was supposed to, well then I would be right as rain. I really was in love with the bitch. Hopelessly in love with Hope. I smiled, it had a nice ring to it.

CHAPTER 35
Hope

I wanted a cigarette. I hadn't smoked in years but I wanted a fucking cigarette so bad right now. I lifted my glass and took a drink, sniffed and set it back down. I was pretty much done drowning my sorrows but didn't have any place to go just yet so I figured I would knock back a few more and maybe if I got lucky something would present itself. I wasn't exactly a stranger to picking up men in bars... except I didn't want that anymore. I wasn't up for a one night stand. I'd had a taste of something better, and I just wanted him now... except now I wasn't sure he would want me.

"Have another?" I asked dully.

A blur of light denim, black leather and beneath that, white cotton dropped onto the barstool beside me. I looked over at ol' blue eyes from Cutter's boat that morning.

"Think you've had enough," the bartender said looking me over.

"I'm inclined to agree but go ahead and give her one more, I got this," Ol' Blue Eyes winked at me and I huffed a half assed snarky laugh.

"Ohhh you couldn't handle me. Trust me, Baby Cakes," I said.

"You got someone who can though, don't you?" he asked and smoothed his hair down in front, so it formed a point between his eyes. It was a style that worked for him. Easy to manage but made him look real nonconformist and badass... of course the raggedy assed leather vest... excuse me, *cut*, he had on went a long way to perpetuate that image.

"Seems that guy can handle a lot of women, doesn't it?" I asked him and nodded to the bartender who set a fresh Cosmo in front of me. I took a sip. Ol' Blue Eyes smiled a crooked panty dropping grin at me which did absolutely nothing for my lady bits whatsoever.

"Reaver," he said ignoring my barb completely and he stuck out his hand before following up with, "Reaver Michaels."

"What is it with you guys and the juvenile," I frowned my brain catching up, "Wait, I thought bikers didn't do last names."

He was shaking my casted hand and I didn't remember giving it to him. He let me have it back, again with that grin, his sky blue eyes sparkling.

"It's my name. Well the Reaver part wasn't always, neither was the Michaels part. I took my road name and my wife's last name when we got married. You met her this morning."

I narrowed my eyes, it was taking way too much fucking brainpower for me to work that one out. I was fucking lit and I knew it. The nice part about being this lit is the rest of it was dulled, the ache was still there but it was less sharp, less raw.

"How about this, Princess? I'm going to tell you a story. You just sit back and enjoy your drink and have a listen." He looked me over and that's when I saw it. Sliding behind his eyes. He really needed me to listen, I just didn't know if I had it in me to carry any more people today. I sighed. Why the fuck not? I was pretty good at being some kind of big damned hero lately.

"Shoot," I told him and waved him on. If he was talking, then I didn't have to, which was probably a good thing.

"So I'm at this wedding, the girl getting married? My wife. Except she was marrying this total douchebag and I was gonna let her."

"You're joking right?"

"Don't interrupt."

I put up my hands and leaned back, I wasn't sure I was drunk enough for this, but he was continuing on, "I lucked out, and I know it's a shitty thing to say, but I did. The douchebag dumped her at the alter."

"Shit, that sucks..."

"Don't interrupt," he said.

"Sorry, except, you know, I'm not." I giggled. For some reason I thought that was hysterical. He grinned too, and shook his head and kept talking anyways.

"So I put her on the back of my bike and took her to her

honeymoon destination, figured she needed the dust to settle and the vacation was already paid for, so what the fuck? Why not right?"

He paused so I figured it was okay to speak, "Lemme guess, destination here?"

"Destination here," he said with a smile. Let me tell you something, for a guy I didn't know, Reaver told me a lot of shit. Enlightening shit…

"You did what?" I asked abruptly, I wanted to make sure I'd heard him right.

"We shared her. Take it you're not a fan?" he said.

Reaver let me stew for a minute, mulling things over. I'd never done two guys at once. Not that the notion didn't appeal to me, it was one seriously hot fantasy. More like the guys I had been with, I'd never been with long enough to find out if sharing was an option. Or if it had been, I'd never found another guy at the same time I was with one, that would share to make the fantasy a reality.

"Okay, so you guys shared her, you went home and did what? Got hitched?"

He nodded then said, "This is where shit gets real," and he didn't sound one bit happy about it. Something told me I wasn't going to like this and today had really been a shitty day, aw, what the hell? I waved him on. Maybe listening to this would make my damage seem like less.

The shit got real. Reaver spilled it, about being shot, about faking his death to get the women of his club to agree to stay out of harm's way, and how Cutter played Captain-save-a-ho, taking them all in. Including Reaver's wife… who thought she was a widow.

"What the fuck?" It was a rhetorical question but he shrugged laconically and sighed

"Listen, Sister. Six months was a long time for him to keep my secret and to take care of my Doll while she was falling the fuck apart. He told me he'd fallen in love with her, that he did love her, and when he gave her back to me, he told me I was a lucky bastard, which don't I fucking know it? Feelings like that don't evaporate overnight. Hell it's only been three months since I showed up down here very much alive, if not well." He lifted his shirt under his cut and exposed some pretty serious scars on his side. An entrance wound, with several surgical scars radiating out from it.

A pair of dog tags was also revealed but he wasn't military, never had been and never would be. I pointed at them, "And who do those belong to?" I asked.

"My best friend Trig, he and Sunshine wanted to come down too but their shop is too busy."

"Why? Why did you come down here? Why did he want you to come down here?" Something felt like it was missing.

"Cutter called, said he was in love with this woman, that his crew just went all rescue black ops mission to New Orleans with her to save her sister. Said the sister was in bad shape... heroin, and he needed Doc's help with getting her straight physically, so one of his guys could help her detox. Trig and I know something about that, detoxing I mean. Trig man, he couldn't come down, but like I said, I owe Cutter for what he did. Keeping my woman safe for me, giving her back to me... I would do just about anything to repay that debt so here I am."

"Here you are..." I twisted my lips back and forth and stared at the melting ice in my glass, which had emptied its self. The world swam around its edges from my drunk and I didn't feel one damn bit better. I just felt tired, angry, hurt, and... alone. I licked my lips and bowed my head and sighed. I was so fucking tired of being alone and for a brief, shining moment, Cutter had shown me I didn't need to be... Then she'd crashed into him and the illusion that I might finally have something did some crashing of its own. Crashing and burning. I wasn't blind. She was pretty... there was history...

"Hey, look at me."

I did it without thinking, concerned blue eyes roved my face and I blinked.

"Let me take you back to the boat. You and Cutter can talk, sitting here drinking yourself stupid isn't helping, I can see it isn't," he leaned back on his stool and looked me over.

"Can I get another?" I asked the bartender, who gave me a kind if slightly nervous smile.

"Sorry, Sweetheart. You're cut off. I think you should do what your friend suggests and get on back to Cutter, I've known that guy a long time. He's stand up and I bet you he's worried about you."

"He's got this whole damn town in his pocket doesn't he?" I asked the bartender point blank.

He gave me a smile and didn't even try to deny it, "There's a reason for that, Honey. He's done right by this town in a lot of things, in a lot of ways."

I huffed out a sigh, "Saint Cutter," I muttered.

"Come on, I'll walk with you. Don't even have to talk, but I bet some clean air will do you some good," Reaver looked me over and frowned a bit, "And food. Food too. It's waiting back at the boat."

"He's there with her, huh?" I asked.

"Come on, here we go," he paid for my drinks, took my uninjured hand, and helped me to my feet. I swayed, dizzy for a moment and his arm went around my back until I was steady.

"You good?" he asked softly.

I snorted and laughed, and the laughter built until I had tears rolling down my cheeks. I was fucking losing my shit, and all Ol' Blue Eyes did was stand there, a serene little smile on his lips as he watched me fall apart, waiting for the laughter to subside so we could get under way.

"Oh that was good, I needed that..." Except I didn't. My words were a lie, this wasn't a much needed laugh when the going got rough this was me barely holding on by my fingertips. I pretended everything was okay. That I was good. Nothing was bothering me! I was a happy drunk... when really all I wanted to do was slide down some wall somewhere into a corner and cry.

I wanted to scream my injustice into the night and I didn't want to quit screaming until somebody heard me and I really, *really* wanted that somebody to be Cutter. I knew just how pathetic and weak that sounded and I would pull myself up by the boot straps in a minute. No one would know. No one would ever know these things and that is what made me stop in my tracks along the boulevard and take in several deep breaths. I stared out over the water. The sun was down, but the sky still had that fiery light in it, the orange globe having just dropped below the horizon.

"What's up chick?" Reaver asked and I shook my head.

"Dizzy," I lied.

"Yeah, right. Look, you don't have to tell me and you don't know me and can tell me to fuck right off if you want, but I really want to ask you a favor."

We resumed our sedate pace back towards the marina and I held my breath for a moment, "Yeah, what's that?" I finally asked after a long exhale.

"You're drowning on the inside and for whatever reason, I think you were letting Cutter in and I *really, really* don't want to see that dude shut down or shut out because of me or my Doll. It'd crush her and she doesn't need or deserve any more hurt. She didn't know about you when we got here. She feels bad, I hate seeing her hurt."

I stopped him, "Were you going to actually get around to asking me something anytime soon?" I asked wearily and yeah I know I sounded like a bitch.

"Don't shut him down or shut him out just yet, please?" he asked and I looked up at him. His face was somber and I thought about it…

"Ever hear the whole 'it's not you it's me' line?" I asked.

"Yeah," he smirked wryly.

"Yeah. That." I trudged along wordlessly beside him for a minute or so before he broke the silence.

"I come from a screwed up background. So do a lot of the dudes that land in this life, typically they're looking for a place to belong when no one else will accept them…" he cleared his throat, "Cutter, his crew… I don't know what you did, but they accept you. Cutter put out the call that you were missing and I was there, not a one of his guys argued. Every one of them dropped what they were doing to go out and go look. From the sounds of it a couple of them got in Cutters ass about it too. Wanted to know what he'd done to fuck up."

"Nothing," I said, and it was true, "He didn't do anything."

No it was all me. Screwed up, isolated, stubborn and set in my ways looking for the slightest flaw. It's what I did. Look hard enough, look long enough you find a loose thread. Pull it and the whole pretty lie unravels. Except when you're me, you do more than just look. When I can't find a loose thread, I end up making one.

"He's not going to give up on you that easy you know," Reaver said and again with that grin. I sniffed and looked at him.

"Eventually, I'll make him," I said and shrugged a little hopelessly, "It's what I've always done. It's what I do." It was how I saved myself from letting them break my heart. I did the breaking first.

Reaver turned and stood in front of me, blocking my path. He looked down at me and gripping my shoulders lightly gave me a little shake, "So if you know that, why don't you knock it off? You're the only one who can."

I blinked up at him stupidly. I mean he was right... but, I gave a little shrug and he let his hands drop. We were at the marina and I looked out over the boats gently bobbing and swaying in their berths.

"I don't mean to be a pain the ass, I just don't know any other way to be," which was both honest and true. The first of many waves of humiliation washed over me.

"Hmm, why is that?" he asked.

"You tell me, Dr. Phil," I uttered and yeah my resting bitch face was back but I think that had more to do with the fact I was sobering up and was feeling pretty fucking embarrassed about my craptastic behavior of today than it had to do with anything else. So of course what do you do when you're embarrassed by your shitty behavior but are a prideful bitch like me? Why make it worse of course.

Goddamn it I was a mess.

I struck out across the parking lot towards Cutter's berth, Reaver shadowing me silently, hands buried in the pockets of his jeans. I didn't want to do this in front of them. Either of them, meaning Reaver and his wife. There was nothing for it though. Not like they were going away. I steeled myself and stepped onto the wharf following it down to Cutter's dock. He was at the small grill on the stern of his boat. She was setting places at his small deck table.

I climbed aboard and stopped, uncomfortable with only myself to blame. He set aside his spatula and she stopped, plate between her hands and peered at me from behind him. I suddenly felt just so damned tired. Like all I wanted to do was crawl into a bed somewhere and sleep for a thousand years.

Cutter closed the distance between us and cradled my face between his hands and the gesture was so sweet, coupled with the concern and yes, maybe even fear radiating out of his warm brown eyes, I felt so incredibly guilty...

"I'm sorry," I mumbled and the smile he graced me with was so perfect, sad but perfect. He pulled me into the circle of his arms and the cracks in my veneer finally became too much. I closed my eyes, took shelter in his arms and let myself cry.

CHAPTER 36

Cutter

She folded against my chest, into my arms, like she was meant to be there and she was. I held her tightly, fingers sliding against her slick, shiny hair, so warm, and alive as I tucked her head beneath my chin and just stood there, letting her let it out. She clung to me and cried and I think it was the first time she'd really *wept* in a long time.

Reaver, motioned for Li'l Bit to join him and she slipped past us, giving me a sympathetic look as she joined her man, who took her below deck. They were giving us privacy. I could appreciate that and I'm sure, if she were more with it, Hope would too.

I kissed her head and huffed out a sigh. I wanted to fix it. I wanted to put it all back together for her, see her happy, I mean for fuck's sakes the woman busted her ass for those two girls, to support them, to love them, to provide for them and when it came down to it, to find one of them and I was starting to realize, she'd been doing this for so long, by herself with no one there beside her... God. It was amazing she was still standing at all.

"Shh, I've got you Sweetheart," I murmured in my best attempt to be soothing. I'd never been awesome at being the supportive type in these kinds of situations and as shitty as it sounds, I couldn't stop the wave of relief from overtaking me when the crying jag she'd gone on was blessedly short lived.

Her tears dried up but she hadn't moved or pulled away yet and I was real grateful for that. I loved the feel of her in my arms, tucked close. I inhaled her flowery sweet fragrance, somewhat hampered by the smell of alcohol coming off of her, but intoxicating its own right anyways. She tugged back from me gently and I led her to one of the seats near the grill. She sank into it and I saved dinner from burning.

That done, I turned and knelt at her feet, placing my hands on her knees. We were eye to eye this way or just about. I searched her sad and sullen face and smoothed some of her long, dark locks behind her ear.

"I lose you?" I asked her point blank, steeling myself for the answer I didn't want to hear.

She searched my face, "No," her voice was small, low and dewed with her tears. I felt myself relax.

"Just tell me what's going on in there, huh Baby?"

"I don't know," she sniffed, breath hitching, I gave her my best look like she knew that wasn't true and she sighed out.

"A lot, there's a lot..." she said haltingly, "Just so much has happened in such a short amount of time and I," she bit her lips together and her eyes welled up fresh. I reached up and thumbed the new tears out from under her eyes. Overwhelmed didn't even begin to cover where my girl was at.

"One thing at a time," I said soothingly.

"I was jealous, and it's shitty and not fair and I don't have any claim on you, I mean you've already done so much and," I put a finger to her petal soft lips silencing her. She watched me, dark eyes inquisitive and that was good, that was real good.

"You listen to me, alright?" I raised my eyebrows and waited and she nodded slowly. I took my finger away from her mouth and took a cleansing breath.

"If roles had been reversed, if some dude I didn't know came up to you, right now, and put his lips on you, I'd knock his fucking teeth in," I told her. She and I stared across the short distance between us, silent. I leaned forward, brushed her lips with mine, "You're my woman, and this is a two way street, Sweetheart." I kissed her slow and let it build into something deep that I hoped touched both our souls.

I drew back carefully, and had to smile. Her eyes were closed, her face lax with something akin to peace. Her breath escaped her in a soft and gentle sigh and I'd be lying if I said I weren't hard but I needed to ignore my dick. Get to the bottom of some things.

"What else, Sweetheart?" God I just wanted her to give me

something, anything, I could *fix* right here and right now. Something to make her feel better. Something that would make her realize that I would do anything for her. There wasn't any 'just about' in there. I would. I would do anything for her. To wipe the ugly hurt from her eyes, to sooth her down into a place where she could open up, put some healing on *her* hurts.

"I feel, I don't know… I just,"

"Shh, slow and easy, Sweetheart, come on. Don't get worked up on me now. What else?"

"I feel guilty."

"Water under the bridge, Babe. It's okay," I told her. She closed her eyes.

"No, I didn't mean… I meant about Faith. I'm trying. I really am, but I *lost* her, I lost her and then I found her but now I've *found her* and she's with someone *else* and I'm trying, I'm trying so hard to give her," she swallowed hard, more tears threatened, and with a soft gasp she pressed on, "Her space and do what she wants but I feel so guilty, like I should be there and like I'm failing her all over again."

She looked at me and her dark gaze willed me to understand, but I couldn't. Not really. Not this. I had never been a parent, and even though those two girls were her sisters, Hope had been responsible for 'em for so very long she might as well have birthed them herself. It was suddenly easy to see why she underwent such an extreme form of birth control, opting for the permanent surgical option.

"Okay," I said and nodded, "Okay, this is what we're going to do. I'm gonna bring Reave and Li'l Bit back up here and you and Li'l Bit are gonna relax and get to know each other. Can you do that for me?" She nodded, she didn't look *happy* about it, but I needed her and Li'l Bit out of the way some. I had an idea, and when I had one of 'em like I did now, wasn't anything going to stop me. I kissed her one more time and went and got Reave and Li'l Bit from below decks.

"Yo, Reave. You remember how this works?" I asked and indicated the sails and the like. He let out an explosive breath.

"Kinda," he said.

"Kinda is all I need."

I went to the radio up by the wheel, "Harbor Master this is the Mysteria Avenge…" dinner would be cold, but who cares? I could reheat it and some things were more important.

CHAPTER 37
Hope

I focused on the small woman who was huddled in her man's black hoodie. It made her look smaller. She was short, but had some curves, unlike me. She sat down in the chair at the table next to me and blushed.

"Hi," she said.

"Hi," I echoed back. She laughed nervously. God this was fucking ridiculous and awkward. I didn't want to sit here, drunk after making a total asshole out of myself in front of these people, with these people –

"Harbormaster this is the Mysteria Avenge," I looked up sharply and narrowed my eyes. Cutter grinned down at me as the radio squawked a return in his hand.

"We're going out?" the woman said excitedly.

"You two just try to get to know each other and bury the hatchet," Cutter said and he was up, leaping to and fro, unhooking this, untying that and I just… well shit. It was much easier doing what he asked.

"I'm Hope," I said.

"Hayden," she returned carefully.

"So, um… not sure where to go from here," I said, "I mean it's obvious we've both fucked the same man," she laughed and colored in the weak light from the harbor. The engines thrummed to life and the lights out here on deck flared to life. I blinked and put up a hand.

"Sorry, Sweetheart," Cutter grinned down at me and it was obvious he wasn't sorry in the slightest.

"Where are we going?" I looked at him speculatively.

"You trust me?" he asked and suddenly I was the hard focus of three pairs of eyes.

"You know I do. If I didn't I would be with my sister right now."

"That just shows you trust the dude that's with her, doesn't it?" Reaver asked, coiling one of the lines off the side of the boat.

"No. Cutter asked me to trust him, I trust Cutter, so Marlin's with my sister," I shrugged. It made sense in *my* head.

Cutter gently barked orders and Reaver followed through and in a few minutes time Cutter had us moving, out into the open waters. I looked up, the stars were beginning to come out, twinkling in the clear skies. Soon, the act of looking up, coupled with the rise and fall of the boat, well, my stomach roiled a bit. I was pretty sure my Cosmopolitan binge drinking didn't help, like at all, and my inevitable heaving over the side while my current man's ex-lover held back my hair just made my humiliation for today complete. Still, once I puked, I felt much better. Funny how that worked.

Hayden stood near me, face crumpled into lines of sympathy as she held back my hair, smoothing it back from my face, petting it really. She was just generally being a comfort while the guys steered us towards the unknown destination Cutter had in mind. All I had a mind to do was kneel on the bench running around the perimeter of the aft deck while I heaved into the churning waters off the side. Yep. Abject humiliation, full and complete, and I only had myself to blame. Fun times.

"Better?" Hayden asked and I spit.

"Not really, God I am such an *asshole*," I groaned. Hayden huffed a small laugh.

"It could be worse," she said and shrugged.

"Not sure how."

She was silent and when I straightened her hands left my hair and she stood, mouth firmly shut, eyes sparkling with good humor. She really was a pretty girl. I could see why Cutter had been hooked. Still, aside from sharing hair color she and I were worlds apart which made me wonder what in the world he saw in me.

"Oh, hey," she said and reached out halfheartedly when I turned away. I wasn't used to being so all over the map emotionally. This shit seriously sucked.

"Sorry. I just, I don't know, I just don't get it," I said shortly. She sank down on the bench next to me.

"Don't get what?"

I didn't say anything, just turned my face into the breeze. Hayden sat silently with me and Reaver came around with a toothbrush loaded with paste and a bottle of water. I accepted these things gratefully and scrubbed the gross out of my mouth. Hayden didn't push me to talk and the guys were kept a little busy. Cutter had turned off the motor and the snap of canvas and clink of catches and fittings filled the sultry evening air.

"Where are we *going*?" I asked. I didn't like leaving things in the air like that, Cutter just laughed.

"You'll see."

"Better question is what will we do when we get there?" Hayden asked. I nodded. She had a point there.

"Finish up some dinner, we're almost there. I think we're about five minutes out or so. If fuel weren't so damned expensive I wouldn't have even bothered with the sails but we got a good wind," he shrugged as if to say, 'so fuck it,' and let the ship's wheel slide through his hands. I rinsed the toothbrush over the side and wrestled with my impatience.

"So um, what do you do?" Hayden tried.

"I'm a defense contractor," I said and at her uncertain look, dumbed it down for her, "I train police departments how to disarm suspects without killing them."

"Oh, sounds exciting," she smiled.

"It's a lot of paperwork," which was true, "What about you?" I had to make at least some small effort, I mean right?

"Interior design," she nodded, blushing faintly. Probably worried I would judge based on its excitement level or lack thereof as compared to my line of work.

"What about him?" I asked instead, sidestepping the mess entirely.

"Drywall install. We actually kind of go together," she smiled.

"Like peanut butter and jelly!" Reaver crowed, proving he was shamelessly eavesdropping from the other side of the deck. Hayden turned and the smile she had for him lit her up from the inside out. Wow.

"How did you get into, uh, defense contracting?" I hated that question. Really hated it, but she didn't know. I looked over at Cutter who winked at me.

"My sisters' dad, he," I cleared my throat, "He never went after them, I mean, they were his and I guess that grossed him out but me… I was a different story. My mom didn't believe me. A friend of mine, her dad put her in martial arts and we were thick as thieves. They had money so they asked my mom if they could put me in with her and my mom, the hippy, said no of course. I had to beg and plead and yeah," I laughed a little bitterly.

"It was my stepfucker that talked her into letting me go. I took to it like a fish to water. He stopped coming into my room when I was fourteen and nearly caved his nuts in. Mom couldn't really ignore it after that and kicked his ass out. Though to be honest, I think it was his drugging that got him kicked out more than anything."

Three sets of eyes on me, I didn't know what was making me say any of this. Like everything else, I didn't generally talk about it but you know me! All in, as always.

"I stuck with the martial arts even after they split, my friend never made it and my instructor, he had a soft spot for me I guess. He let me keep coming. When I graduated high school, my mom was in real bad shape and died, I had Faith and Charity who were like ten and seven, my grades… hell, no money for college," I sighed. "I had to support them somehow so I enlisted, the Army took what I already had and built on it. They found I had an aptitude for teaching and the rest is history." I shrugged and for a long minute the only sound was the boat cutting through the water.

Reaver cleared his throat, "Damn. That's fucked up."

I shrugged, "Worse has happened, I think I turned out pretty okay all things considered."

"Reave, man, need you to get that line," Cutter said and his tone was dark, ominous even as he tried to get a handle on whatever he had going on inside.

Man, wasn't I just one giant freaking ray of sunshine today? I turned to Hayden and scoffed a laugh, "Ever wish the day had some kind of reset button like some video game console?"

"I think we all do, but yeah, I've had some doozies."

The boys dropped the sails and tucked them away, Cutter lashed the canvas down and dropped anchor so we wouldn't drift. I looked around. The coast was off in one direction. Pretty close, actually. The lights from beachfront houses glimmered and though we couldn't see anyone moving around in them, we could see the blue glow of a television here or the warm lights on the ground floor there. People were probably having their dinner.

"C'mere, Sweetheart." Cutter held a hand down to me where I sat and I took it and got to my feet, he led me to the side of the boat, closer to the shore and brought out his phone. It started ringing on speaker.

"Hello?"

"Hey Marlin, how's our girl?"

"Sleeping, she's rough. I think she'll get through it. She's strong like her sister, just in different ways."

"Thanks," I said sardonically. I didn't feel strong. Not in the slightest.

"Hey man, come to the window and give the signal," Cutter looked down at me and I looked up, a light winked in one of the upstairs windows of an otherwise dark house. I blinked.

"Is that...? Are we?"

"Thanks, Marlin," Cutter said.

"That you bobbing out there, Cap?"

"Yep."

"Oh, cool. Night then."

"Night," he hung up and pulled me back against his chest, "You're just a five minute swim away, Baby. Now you both get your wish. She gets her privacy and you get to be close anyways."

"You seriously just sailed us to my sister's back door," I sounded incredulous. I *was* incredulous.

"Technically it's *my* back door. I mean it is my house..." I slapped him hard in the chest with my uninjured hand and he said "Owe!" and put up his hands to guard himself, though he was laughing, eyes smiling again.

"Why would you do that?" I asked and I was dead serious, I needed to know why.

"Oh hey," he pulled me into his arms, "I love you, that's why. Now when you gonna figure out that I'm in this? I want you in my life, to see what the hell can happen when this shit storm dies down. I love your feisty, that you can keep me on my toes. I love that you're messed up, that no matter how screwed up it gets that you can hold your own," I snorted and he paused.

"I've been doing a damn fine job of that today," I said bitterly.

"We all reach our breaking point, Baby. You, me, your sister sure, but I like you… *we* like you and raggedy ass bunch of misfits or not, you take a look around at each of us and we all got one thing in common, me, you, Reave and Li'l Bit here… any one of my boys…"

"Yeah, what's that?" I asked softly.

"We don't give up. No matter how high the shit piles on, we don't quit and I *need* a woman like that, a woman like *you* in my life to help me keep these fuckers in line." He pressed a kiss to my forehead and I swallowed hard, my heart giving a sharp ache where it felt fractured and splintered.

"Yeah, but why me?"

"You're beautiful, you're challenging, and mm, I'd be lying if I said your pussy wasn't some of the sweetest I ever had," I choked and laughed.

"Way to ruin it, Casanova."

Cutter smirked and chuffed a slight laugh, "I'm a rough-around-the-edges bastard."

"Me, too," I said and tipped my face up for a kiss, which he gave me.

Reaver cleared his throat, "We good? This mean we can eat, because I'm fucking starv – owe! Hey!" His little Mrs. was slapping him in the chest and shoving at him playfully like I had Cutter the moment before. I searched Cutter's eyes by the dim light from the boat and he smiled.

"Isn't there a rule against feeding the animals?" I suggested, arching a brow.

"Yeah, but I don't really live by civilian rules," he said and his look held meaning, carried weight.

I dropped my voice and self-consciously glanced at the other couple who were going about getting the gas grill reheated and straightening the place settings from our impromptu sail.

"I busted down the door with the lot of your men and murdered a bunch of human traffickers something like two days ago. I think we're way past pretending I play by your so-called 'civilian' rules at this point, don't you?" I asked. Cutter smiled broadly.

"Wine with dinner?" he asked.

I scowled, "You asshole."

He laughed, long and loud and deep and Reaver and Hayden turned to us smiling, their own banter forgotten for the moment. We had a nice meal, and some good conversation, my eyes drifting to shore and just having that house within sight, it did amazing things for my frayed nerves. It really did. Cutter held my casted hand beneath the table, his fingers finding the spaces between mine, like they were always meant to be there. I still couldn't fathom that this man wanted me but his grand gesture had left little room for doubt. I think it was the thing that tipped me hopelessly over the edge, pitching me into the yawning chasm of being utterly in love with him right back.

I mean if what they say is true, if love means seeing someone and what a mess they can be, how moody they can get, and can handle you no matter how hard you can be to handle? Still wants you in their life anyways? Shit, then whatever was happening was the real deal now wasn't it? I needed to stop poking at it, stop waiting for the other shoe to drop I mean, I'd earned this a little hadn't I? Being loved by someone, loving them back, even with the major shit storm of fucked up going on around me and my little family of three?

Cutter shook my hand a bit and I looked up into his warm brown eyes. He smiled then, and in that smile it held such warmth and laughter and light and it said to me, *yes*. Unequivocally *yes*, and I knew then right there that in Cutter I had found my match, my soulmate, if there was such a thing… and I would be damned if I was going to let that go. No, no, no, no, no.

CHAPTER 38
Cutter

"Hey Reave, let the girls deal with clean up, I need your help man." I waved him over and opened the storage hatch. I was gonna let him and Li'l Bit have my cabin. It was a nice night, we were in sight of the shore and I figured Hope was tough enough to spend the night under the stars with me. Still, setting up the hammock was much easier with two sets of hands on deck rather than just the one.

Reave set down the stack of plates he was handling and came over. Li'l Bit smiled behind his back and gave me this look with this deep romantic sigh that plainly communicated her love for her man and her happiness for me. I gave her a smile back and caught Hope, watching the exchange, her deep, dark eyes calculating, considering. Finally, she locked gazes with me, and face still neutral, gave me a nod. She was still trying to come to grips with Li'l Bit and what she may or may not mean to me and that was okay. She was doing a pretty fucking stellar job all things considered.

"Come on. I'll wash, you dry." Hayden smiled at Hope and led her below decks while Reave and I wrestled the canvas open and laid it flat. The hammock was a big bastard and meant for two and when hooked up right, between the two masts, stable enough to fuck on. I'd done it. I just didn't want any tonight. No, tonight I wanted to try intimacy with my woman. I think she needed something a little deeper than a few inches of my dick in her puss.

Laughter accompanied the sound of running water out my little galley window and it did my heart some glad.

"She's kind of a hot mess, you sure?" Reaver asked, but he was smiling, his mannerisms affable.

"I'm sure," I said, steady and on an even keel, that's what I felt when I was with Hope. Like there wasn't anything that could stop us and I was pretty damn sure there wasn't. We evened each other out, I think. Give and take, push and pull, I was the water to her shore. It was comfortable, even when it was crazy. Okay, it'd been crazy from the word go but I really wanted to see how well we'd mesh when the shit finished dripping from where it'd hit the fan. I saw such a wild potential in 'us' and I really wanted an 'us' to happen but I'd have to get through those walls first. I could do it. I'd already made it through the first gate.

Reaver and I finished setting up the hammock talking easy about life up north as I caught up with all of the goings on up there.

"Red have her baby?" I asked. Reaver grinned and Li'l Bit squealed from the hatch.

"Oh my God, I forgot to show you!" She came tromping over, bare feet slapping the deck and Hope hung back a little dubious. She wasn't used to the easy familiarity Li'l Bit exhibited. The casual touching and cuddling us three, Li'l Bit, Reave, and I were into. I held out my hand to Hope and she came to me, almost reluctantly. That hurt a bit. She peered down at the phone with me as Li'l Bit scrolled through pictures of Rev and Red and their little bundle of joy in what appeared to be her pink stocking cap.

"Eden Lorraine Alexander, eight pounds thirteen ounces of adorable baby cuteness," Li'l Bit was all glowing and excited for her friend and Red looked perfect, happy tears in mama's eyes while a proud papa looked on.

"She got her dad's black hair and her mom's hazel eyes," I said smiling.

"Mm! I think they're already working on number two, Rev wants a little slugger. He's dead set on Dante for the name." Reaver grinned and leaned against the mast

"She's such a good baby, too! Let's mom and dad sleep through the night for the most part," Li'l Bit put her phone away.

"That won't last," Reaver said and laughed, "Connor did that too the first month or so then it was like someone flipped his switch."

"You have a kid?" Hope asked, looking from one to the other of them.

"He does, I don't," Li'l Bit gave Reaver a charmed smile.

"Connor's eleven, and if you'd hurry up and get knocked up we'd be good on that front," he winked at his wife.

"You guys are trying? No shit?" I asked and felt delighted for them. Hope was stiff in my arms and I sensed a talk coming on about rug-rats in our future. I'd never really wanted them myself, something told me there was some emotional baggage there but it didn't have to be dealt with tonight, she was under enough strain.

"Trying, yeah. Just started really, Doll insisted we talk to Connor first, she wanted to make sure my oldest boy was cool with a little brother or sister, didn't want to just spring it on him."

Hope's tense posture softened a bit at my side. Ah, ha. Some more of the mysterious bits of my girl were unravelling. I kissed her temple and she softened a little more.

"It's not that late, but it was a long ride and we were up early to make it, I don't suppose you'd mind if we turned in, would you?" Lil' Bit's eyes sparkled with a mischievous light. She knew damned well what she was doing and I was glad for it. I smiled at her.

"Not at all, feel free to take my bunk, I wanted to stay up here with Hope if you don't mind. Keep an eye on the house with her."

"Naw, we get it, Man," Reaver came forward and we clasped hands pulling each other in to tap shoulders before backing off.

"Good deal, man."

"Good night, Hope," Li'l Bit smiled at my girl and Hope nodded. She still looked uncertain and it wasn't a good look for her. I liked it when she was on solid ground and I was pretty sure a good night's sleep would get her on towards that.

She let out a breath once the hatch shut behind my two friends and her shoulders dropped marginally.

"Doin' okay, Sweetheart?" I asked softly.

"God, could I look like any more of an asshole?" she groaned palming her face.

I laughed softly, "Probably, but Reave and Li'l Bit, they get it. What I wanna know is what brought on the sudden bout of insecurity from my girl who's always so sure of herself?" I tugged her gently into my arms and she pointedly wouldn't look at me, her eyes fixed on the darkened house in the distance.

"Maybe I'm not so sure, Cutter," she swallowed hard.

"Well, if there's one thing I *need* you to be sure of, it's that I'm not going anywhere."

"Yeah, why is that?"

"Strip and I'll show you," I teased. Hope huffed a laugh and her smile made me smile.

"Truth, that's why…" I murmured. Her brow wrinkled in confusion.

"What's why?"

"You smile and I can't help it, I have to smile too. Now, I was only half joking, I mean it. Get naked. Time for you to relax."

"Make me," she challenged, and I smiled again.

"That's my girl." I pulled her roughly against me and before she could skate back out of reach I gripped both sides of her short little black shirt dress and pulled, buttons pinging off the deck. Hope groaned and I let the material slide off her body. She wasn't up for a fight, so she didn't fight me, which was good.

I placed a palm in the center of her chest and pushed her down, my arm behind her back, lowering her gently to the wide hammock. I knelt between her thighs and had myself some dessert, licking her until she came apart something like twice. Until she gazed up at me, dark eyes hooded with desire and I could sink myself balls deep inside her. But I didn't want that, no. I wanted her hot mouth on me. I wanted those lips wrapped around my cock while I pressed into the woman's throat. I wanted it bad, like back in New Orleans.

I pressed my thumb against her mouth and past her teeth and she let me, her tongue hot and velvet. I groaned and grew that much harder as she sucked.

"Fuck Baby, that's nice…"

"You want me to suck your cock, don't you?" she asked.

"Yeah, yeah I do… but only if you want to."

"Yeah, I want to, but there's a rule this time," she swallowed nervously, "Don't force my head down on you, or I swear to fucking Christ I'll bite you."

I froze, *shit*, I think I just stepped on a landmine, the echo of an earlier conversation loud in my ears… Her fucking stepdaddy made her cop oral. I'd bet my next haul of Cuban cigars on it.

"Baby, why didn't you tell me any of this in New Orleans? In the hotel that first time?"

"I was trusting you, and I don't always think about it. I was caught up in the moment and the moment was perfect, but now... It just feels like it needs to be said. I'm too close to those memories and I just need you to not force my head. Okay?"

"Wouldn't dream of it, Hope. You don't have to do anything you don't want to," I'd lost my wood. She gently cupped me in her hand and smiled. I cupped her face in my hands and looked deep into her soul.

"I want to, now shut up and let me," she said.

I let her go and she resituated herself so she lay on her stomach while I still knelt by the hammock, I walked forward on my knees and made it easy for her, she undid and peeled back my shorts and my cock started to get back with the program. It was a damn fucking shame it was sometimes gonna be hard for her to cop a blowjob. I was pretty amazed she hadn't had much practice at it, that she was a fucking natural. Her mouth on me, Jesus, you would never know such a hard-assed, kickass woman was doing it. She was slow and gentle this time, reverent with how she worked me and it was really nice.

She didn't blow me like back in the hotel, she didn't blow me this time like she liked to fuck. She liked to fuck hard and fast until I wore her down into something more sedate and loving. Except right now, she was as gentle as a lamb and made love to me with her mouth from the get-go. I gazed down the length of my body. Watching this was half the thrill, after all, but her hair was in the way. I gently touched her head and she flinched but I could fix that easily enough.

"Oh yeah," I groaned, "Your mouth is so fucking perfect, I wanna see, Sweetheart, so I'm going to touch you, I'm gonna gather up all this long, satin soft hair, and I'm going to watch you make love to me with your mouth, because that's what you're doing, isn't it?"

"Mm," she moaned around my shaft and the vibration of it had my balls tightening. I was going to blow way too soon. This was something. Watching this wild woman do something so sweet, so submissive, without me having to make her…

"Hope, I'm going to come, lover, I'm going to…" I grunted and came and she rolled those dark eyes up my body as I did and that vision is forever burned into my brain. Holy god almighty. She was so fucking perfect. She drew off me and got up, went to the side and spit and I was cool with that, if it was what she needed this time, that was cool.

I knelt and breathed out and she came back to me, standing in front of me. I wrapped my arms around her legs and placed a reverent kiss next to her navel, turning my head and cuddling into her. She raked her nails gently through my hair, against my scalp and I shivered.

"Thank you," she whispered.

"For what?" I asked. Was she for real?

"I've never been able to make a man come from that, not since… and now I've done it twice."

"Mm, Sweetheart, I don't know how anyone could resist or hold off," I told her truthfully.

"Anyways," she said, my words making her uncomfortable, "Thank you."

"Thank *you*, now I'm gonna need you to lie back because I need inside you. I really do…"

CHAPTER 39
Hope

I opened my eyes. It was still deepest night, so late as to probably be early, the air just had that smell to it, you know? I was warm enough, the night sultry and warm and I was snuggled up close to Cutter's warmth, my head on his shoulder, leg draped over his. So why was I awake? I blinked and held very still beneath the single flat sheet draped over us and waited. Water lapped against the hull, there was an odd creak from the wood or one of the ropes but nothing seemed amiss or out of place.

So why was I awake?

Cutter sighed out into the night, his arms tightening around me, and I looked up, his eyes were closed but a small smile played on his lips. He was sound asleep so I wondered what it was he dreamed. I settled, laying back down, closing my eyes to listen to the waves lap in counterpoint to the cadence of his heart. I liked it here, in his arms. I liked it here, in this town and I realized I was sick of having no place to put down any roots. I was tired of having no life, and as much as I loved my sisters, my heart wrenched when I realized I would always love them, I would always be here for them, but the apron strings had been cut. They were standing on their own now.

I mean, Charity, the youngest, she'd been standing on her own for quite a while. She was on the very verge of graduating, of finding a career, of finding a man and starting a family... Faith, the middle child had always been shiftless as the sands along the beach out there. Never settling but always travelling in the direction I'd pushed her. God, I felt so *guilty*. I'd always pushed and pulled her in directions she didn't want to or *wasn't meant* to go. She'd always been the free and artistic one... but I'd pushed and pushed and pushed and finally she'd given in and gone to that damned school when if I'd just *helped her* financially she could have lived on campus but no, I had to be stubborn. I had to teach her to stand on her own and look what I'd done.

I'd made her an ever loving target for that carrion eater and my baby sister had suffered the ultimate price. My bright eyed and innocent Bubbles had –

"It's not your fault, Sweetheart, no one blames you…" Cutter's voice was at once soothing and sympathetic.

"*I* blame me. *I do*, okay?"

"Shhh," he held me as my bitterness poured out and it was just what I needed to do. To purge, to get it out and take some deep cleansing breaths and to try to find my center again. I was horribly off kilter and bound to self-destruct if I didn't, and all grown up or not, my sisters still needed me to be the strong one.

Cutter kissed my forehead, his lips warm and soft and my eyes drifted shut unbidden. It had been a cathartic cry, and I felt steady despite the gentle rocking of the boat, as he held me close and let me borrow his strength.

"I can't do anything for her and it *kills* me, but she can't know I'm crying about it like a little bitch either. I don't fall apart in front of them, I never fall apart in front of them," he hushed me, hand cradling my head, thumb against my lips and I stilled.

"You do what you gotta do, Sweetheart, but when you're with me, you do you. I got you. You ain't gotta hide from me, or pretend that it's okay when it's just you and me because it's not. I get that, and there's no judgment here. We make a good team, good partners and I like that, Babe. I like it and I want to keep it, and I want you to find some happy and if that means you gotta be unhappy then we'll do that. You get me? I'm not going anywhere and I damn sure don't think less of you. I'm amazed you've held it together this long."

He soothed me, with gentle touches and his deep rich voice, like no one ever had before, or could. I found strength in him, I found calm when I needed it and fuel for my ire when I needed it instead. I cuddled into him and let him soothe some of my misery away and as we drifted, tethered only by the boat's anchor, I stared across the strong planes and angles of his chest, over the water at the lightening sky behind the houses and sighed.

"Promise me you won't give up on me," I said suddenly, well aware of what a squirrely mess I was right now, unaware of how long it might last.

Cutter chuckled, "You're stuck with me as long as you can tolerate me."

A long, feminine wail drifted out to us from below decks and the both of us laughed, stifling our giggles behind our hands, snorting and just generally trying to keep ourselves from being heard.

"I wondered what woke me up," I said dryly.

"They been at it more 'n an hour," he chuckled.

"Sounds like us," I said softly.

"Hmm, yeah, you know what? It sounds like a good idea," he drew my leg higher on his body and turned, a few awkward thrusts of his hips and he found me, sinking in slowly, working himself back and forth until just by virtue of starting in on me, I became wet enough to ease his way.

"Not going anywhere, Sweetheart. I promise, you'd have to fight me to make me let you go anyhow."

"We all know how that turned out last time," I whispered.

"Damn right... god you feel so fuckin' *tight*."

I kissed him, the angle we had was awkward but working, and I let him make love to me as the sun rose slowly in the sky. It was beautiful.

CHAPTER 40
Cutter

"What is the big, god damn, emergency?" I demanded. Hope had been *pissed* when I told her to relax and chill back at the Mysteria Avenge and had vaulted the side and swam for shore, dry clothes sealed in Ziploc bags along with my other essentials, trailing in a dive bag.

Reaver didn't help, laughing his head off at the expression on her face as I'd gone over the side. She couldn't follow with the cast on her arm.

"I'm kicking you in the balls when you get back!" she'd shouted at me. Only got pissed off even more when I'd shouted back that no she wouldn't, she'd need them that night. Hayden had given her a sympathetic look and Reaver had fallen on his ass he was laughing so hard. I hoped like hell that my girl didn't kick *him* in the balls. I'd come back to find a hole in her.

I hadn't had time to worry about it. I was making way to The Plank to answer my secretary's nine-one-one text to get my ass to shore. Now I was glowering at my whole assembled crew minus my VP and I had a sinking feeling…

"Easy, Captain." Pyro said affably and it was the fact my best friend and first mate aboard our salvage boat was at ease that put my raised hackles down.

"We wanted to talk to you," Atlas said.

"Yeah, we put it to a vote," Nothing said grimly, but that was Nothing for you, he was always a grim bastard.

"You vote me out as your Pres.?" I asked, half expecting the worse. My girls gloom and doom was wearing off on me a little I guessed. The boys all busted up laughing.

"Fuck no! We took Marlin's vote by proxy, man." Atlas said, wiping tears out of his eyes.

"What the fuck is this about!?" I demanded. I was as lost as a whore on her way to church.

"Have a seat, Cap," Lightning suggested. I went to my electric chair and dropped into it.

"We need to ask you something," Pyro said, "You give any thought about making Hope your Ol' Lady?"

I eyed my friend, "Uh, yeah," I nodded.

"And?" Atlas prompted.

"Have to ask her, not sure how my rag would go over."

"Yeah that's what we voted on," Radar pulled out a plastic grocery sack from under the table, I raised an eyebrow.

"Dude, I looked, it's not exactly in our by-laws but it's not exactly *against them* either..." Atlas said.

"What did you guys fucking vote on? What did you do?" I demanded suspicious.

Radar pulled a cut, a small, trim one out of the bag and laid it out in front of me. I blinked, stupid. The top rocker read 'property of' like it should, the bottom rocker 'Cutter' like it should but between the two...

"No Ol' Lady's ever worn the club's colors..." I said looking the patch over, the Kraken dragging the ship below the waves.

"Hope ain't just an Ol' Lady, Captain," this coming from Beast.

I looked around the table at all my guys and they all stared back plaintively, "Somebody explain, before I suffer a goddamn stroke."

"Hope can take it man, she stood side by side with us as good as any brother and if she were a dude, it'd be no contest... She'd be in. We see she makes you happy, you guys are a good match. She can handle it, and we wanted to show not just you but her that she's got a place here. We want her to stay, too," My best friend and first mate sniffed and propped his boots on the table, leaning way back in his chair. He raised his eyebrows, and waited for me to finish processing what my boys were telling me.

"Hope is yours, Man; every one of us can see it, but she's got this club's respect and fuck what any other club says or thinks... Except for our brothers from another mother up North. They think like us anyhow," Nothing shrugged, "That's why we like 'em."

I kind of scoffed a little incredulous and picked up my gavel, "So ordered?" I asked and got a rousing round of smiles and agreement, "So entered!" I brought the gavel down on the arm of my chair with a sharp crack, but my eyes were fixed on the property rag in front of me. There was only one thing left to do, really, and that was to convince Hope to wear it. I had no idea how to go about doing that but at the same time, I knew the time wasn't right. Not right now. She was stressed out enough and add the pissed off to it... nope, it would have to stay here for now.

"I really don't know what to say, boys, except 'thank you', so thank you." I embraced each of my brothers one at a time until I came to Nothing.

"When you gonna ask her?" he asked.

"I have no idea, definitely not until this shit storm has had a chance to calm down."

"I was gonna suggest that, she and the sister doing okay?" he asked.

"I don't know, Man; I really don't know, Hope seems to be hanging on by a thread and you know Marlin, he's gonna do everything he can to protect Faith's privacy and truthfully? That's why I picked him. That poor girl has been through enough."

Nothing nodded solemnly, he'd seen quite a bit of shit back when he'd been an EMT or Paramedic or some shit. I knew it was one of the two and that they weren't exactly the same thing. Didn't care enough about the distinction.

"Well, you know we're all here for you and Hope, Captain. Just call." Atlas said from over Nothing's shoulder. Nothing turned, nodding back in agreement to what my secretary was saying.

"A man couldn't ask for a better band of brothers," I told my men and it was true. I looked down at the table, at the leather bodice-like vest the boys had gotten my woman and I felt a surge of emotion. A lot of things, so many things at once I couldn't even begin to describe it if I wanted to.

"Get on back to Hope, Captain, we all know you want to, we'll call you anything else needs attention," Pyro nodded to me and I looked over all my men in turn one more time.

"You boys see something I don't?" I asked.

"Yeah, she's your 'one', dude. Now get going!" Lightning winked from the back of the bar and I huffed a laugh.

"Okay, I'm going," and I went, still marveling at what my boys had done for me and her.

I got back to the house, tucked my clothes back into their Ziploc bags and sealed them tight. I switched back into my dry shorts, the sun having worked its magic on 'em while I'd been at The Plank and the material had lain out on the back patio's retaining wall.

I hadn't bothered to go in the house either coming or going, I'd just gone around it, and had taken the Crash truck back and forth. I looked over my shoulder as Marlin slipped out the back slider.

"How's she doin'?" I asked.

"Rough. She's hurting, Jonesing hard for a fix that I ain't got shit to give her," Marlin bowed his head and palmed the back of his neck. "It's worse somehow, you know?"

I did know. His brother had been on the shit of his own volition, Faith wasn't a willing addict, this had been done to her...

"Yeah, man. I know."

"Thanks," Marlin nodded and sighed going back for the door.

"You need to talk, you can reach out." I called after him. He nodded, a haunted look in his eyes and I knew that look, it was bad in there, whatever was going down and I had mad respect for my VP handling it like he was. If it had been Hope, I could do it. I would do it... but it wasn't and I didn't know the first thing about getting a junkie off of that shit. Probably wouldn't have the patience for the whining and tantrums he was about to endure, but Marlin was good at that... enduring. His brother had been a cross of his to bear for a long while. Damn fuckin' shame that had turned out to be.

I slung the mesh dive bag with my pile of sealed essentials in it over my chest and made the long walk to the water's edge. I could see two heads bobbing in the water alongside the Mysteria Avenge and smiled faintly to myself when I caught sight of Hope on the hammock, she'd raised her arm to shade her eyes and the motion caught my attention.

I trudged into the surf and made the swim back out easily. Reaver and Hayden waved, masks and snorkels in place and I waved back. I wanted a minute with Hope alone. I climbed up the ladder off the side and hauled myself onto the deck, dripping. Hope lazed in the sun, her bronzed skin gleaming with oil, the smell of coconut and lime perfuming the air.

"Hey," I said.

"Fire out?" she asked.

"No fire," I unslung the bag and let it drop.

"What was the big damn emergency then?" she seemed like she was back together and I smiled.

"Tell you about it later," I said and she glanced out at the water and nodded and that right there must have been what my boys saw in her, or part of it.

"I ain't letting you go. Call me creepy, or a fucking stalker status asshole all you want, but you don't find this but once in a lifetime, Babe." I dropped to the deck, sitting beside the hammock and crossed my ankles, propping my forearms on my knees. I looked at Hope who looked at me plaintively through her big bug eyed sunglasses.

"Good to know we're on the same page," she said quietly and evenly but her voice was almost too steady, too careful.

"I'm in it to win it here, Sweetheart. You and me and living this life of mine. You make my world complete. You make it perfect and I want that, I want you so hard…" I shut my mouth and shook my head.

"I'm a mess," she said softly and I shook my head.

"No, you're *my* mess," I said and she nodded carefully.

"My sisters…"

"Will sort themselves out with our help. I get it, you're a package deal and I really am okay with that; I mean, haven't I proven that by now?"

"Yes,"

"So stay with me. Move in with me, say you'll be mine."

"Only if you say you'll be mine too…"

"Two way street, Sweetheart, I'm down with that. I really am. I want you, and to be clear, that means only you. I don't want anybody else, I – " Didn't get to finish what I was saying because she rolled off the hammock lightning quick and flattened me to the deck. I put my hands on her hips where she straddled my waist and she pulled off her sunglasses, searching my face for any bullshit. There was none, and finally satisfied that I meant every word I was saying she kissed me.

I held my woman in my arms under the warm sunlight and felt a burden on my soul lift. I had a partner, I had a Queen for my little seaside kingdom, finally and whatever lay on the road ahead I knew we could handle it, just like we'd handled everything to this point.

"I love you," she said against my mouth.

"I love you too, Sweetheart. No insecurities, no worrying nothing to be afraid of. We got this," I promised her and she laughed, and it was one of the freest sexiest sounds I had ever heard come out of her. Her arms went around my shoulders and mine went for my fly. I couldn't get enough of her, I would never get enough of her; I loved her just so damn much. Everything else was just a fucking formality in the face of that and not me, not her, and none of mine stood much on formality.

"Oh God," she gasped as I moved her bikini bottom aside and sank into her. I smiled up at her.

"I like the sound of that, you can call me that any time you like, Sweetheart."

Hope threw back her head and laughed and I swear on everything, it was the sweetest and sexiest sound I'd ever heard, and I wanted to hear more of it. A lot. Until the day I died.

Amen.

EPILOGUE

Faith

The house in New Orleans

I watched him rape her, the other girl in my room and I couldn't close my eyes. The men out front were at their loud video games again, or so I thought. They sounded louder, realer somehow... wait... was realer a word? I didn't know.

Whirling, the room started spinning, and if it were possible to be sick of such a thing then I was, this euphoria they pumped in my veins, the sluggish feeling it gave me... I hated it. I loathed it, and I would give anything for it to stop.

I stared at the leather band around my wrist, finally able to drag my eyes from the rutting on the stained mattress on the other side of the room. *Boom! Bang, pop, arugh!* The sounds of violence intensified and I squeezed my eyes shut and tried to remember the nice boy, the sweet boy who had looked around my storage locker cell, who'd taken pity on me, who had spoken so sweetly and given me his bracelet... the first glimmer of kindness in so long... so long...

Crack!

The door exploded inward on its hinges and a woman, an avenging angel, a superhero strode through. Except angels didn't have hellfire in their eyes did they? Avenging angel? I couldn't remember... I closed my eyes and sighed out. I'd dreamt this before, hadn't I? A thousand times and more... my sister, Hope, coming to my rescue, except it hadn't happened then and it wasn't...

"Faith," my sister's voice. I sat up, drawn by strings, this was the cruelest dream yet, she'd never spoken in the others...

"Faith?" she tried again and I looked up...

"Hope, is it really you?" I asked and the avenging angel, the hellfire was gone and all that was left was my sister's face set into deep lines of regret, deeper lines of grief. I reached out with my arms like when I was small and I wanted Hope to pick me up and she was there and I breathed in deep the smell of my sister, my family, my home, and she spoke...

"It's okay Bubbles, I got you. I got you now, I always got you Sis," and I collapsed into her arms and clung to one thought... *Real, this is real, Hope is here; Hope has found you.*

We were in another room then, death and destruction and chaos and shouting. A man with long brown hair and soulful brown eyes shouting, bellowing, making me flinch and then *he* came... I blinked and shook my head and blinked again to try and clear the illusion but it wouldn't go away.

Golden hair and rich, sky blue eyes, I stared I couldn't help it, and then he picked me up and for the first time in so very long, I knew... I just *knew* what it was to be safe in a man's arms again.

What was going to happen to me?

From the Author of
SHATTERED & SCARRED
THE SACRED HEARTS MC

A J DOWNEY
MARLIN'S FAITH

Other books by A.J. Downey

THE SACRED HEARTS MC

1. Shattered & Scarred
2. Broken & Burned
3. Cracked & Crushed
3.5. Masked & Miserable (a novella)
4. Tattered & Torn
5. Fractured & Formidable
6. Damaged & Dangerous

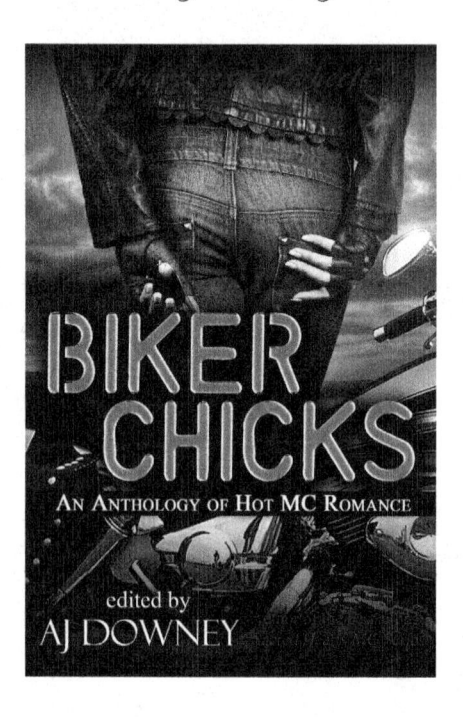

Paranormal Romance
I Am The Alpha (with Ryan Kells)

About the Author

A.J. Downey is the internationally bestselling author of The Sacred Hearts Motorcycle Club romance series. She is a born and raised Seattle, WA Native. She finds inspiration from her surroundings, through the people she meets, and likely as a byproduct of way too much caffeine.

She has lived many places and done many things, though mostly through her own imagination… An avid reader all of her life, it's now her turn to try and give back a little, entertaining as she has been entertained. She lives in a small house in a small neighborhood with a larger than life fiancé and one cat.

She blogs regularly at *www.ajdowney.com*. If you want the easy button digest, as well as a bunch of exclusive content you can't get anywhere else, sign up for her mailing list right here:

http://eepurl.com/blLsyb